Joe Zeppetello's *Intimate Disconnect*, true to its title, is a close peregrination through a thirty-something's world of achievement and talent thinly balanced in an equilibrium of explosive proportions spun out within the metaphor of divorce. The story follows two ambitious yet self-doubting friends, one the CEO of a successful purveyor of high-end toys for customers with money to burn, the other her friend and busy divorce lawyer who takes on the CEO's own divorce from the adolescent inventor of the company's products, the latest a floating cold drinks tray for hot tubs. The author's exploration of the details of these lives and the flighty-to-paranoid characters they have to deal with, including a few old and new lovers thrown in, is a marvel to behold.

~Vernon Benjamin, Author of *The History of the Hudson River Valley*.

Intimate Disconnect

Joe Zeppetello

ALL THINGS THAT MATTER PRESS

To Karon
Sorry we missed you
Best wishes
Joe Zeppetello 8/13/22

Intimate Disconnect

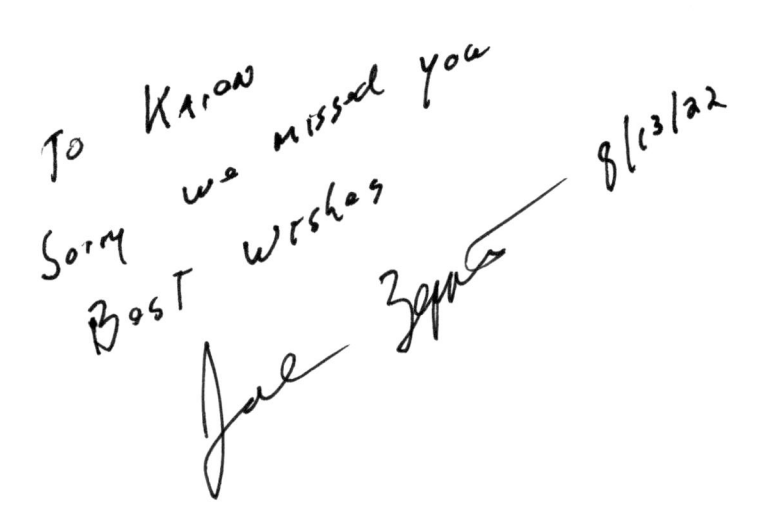

Copyright © 2020 by Joe Zeppetello

All rights reserved. No part of this book may be reproduced or transmitted in any form or by any means without written permission of the author and publisher.

This is a work of fiction. Any resemblance to actual persons, living or dead, is purely coincidental.

ISBN 13: 9781734685527

Library of Congress Control Number: 2020941041

Cover Photo By: Lyza Zeppetello

Cover layout © by All Things That Matter Press
Published in 2020 by All Things That Matter Press

Dedication

To my two sons, Eliah and Noah, who taught me patience.

Acknowledgements

I wish to thank Vicki Sarkisian and Ginny Perrin for reading and commenting on earlier versions of this work. I would also like to thank Annamaria Maciocia, Esq. for all the great hallway conversations we've had about law, politics, and life in general.

1

Monday, October 1, 10:30 AM

"Hello, Eric," Anne said as calmly as she could.

"I came to protect you," Eric said.

"I know. That's very nice of you to think of me."

"They're not being fair to you, Anne. They don't know you like I do."

"I agree, Eric, but you didn't need to bring the gun. Maybe you should put it down?"

"How else will I be able to protect you? How else will you know that I love you? That's my job. You've been asking me to protect you for all these months. I saw it in your eyes."

"I know, Eric," Anne said. He listened to her and something relaxed in him for a moment. He dropped his guard and lowered his weapon.

"Jesus Christ, Eric," April said. "You're a dammed idiot if you believe that. She's bullshitting you and you can't see it?" She had gotten her Walther PPK out of her handbag and was pointing it at Anne. "You can't see that she's playing you to save her own skin? She doesn't give a shit about you. She's just waiting for the police to get here, which is going to be very soon, judging by all the noise downstairs." Eric looked confused. Anne was astonished.

"I'm here to protect Anne," he said after a minute.

"Get real, Eric. You're such an idiot." April paused. "You need to shoot her. Can't you see that?" April said. Anne was still dumbfounded. April looked directly at Eric but was misreading him in a very dangerous way. "You shoot her, or I will, and they won't even suspect me," she said. "You're the nut with the gun in here, not me." She looked at Anne, who was completely paralyzed.

At this point, much to her own surprise, April's gun went off.

***

Nine Months Earlier

"They like their reality served cold in this apartment," Zoe Peters said to herself as she pulled on a sweater over her nude body. Fresh from the shower, she slipped the damp towel to her waist in her cold bedroom. She was talking softly to her boyfriend, Nick Mason, who was still asleep in bed. He'd spent the night, even though she'd hoped he'd go back to his place. Zoe was thinking seriously of making him her ex-boyfriend. He had accumulated far too much baggage over the past year for her to deal with, having already left a husband who had plenty of his own baggage, she needed to get ready for work. She shivered as she finished getting dressed.

As an attorney not long out of law school, and not the youngest in her graduating class, she went into family law, a euphemism for "nasty damn divorce." She remembered deciding to specialize in this field because of her own divorce that was triggered by her acceptance into law school. It had been made acrimonious by the attorneys who represented her and her ex-husband. Zoe decided that she would try to work out divorces that were mature, where the two parties sat down across from each other and worked things out in a calm and grown-up fashion. So far, she hadn't met with much success. The system was built to be adversarial, and that's how things usually went. While adversarial might be a good thing in criminal court, it tended to get "ugly for the sake of ugly" in family court. Zoe had notes for a particularly disagreeable pre-trial-hearing coming up later this morning sitting on her nightstand and had wanted a good night's sleep—alone. Nick had vetoed that, and she was a little angry with him, although the sex was always welcome.

Her coffee was too sweet this morning—she had forgotten about the spoon of sugar already in the cup and put in an extra one. She dumped it down the sink, made another cup, and sipped it while looking at the screen on her notebook and riffling through her handwritten notes checking the facts of the case. The case itself wasn't as bad as dealing with the opposing counsel who had a tendency for the dramatic, which was a little foolish, as the divorce laws in this state were clear and current. There wasn't a tremendous amount of room for negotiation. Sipping coffee, she reviewed the case again: there were two children, so the formula for child support was pretty clear, custody had already been determined, and there was some property that was held in common. However, Zoe knew that the husband was hiding a lot of income, and that's what the hearing was all about. Her forensic accountant had found more than one discrepancy, and she needed to get this on the record. The two clients owned a restaurant in common, and the main issue was how much money the restaurant made. It had given them both a good lifestyle, vacations in the Caribbean, private school for the kids, an enormous house. All of these were now on the table. It was like moving chess pieces in a game where the rules weren't always followed, and the cheaters didn't always get caught.

Her car was cold and damp. She had bought down, as her brother had put it. He wanted her to buy a Lexus or a Mercedes, something prestigious. Instead, she had bought a small hatchback because it got great mileage; it suited her. Her brother, Chris, drove a Ford pickup and worked in construction. "No one will trust a lawyer who drives an economy car," he had said. "They'll think you're not very good." She liked small cars because she was small. Her brother had gotten all the height and the size in the family. Chris was well over six feet tall, Zoe had gotten her mother's slim and petite figure, dark hair, and brown eyes that were almost as dark as her pupils. The joke was that her car stayed in the parking garage under the firm's office building. No one ever saw it.

She drove toward downtown, getting off the highway a few exits early. It was a lot faster to deal with the lights on Main Street than with the usual morning traffic jam on the highway. After swiping her card at the gate to the garage, she found a parking place near the main elevator and was in her office a half-hour before the firm opened. The only other person in the office was the office manager. She was sitting behind the reception desk checking the calendars for the attorneys and paralegals for the day on her massive monitor.

"Hi, Ms. Peters. How are you this morning?"

"Fine," she replied, "Holding down the fort I see."

"Yeah, someone has got to do it. You have a pre-trial this morning," she said, looking up from the screen, "with … oh!"

"Yes. I know."

"Sorry."

"Someone has got to do it," Zoe smiled and went to her office. Sitting in her leather chair, she pulled out her notebook and connected it to the office wireless. Most of the notes about the case were in her head already, but she pulled up a few documents that were still on the server.

"You here already?" Jimmy, her paralegal said as he arrived. He was fresh out of college and juggling more than one boyfriend. An excellent paralegal, but he tended to party, with his weekends starting somewhere around Thursday night. He had an extra dose of cologne on this morning, which meant he had probably gotten lucky last night and only had enough time to wash up this morning. "Morning, Zoe."

"Hi, Jimmy. I hope you weren't out too late last night. I'm counting on you."

"I'm fine," he said, holding up a huge disposable paper cup of coffee from a national chain store.

"You'd better be." Zoe went back to looking at the document on her screen and then printed it out. She had more than one strategy for today and this would be her backup plan. The two prepared for the hearing.

Their client arrived a few minutes early. She had dark rings under her eyes.

"Susan, would you like a cup of coffee?" Jimmy asked. She shook her head.

"I just want this over."

"If things go well today, it'll be downhill from here," Jimmy said. She sat in a chair and waited, holding a magazine, but not looking at it. Zoe called her into the office and went over some of the strategies.

"You know they're going to bring up the fact that you take antidepressants and that you've had psychotherapy. Let me respond to that, or simply say that you had some issues with depression, but that you had treatment and you're doing fine now. What we don't want are surprises. Any surprises you can possibly think of?"

"No. I went to a therapist for about a year after our youngest was born. I had problems with postpartum depression."

"Good. You say that, and don't volunteer anything else. They have to take our word for this because the records are private. The less on the record the better for us."

Jimmy knocked on the door and then poked his head in. "They're here, ladies."

Jimmy, Susan, and Zoe went to the conference room. A stenographer was setting up, getting ready to take notes. They had all met before so the introductions were a formality, and Susan just barely acknowledged her husband Frank. He looked away when she looked in his direction. John Raymond, opposing counsel, led off. He presented some medical records.

"Are these your records?"

"Those are privileged and private information," Zoe said.

"Not when your client signs a waiver." He produced the waiver. Zoe looked at it, and raised an eyebrow to Susan, who was staring at the desk, not making eye contact.

"Are these your records?" Raymond asked again.

"Yes," Susan nodded.

"Do you know what they say?" Susan nodded and started to tear up. "You need to speak up."

"Yes."

"Can you explain why you were under treatment for depression that left you in an almost catatonic state? This was at a time when you had three little children at home?"

"Postpartum depression. I believe it says so on the diagnosis." Susan was getting her voice back.

"For over a year?"

"Was that a question you want answered?"

"Is this a photograph of you?" He threw a 4x6 photo on the desk. Susan picked it up and turned white.

"Yes." Zoe looked at it. The photo was of Susan. It was grainy and probably had come from an Internet social media site. It was obvious she was smoking a joint.

"That photo was taken a month ago when you were at a party. Do you remember it?"

"Yes. I didn't think anyone was taking pictures for God's sake! It was a party."

That was the second surprise in ten minutes. Zoe was getting angry. She picked up the photo.

"It could be a cigarette."

"I know for a fact it wasn't," Frank chimed in.

"Really? How?" Before his attorney could stop him, he answered.

"Because a friend of mine was at the party. He took the picture and then put it on his Facebook."

"We'll need his name."

"Why?"

"Did he call the police?"

"No."

"Did you?"

"No."

"Why not? If you're so concerned that she has what looks like marijuana, and your whole case so far has been to try to show my client is an unfit mother, why didn't your friend or you report this crime? Why didn't you get the kids away from her right then and there?" Zoe paused. "Maybe you didn't because then you'd be stuck with them?"

"Is that a question you want answered?" Raymond asked.

"Maybe later. This photo could easily be bogus. It could have been Photoshopped for all I know. And since his friend posted it on his social media site, maybe there is some collusion going on here. Who knows?"

"I insist on entering it into the record."

"Do what you want. And I'll insist on getting an affidavit from the photographer, and then I'll insist that he and your client both be charged. If they were so concerned that people at that party were doing drugs, they should have called the police." Of course, she was bluffing, but the photo could sink her case. The judge they drew for this case, Franklin Barnum, was a distant relative of Ben Franklin, and he never passed up a chance to explain it after telling people his given name. The Barnums were part of a long convoluted genealogical bush that was more or less parallel to the offspring of one of the founding fathers, which led to the rumor that they were not exactly the legitimate heirs of Mr. Franklin, a man who was well known for his ability to seduce. In any case, Zoe knew that Barnum was an arrogant bastard who would flip out if he saw that picture, even though he'd been twice disciplined for being drunk on the bench. Once, she heard that he'd passed out and fallen off his chair, landing on his clerk. It was announced in the local paper that the judge was "taking a leave of absence for health reasons." The short article was just above the Police Beat that regularly announced all the people who'd been recently arrested for driving while intoxicated. Apparently, she thought, "Judging While Intoxicated" wasn't illegal.

"We'll take this off the table for now," Raymond said, and he slipped the photo into his thick file. Zoe knew that he couldn't be trusted. She was sure that the photo would probably end up in the file that went to the judge. There wasn't anything she could do about it now, but she made a note of it. Raymond went on for another hour or so with the evidence that he had. He was obviously trying to prove her to be an unfit mother as a way to bargain for custody rights, or to get her client to take less than she was entitled to for fear of losing her kids. Children made the best bargaining chips. Zoe had seen more than one client agree to some awful deals in order to get or maintain custody. Raymond was also trying to show that Frank was financially strapped because his business soaked up most of his capital, something the forensic accountants didn't agree with. They took a twenty-minute break after he was finished; Zoe was then to start her questions. Despite the three long hours of testimony, Raymond hadn't established anything that they hadn't already anticipated, except for the photo. Zoe was going to have a talk with Susan about that and a few other things, but this wasn't the time for that.

They began the session, and Zoe asked Frank a few quick questions about his finances.

"Is it true you own a house near Burnett Park?"

"The bank really owns it."

"According to the records, the mortgage is almost paid off."

"Well, it still costs money. The taxes are high."

"You claim you make less than thirty thousand a year from your business."

"That's about right. That's all I pay myself."

"Who pays your mortgage?"

"What?"

"Isn't it true that your mortgage, your children's school tuition, and your car payments all come out of your business, the Bourbon Street Café?"

"I wouldn't know."

"Well I do." Zoe produced a report that came from the accountant. "This shows that the thirty thousand you draw is basically spending money. Every other expense is paid for by your business, including three trips last year to your house in Aguadilla, Puerto Rico. Incidentally, your wife and kids didn't go with you."

"I had a lot of stress. Needed to get away." Frank was starting to sweat.

"I didn't ask you a question," Zoe said. She paused and let him squirm a little.

"Now, I want you to look at this. Let me know if this is your signature." Zoe produced a copy of a bill of sale. Frank looked at it, and his eyes narrowed. He sat back. Raymond looked puzzled.

"This is a bill of sale for a brand new Corvette. Notice it says, 'paid in cash.' The dealership had to file a report for such a large transaction. Didn't you know that? The government requires any transaction of over $10,000 to be reported."

"That is a company car. It was bought with company money," Raymond said as he tried to limit the damage.

"A $75,000 Corvette is a company car? I'll let the judge figure that out. I guess you must use it to deliver pizzas. By the way, here's a copy of the withdrawal form. It came from Frank's private account, not the business account. He's certainly saved up a lot of money for someone who only makes thirty thousand a year." She paused. "One more item we need cleared up," Zoe said, moving on to the document she'd found this morning. She pulled out a loan application. Is this your signature?" Frank looked at it and nodded. Again, Raymond was puzzled.

"This is an application for a $500,000 equity loan against the property in Burnett Park. Is that property co-owned with your wife, Susan?"

"Yes." Frank was noticeably quiet.

"Is this her signature on the application?" Frank looked closely, trying to find something to say. "It looks like hers."

"Not really. In fact, she was visiting a friend about 200 miles away on this day. We know because you tried to renege on your visitation with your kids after she'd made her travel plans. I have an affidavit from the bank officer claiming that the woman who signed this paper is a tall brunette, who bears a strong resemblance to your girlfriend, Amy. The same person who, it seems, has been driving your new company Corvette around town. Is she delivering pizzas now? Need I tell you that forging a document like this is a felony?"

"I didn't get the damn loan anyway," Frank said.

"Thank your lucky stars. The bank would have had you arrested for fraud if you did—both you and your girlfriend." The rest of the pre-trial went routinely. Zoe caught Frank in a couple of more flat-out lies, but Susan hadn't helped her case either, so they were just a little ahead when they broke in the late afternoon. Zoe had wanted a slam dunk, with Frank ready to sign on her terms. They weren't there yet. In her office, Zoe told Susan to close the door.

"I had asked you about any surprises. Why didn't you tell me about the therapist's hospital records?"

"They told me I had to sign the release for my health records, or I wouldn't be able to see my kids and that I could be sent to the State Hospital for observation."

"Who told you that?"

"My first lawyer. Before I hired you." This wasn't the first time Zoe had picked up a case from an incompetent attorney. In fact, a twenty-four hour observation could have helped her case right now, would have gotten the whole depression issue on the record in a more favorable light than it was. People with mental health issues should seek help, but if they do, it's the first thing used against them in a divorce case, or in a job search, or in any other way the people can use it.

"And the party?"

"It was stupid, a weekend that Frank had the kids. I needed to relax. I was with a bunch of friends that we have in common. Frank wasn't going to be there, so I thought it would be okay to let my hair down."

"You can't relax. You can't let your guard down, not for a minute, not until this is over. I can do some damage control, but you need to get yourself together. Pronto."

"Sorry." She seemed ready to burst into tears.

"Hey. It'll be all right. We just have some more work to do. That business with the car and the loan is good leverage. It gave us some bargaining power. I think they both were floored that we knew. I'll see what Raymond offers us."

9

Zoe was home that evening. Her cell phone rang; it was Nick. She let it go to voicemail. The day had been okay, but still frustrating. She'd hoped that Susan's case would be all but settled by now, but she knew that there would still be some hurdles. Well, she thought, I've done all I can. I can't take the work home with me. She poured a glass of red wine and turned on the TV. She wanted to be alone tonight, maybe watch a stupid movie on TV and just relax. She texted Nick and told him not to come over and got an immediate reply: "Y?" She sent back to him that she was too tired and wanted to go to bed early. He texted that it was "K." For some reason this pissed her off. "It damn well better be okay," she said out loud. "It's the way it's going to be. God, when did he get so … weird? He used to be fun." She sipped some more wine and gazed at the movie. It was an old black and white, but not a good one, an overly melodramatic film noir from the 1950s, so melodramatic that it was accidently funny by today's standards. This was fine with her. She wasn't too choosy tonight, just didn't want to think about anything. Zoe fell asleep on the couch, her glass of wine still half full on the coffee table.

2

Nick Mason had been listening to the radio on the drive to work. He knew Zoe was mad at him but wasn't sure why. She'd had a case that was really getting to her, and he was trying to be supportive, but she had been remote and didn't pick up last night when he'd called. Her text was almost rude. He knew she didn't want to be crowded, but he'd only gone over once last week and had been away on business the week before. He couldn't help it if his schedule only left him a couple of days to be with her; they always seemed to be the wrong days. Things had been fun at first, basically dinners, movies, and sex, but he knew they'd changed in the past few months and wasn't quite sure why. He went to his office and noticed the light was flashing on his phone, and his e-mail box had a load of new messages. He'd been ignoring his messages this morning as he had needed to sleep in a little later than normal and wanted to eat breakfast in peace.

Now he had to deal with panicky clients who'd been leaving him messages since late last night. Nick had been the top salesman for TrendInventions before they'd put him in charge of all the sales representatives for the company. He still had his own clients but was also responsible for making sure the other reps were making their quotas and pushing new products. Nick was a born salesman. He made you feel good about buying from him and could easily talk a client into doubling an order. As he breezed through his email and messages, he wondered how some of the people in charge of multimillion-dollar businesses had gotten there. They seemed to panic at the least little issue but ignored important problems or explained them away. They certainly had all been to the same school. It didn't take too long to straighten up the few real problems and to smooth over the stuff that didn't matter anyway.

He checked to see if there was any snail mail in his box in the mailroom. There were a few promotional brochures for equipment he never used or didn't need, and he found two letters from clients who still used the mail instead of email or messaging. He had to schedule some meetings with the staff to bring them up to speed on the new products for the season, but that could wait.

"Anything good? Any checks?" Eric, the computer expert from the CFO's office, was looking over his shoulder.

"No. Never any checks here, just bills. How are you doing, Eric?"

"Fine. They've been riding me hard and putting me away wet this week. It's the end of the fiscal year and everyone wants to spend down their budgets."

"That reminds me," Nick joked.

"Oh God, not you, too?"

"No. I'm set for the time being."

"You have any lunch plans?"

"No. I thought I'd meet Zoe, but she's busy today." Nick didn't want to tell him that she hadn't returned a message since yesterday.

"Lawyers are always busy. Nature of the job."

"Yeah. Where do you want to go?"

"Lindy's? It's good and cheap enough for a lowly office drone. You used to be one of us before you went over to the dark side, management."

"I eat there all the time. See if anyone else wants to go. I haven't seen the old gang for a while. The dark side doesn't pay that well, either."

"So you say." Eric laughed. He left, and Nick went back to his office to attack the pile of orders on his desk.

***

The restaurant wasn't that busy. There had been a bunch of layoffs in many of the businesses in the area, and people who still had jobs were being thrifty. Nick saw Eric sitting at a booth and could see the back of Anne's head, the CEO/CFO, and the owner of the company. He had hoped for a men's club for lunch, but Anne was also a pleasant surprise. They'd been good friends from when he'd first started. She'd encouraged him to apply for the sales director's job when it had come up and had been far less surprised than he was when he'd gotten it. Although Anne was his age, she carried herself as if she were older. Fair-haired, blue-eyed, and attractive, she had spent most of her life working against the classic blonde stereotype, and more than one person had found out the hard way to not underestimate her. She'd liked Nick immediately because he'd never played that game with her. There were still plenty of men who had problems with women bosses, especially women CEOs; Nick wasn't one of them.

"Hi, Nick. How's it going?"

"Fine, Anne. I see you haven't fired Eric yet."

"He's been doing fine—so far."

"Gee, thanks you two," Eric said. Nick sat down and looked at the menu. It never changed, even though he'd not been there in over a month. He spent most of his time in his office or on the road and lunch out had become a luxury. He knew that Anne wasn't here by accident, either. If anything, she was even busier than he was. They ordered food and made small talk. They chatted about the things that friends from work talk about, office gossip, work, family, and friends. Their meals arrived, and they continued making small talk, and Nick was beginning to wonder if he had misread the whole thing and that maybe this was only a lunch with friends from work.

"I was wondering if you could do me a little favor," Anne asked. Her eyes shifted a little and seemed to change color slightly.

"I might. What's up?"

"I'm thinking of leaving Michael."

This wasn't news to Nick. Their problems went way back to when Nick worked more closely with her. The biggest problem, though, was that they each had a huge stake in the company. Michael oversaw project development, and the two of them had founded TrendInventions together. Michael was an inventive wizard who had a knack for dreaming things up that people didn't even know they needed. The kinds of items you would find in SkyMall, Hammacher Schlemmer, or Sharper Image. Anne had been the one to secure funding and make sure investors left Michael alone to invent, and that no one stole their designs. They made an excellent team.

"So?"

"I was wondering if you could talk to Zoe. She's the best. I don't want this to get messy, and it must be handled quietly. It could chase away investors, and we don't need that right now." Nick knew she was right. The company was quirky at best and had run counter to almost any reasonable business plan; investors would run if they thought that the "dream team" was breaking up. "I have no plans to go anywhere. I just want to get out on my own. I love Michael, but I can't live with him anymore. This has to be very discreet. I don't even dare go to Zoe's office right now. No one can find out until it's over."

"I'm not sure if I have that kind of influence with her. In fact, I'm not sure if we are still going out. But I will talk to her." As soon as she returns my calls, Nick said to himself.

He wasn't going to even bother Zoe for a while, but since he'd promised Anne that he would talk to her, he sent Zoe a text message and asked her if she wanted to go out on Friday for dinner, maybe go to a club for some fun, which was, of course, what she wanted to hear. He had come very close to asking her if she wanted him to come over with a movie and a bottle of wine on Friday, which would have gotten no response at all. She simply replied with the letter "K," leaving the rest of what she might want to say unsaid. There were times she much preferred communicating with a text message to a phone call. For one thing, it could take up a lot less time. If she really wanted to talk to someone, she was not shy about sitting face to face and letting someone know exactly how she felt. The short reply was not lost on Nick, and he still wondered what he could have done to make her so angry. He resolved to ask her point blank on Friday night what was wrong.

His desk phone rang, and he had a slew of e-mails that had arrived while he was at lunch. He also had a dozen new text messages on his cell, and a client from Europe wanted to video chat, and it was already getting late over there. The afternoon was going to be busy.

3

Zoe was working late in her office. It had been another marathon day, and she had just about finished for the week. She had a date with Nick tonight, and she didn't want to be late. They needed to have some fun together, even though she wasn't sure what she wanted from him. She put the files she needed to finish by Monday on her notebook and logged off her office server. No one was in the office; Jimmy had left early. He was enthralled with a new boyfriend. When she got to her apartment, it was almost time to meet Nick. She showered, dressed quickly, and then drove to the restaurant. They always took their own cars and met wherever they were going. She thought of this as a form of insurance, and she was sure that Nick did, too. The restaurant was crowded, and she saw Nick at a small table in the corner. She waved off the hostess and walked to the table. Nick smiled when he saw her, got up, and pulled out her chair. She liked it when he did that, although her mother, a second-wave feminist, would have had a fit at such chauvinism. The waiter came right over, and she ordered a gin and tonic. Nick looked surprised; Zoe usually started an evening with white wine, or champagne.

"How's everything?" Nick asked while sipping a glass of red wine.

"Not bad. I think we finally caught a break in the case."

"Really? Raymond stopped being an asshole?"

"No. That wouldn't be possible. He was born that way, it's terminal."

"A terminal asshole?"

"Yeah. Anyway, he called up and made us an offer that's not too bad. I just want them to back down on the house issue. He wants to let Susan live in it until the kids are over twenty-one and then sell it and split the proceeds. I think she should get to keep it since she helped with the business until they started having kids. Everything else they gave us, and they backed off from the unfit mother nonsense."

"You must have scared the shit out of them."

"A possible charge of fraud and the fact he might have to sell his girlfriend's new toy really moved them along."

"Good. Sounds like this one might work out, too." He lifted his glass. "If I ever get divorced, I want you to be my attorney."

"You need to get married first."

"True." He tipped his glass to her, and then sipped more wine. The food began to arrive. They were both hungry, so they ate and made very little conversation. Nick ordered a dessert, and Zoe ordered a cup of coffee. At the end of dinner, he mentioned Anne, and the fact that she wanted Zoe to handle her case.

"No way! I'm not ready for a case like that. It's a multimillion-dollar business they have, with a bunch of private investors."

"You could do it," Nick said, eating his dessert.

"I'm not that sure. I'm not even sure the partners would let me take the case. This could get tied up for a long time, cost a lot of money and resources. We're not that big of a firm."

"Well. You don't have to decide right now. This has been an ongoing issue since I started there five years ago. She might even change her mind. Although I think this is for real now."

"Why do you say that?"

"Because she and Eric had been having an affair for over a year, but they broke up a while ago. Not Eric's idea. He looks like a lost puppy when he's around her. However, their affair lasted a lot longer than the affair she had with me." He smiled. "Eric's a lot better looking, though," he said while finishing the last bit of dessert and coffee. "You want to go check out a movie?"

"No, he's not, and yes, a movie sounds fine. That's a bit of a shock."

"Not really, not if you've ever met Michael. I'm astonished they even got together in the first place. Love is blind," Nick said, and signaled for the check.

They rode over to the Cinemaplex in his car. If she had driven over herself, it would have meant she'd decided to go home alone after the movie. They drove for a while in silence.

"I thought we'd talk about us during dinner," Nick said.

"We neatly avoided that, didn't we?"

"Well we can't avoid it forever."

"You're right," Zoe sighed a little. "I've been a bit preoccupied with this case, but I also don't want to be crowded. My ex-husband was the king of passive aggressive crowding. He would have crowded me out of my own life had I let him. I don't want a needy relationship. You pissed me off when you stayed over the other night."

"I know. But I hadn't been around for a week. I don't see that as crowding."

"Yeah. Bad timing. Just leave me my space, you know. I don't want any baggage at all. That was our agreement: dinners, movies, dancing, and sex, no commitment, no family, no complaining, and no bullshit."

"Okay. Look, you don't even have to go the same movie I do if you don't want to. I'll just meet you later in the parking lot." He smiled. She hit him on the shoulder.

"Funny guy. You're a really funny guy. For that we have to go to a chick flick."

"Bitch."

"Damn straight."

4

Michael Mali was not normal. Not even in the trendy version of the "new normal," was he normal. Michael was in his shop, a huge room in the basement of their 7,000-square-foot house. He'd been playing with some Legos, strips of plastic, and foam board, testing out a new idea he had. He'd built a few models of a new gadget that would hold a cold drink and a sandwich while floating around in a hot tub. It would refrigerate the drink so the heat from the tub wouldn't warm it up. This would go well with his waterproof TV. Most of his inventions were in support of at least two of the Seven Deadly Sins—Sloth and Gluttony. There seemed to be no end of demand for gadgets that catered to or even promoted vices. He was working hard so as not to think, and he didn't want to think about Anne. He knew she was getting ready to ask him for a divorce. She'd made it clear the other day, but then they both got busy with work. Michael wasn't shocked. He sort of knew it was coming, that she wasn't happy, but still didn't like the idea. He suddenly thought of how he could power the new tray with a rechargeable battery that would last a long time if the cooling coils for the cup holder were shielded with some space-age insulating foam. He drew quickly, making some calculations in his head and then with a scientific calculator. He would have the details sent to fabrication so they could make up a working prototype. Now, he wondered, how big is the average sandwich? Should I refrigerate the whole tray, or just the cupholder?

Later that day Michael sat in front of the swimming pool playing an Internet video game with a group of elite players from around the world. His phone rang. He looked at the number for a minute and then picked up.

"Hi," Michael said.

"Oh. Hi. I was just getting ready to hang up."

"Sorry. I didn't hear the phone ring."

"Do you want to see me tonight?"

"Hmm. I've got a ton of work to do."

"Oh. Okay. I just thought we could check out a new bar. There's one that just opened, and they've gotten some hot reviews."

"No. Not tonight. Sounds cool, though."

"Am I bothering you?"

"No," Michael said, looking at the video game on his screen.

"Okay. Call me back?" There was a long pause. "Okay?"

"Sure. I'll call you tomorrow. Promise."

"Okay. Bye."

"Bye." Michael hung up the phone. It was late in the afternoon and the game was getting full of newbies, people who still hadn't gotten used to the rules and played without any real strategy. As more people came on the server to play, they actually slowed the game down, so he logged off, put on his 3-D glasses, switched to a game he had loaded on the computer, and was fully engrossed when Anne came home.

"Did you eat anything, Michael?"

"I think so. Maybe. Can't remember," he said, while wailing on the controller, trying to launch an attack against the latest adversary the game was throwing at him.

"Maybe you should shut that down."

"In a minute."

Anne sighed and went to the kitchen. Their housekeeper had left a sandwich for Michael wrapped up in the refrigerator. Anne put it on a plate, poured a glass of fruit juice, put them on a tray and took them over to Michael. He stopped long enough to take a large bite out of the sandwich, gulp some juice, and then resumed playing his video game. Anne put her dinner in the microwave.

Work had been exceptionally tough; it seemed that every financial aspect of the company had an issue today. They were a privately held limited partnership and had taken on several investors when they expanded the company, which they needed to do to raise money. However, some of the investors had been getting a little worried lately because the economy had been so bad. One investor in particular wanted her to cut back the labor force. She was fighting against this as they had a very good crew that worked well together, and she didn't want to have to hire and train all new people later on when things got better. As it was, the morale was low because all hiring and promotions were frozen. Some of the partners seemed to think that if they let people go, those same people would sit around waiting to be rehired, like frozen dinners in a freezer waiting to be microwaved. It didn't work that way, not for the good ones, anyway.

She'd had no idea how to run a company when she and Michael had started TrendInventions. Her major in college had been English literature, but she had always had a knack for dealing with people, and she'd learned about the money end of the business out of self-preservation. She had become as good with the finances as anyone with an MBA. Michael was a child when it came to money. Lately, he'd been a spoiled child about nearly everything else, or maybe it was her just realizing it. He could have always been like that, and all she saw, or had allowed herself to see, was the inventive boy-genius part of his personality, not the rest. He was hiding from her and she knew this. He didn't want to even talk about the issues that she had laid out about a month ago. When Michael wanted to avoid something, he simply made sure that he was too busy to engage the problem, too busy doing something, working late, or "busy" with his video games. She was losing patience but was too tired tonight to deal with any more confrontations today.

She remembered when they'd first brought investors onboard that she had been very leery of opening their business to strangers but knew they couldn't go to the next level without capital. The company had suddenly been deluged with orders from big distributors, and they needed to tool up extremely fast. Most of the new investors were content to leave her and Michael alone to run things. The company had made money right from the start, and the return on investment was very solid so everyone was happy. Then the economy went down the tubes with the crash, and now there was one person, a retired surgeon, who was beginning to micromanage, and he was becoming a real pain in the ass. Anne could see his concern if the business had not been doing well, but they had managed to keep sales up for the last three quarters despite the bad economy. Today he'd been taking up far too much time in her office with his half-baked ideas about running the company that he got from his friends on the golf course. She had told him that he was welcome to pull his money out of the partnership, a gamble to get him to shut up, but she knew he couldn't get the percentage return on investment that Trendinventions was paying him. He'd left her office without saying a word, but she wasn't sure what he was going to do.

This was one more thing she really didn't need to deal with. If he pulled his money out and the news got out that she was seeing a divorce attorney, it could make all the other investors bolt. Anne had already started the process of taking the company public, but offering public stock wasn't something she was in a hurry to do. Although the IPO could get them a good chunk of money, the economy was so bad that the stock might not sell even with a good company. She knew that TrendInventions was idiosyncratic, so the investors services might not know how to rate them, and she was very leery of suddenly having a bunch of stockholders to deal with. But they might not be worse than the limited partnership.

She sat down with her dinner and switched on the huge TV. Sound filled the room as a movie came on that she had recorded a couple of days before. She entered the space of the movie and ate her dinner. Michael went to the next level on his video game, uttering a shout and jumping out of his chair. He took a short break to finish his sandwich and wash it down with the rest of the juice, then resumed playing, hoping to beat the game by midnight.

5

Zoe was at the office working out some of the details for Susan's divorce. She was also juggling two more cases that threatened to turn sour. One, the O'Hare case, had started off well, but suddenly her client's estranged wife had started getting very abusive, even childish. Her latest habit was to go into the basement while he was working in his home office and shut off the circuit breakers so his computer and his phones would shut off. Since his consulting business was their sole means of support, this was stupid even for the most spiteful.

Ken O'Hare wasn't sure why his wife suddenly got this way. She had been amicable up to this point especially about his using the home office for his work. He couldn't afford to move out or rent an office someplace else, but Zoe could tell he wasn't giving her the whole story, either. He couldn't afford to move anywhere at this time because the business he had run from his home had not been doing well of late. However, his business had recovered enough so that in another month or so he would be able to afford an apartment. His wife had been content with this arrangement until now. She also hadn't wanted to fight over the house and seemed to be happy with the settlement.

Zoe wondered what was up. Did Kristen O'Hare finally figure out that this divorce was real? Or maybe she had broken up with her boyfriend, or just needed a reality check, or maybe one of her friends told her she could have gotten a better deal even though her arrangement was very generous? Many people who had never seen the inside of a law school, or cracked a law book, were good at giving free legal advice, especially when it came to divorce. And people would believe without hesitation the most counterintuitive, idiotic assertions. One of her clients had maxed out all her credit cards because a friend of hers told her she would never have to pay them off—after the divorce everything would be wiped clean. Someone obviously had divorce confused with bankruptcy. This part of the job you didn't learn in law school, how to be a counselor and deal with incredibly stupid and self-destructive behavior. Zoe knew there were two sides to the story, but was continually amazed at how hard people could make things for themselves and how much money they were willing to pay her to settle issues that they could talk out in an hour or so. Most of what she did was try to talk people into using some common sense. Much of the time, though, it didn't work. Law school hadn't prepared her for that, either.

Jimmy, her paralegal, walked into her office, tapping on her door.

"Busy?" He asked.

"Sure. But what's up?"

"I was going over the pre-trial in the O'Hare case, and I think I came up with something." He paused. "She was really cooperative until two weeks ago, right? We went over credit card bills to get a figure on their debt and who would owe what to whom when the financial issues were settled." He scrolled through the sheets of papers. "This is when she saw his credit card receipts." Jimmy pulled out a sheet of paper, "And she must have seen this." Among the list of charges were bills for a motel room.

"Oh yeah. I guess that would piss her off," Zoe said scrutinizing the bill. It was for a motel on the highway, just outside of town. "A bit hypocritical of the little princess, though."

"You mean because the whole thing started because she has a boyfriend?" Jimmy smiled. "Minor detail," Jimmy said. "Why is it you straight people can't seem to control yourselves? Sex, sex, sex. That's all that's on your minds." Zoe smiled. There was no law against adultery in this state, and no one used it as grounds for a divorce anymore. For this reason, they'd filed under "irreconcilable differences," and no one had really mentioned the boyfriend, but if she thought no one else knew about her affair, she was living in a parallel universe. Maybe she was nice before because of guilt but now felt she could be her real self. In any case, she was costing both of them a lot of money, and she was being an idiot. This is where Zoe was a very good attorney. Instead of letting this go on and bleeding her client dry, she called him on the phone and let him know her suspicions. He'd been a little too stupid himself here, but maybe he could have a sit-down with Kristen before she cost them all of what they had left of the equity on their house and the rest of their savings. She felt there was about a fifty-fifty chance. No one could be more outraged than a cuckolded cheating spouse.

Zoe checked her calendar and got ready for her next meeting. Anne Mali was on her schedule. Jimmy had done his usual thorough job of research. He seemed to already know a lot about this case, even though it had just been referred to her. Zoe had spoken to the partners, and they agreed that the case was big but were willing to give it a try. The partnership was, after all, a business, and this could certainly make a little "rain" even if it was a relatively smooth divorce, not to mention the free publicity when it did go public, which it would. Zoe was still reading the brief when Anne arrived for the meeting.

"We're not a big law firm," Zoe said right after the introductions. "I'm not sure if we're your best bet, especially since there is a pretty large business involved."

"I know. It's just that I want someone who I feel like I know. You're a friend of Nick's, and I trust him," Anne replied, and then said, "It's weird. Maybe you're right. I'm at a loss, really."

"Well. I'll just let you know what I think. If you feel comfortable, then we can draw up a binder," Zoe paused. "We need to decide on the grounds."

Anne sighed, "I'm just tired of being his mom, his nurse, and his big sister all rolled into one."

"Irreconcilable differences would be the best way to go. The law gives you half of all the property, and that's clear cut. Few judges would agree to anything different. There are no children, so no child support. The business complicates things, but everything is on the record, and it's a matter of determining the total worth. Do you want to stay on as an owner, or do you think he should buy you out? Or maybe you can buy him out?"

"I hadn't thought that far ahead. I planned on working. I can't leave him on his own. He'd get eaten alive."

"This can be decided on down the road." Zoe looked at her, thinking maybe the problem of a clean separation wasn't just with Michael. "You first need to agree that I will be your attorney, and then we file. He has a certain number of days to respond. Depending on how he and his attorney respond, things can then start moving along. If no one gets foolish, we can get the paperwork finished in a few months, and then it goes to the judge. This will be a combination divorce and a separation of the assets of your business, even if you stay on as CEO/CFO, so I'll need to hire a lot of specialists. That will get expensive."

Anne got up from the chair and shook Zoe's hand. She agreed to sign a six-figure retainer. It made Zoe a little afraid just to look at the number. She knew that it would require all the help she had and some specialists as she had mentioned, but they also would need to hire a few extra clerks and paralegals just for this case. She also had an odd vibe from Anne. She'd seen relationships like this before, where one spouse acted like the "adult" and the other was the "kid." Usually the adult got tired of the role after a few years and wanted an equal partner, intellectually and sexually, but she'd also seen a disturbing element of enabling. Sometimes the adult partner would purposely infantilize the other in order to make them dependent or keep them infantilized to control them. Zoe knew that if this was the case, then Anne might be one of those who "files, but never finishes." She might use the divorce proceedings as a way to control Michael, like threatening with a big stick—the, "Mommy's gonna leave if you don't behave!" gambit. Zoe hoped that Anne wasn't one who would go in that direction. That could get very messy and very annoying, a lot of work for nothing. She made a note to ask Jimmy to do a little more investigating into their relationship. She wanted to know as much as possible about both Michael and Anne Mali, and their *child*, TrendInventions.

After lunch, Zoe was in Judge Hudson's chambers with the second case she had been working on that day. He'd been the local district attorney for several years until he'd managed to attain a state supreme court appointment, mostly by raising money for the current governor's campaign while he was still the state attorney general. The judge was busy doing a crossword puzzle, and Zoe was trying to focus his attention on a case that had been sitting on his desk for months. He'd just asked her for the second time why she wanted an appointment, even though it had been clear in the letter she'd sent, her numerous phone calls, and was on his appointment calendar.

"Judge Hudson, I was thinking that the Mirin case should be just about finished since we filed it a few months ago. All parties are in agreement, and you said you'd sign off."

"Hmm. Mirin? I'm not sure if I remember that one," he said, while scrutinizing the crossword. "An eight-letter word meaning judge…," he said out loud.

Dickhead? Zoe thought to herself. "Maybe, 'reviewer'?" She volunteered, smiling, and flashing her large brown eyes. Sometimes that worked with Hudson. She should have worn something that showed more cleavage, she thought. He wrote down the word.

"It works fine." He put the puzzle down and smiled back at her, "Mirin case?"

"Yes. We were hoping you could sign the papers so we can close it. Like I said, everyone is in agreement." Even your drinking buddy, Josh Mirin, she wanted to add; the reason why the case had been held up so long, simple spite. Friends of the judge got all sorts of favors. As far as she knew, it wasn't even old-fashioned corruption. He never asked for a dime from anyone, just liked playing the big shot. Some people have power only so they can abuse it, and Judge Hudson was one of those people. Both parties in the case had long since separated, and Mirin's wife and kids were living in another state. She also knew that Josh Mirin wanted to marry his new babe, mainly because she was pregnant, although, that wasn't the impetus it used to be. Zoe had found out about the pending newborn and knew that Josh had spoken to his good old drinking buddy and told him it was okay to go ahead with the divorce only because Jimmy was a genius at getting information. Hudson not signing the papers was simply his playing the bigshot, and, as usual, being an asshole.

"Hmm. Okay. Just have my secretary pull the paperwork, and I'll be glad to sign it."

"I have it right here." Zoe pulled the decree out of her briefcase and handed the judge a pen. He signed it and went back to his puzzle. Like most self-important bullies, since he couldn't be an annoyance anymore, he immediately lost interest. Zoe took the papers herself to the County Clerk's office for filing, a job usually left up to the newest paralegal or office assistant. She called Sarah Rakov, she had already dropped her married name, Mirin, to let her know that the papers were finally signed and filed.

"Really?" She said, "It's almost anticlimactic, but it's great. When will it be official?"

"It's official now. But the certified documents will take a few weeks to get to you."

"What persuaded Hudson to finally sign?"

"Nothing in particular. I think he just got bored and moved on, probably screwing over bigger fish than you, no offense."

"None taken. Maybe he finally figured that I wouldn't sleep with him no matter what," Sarah said.

"No!"

"Yes. He bugged me forever, showed up at all hours right up until the night before the kids and I moved. He came over with a bottle of wine and asked if he could help me pack."

"You're kidding."

"Nope. Just ask Tracey. That's how she got her divorce so fast, even if she happened to have been married to one of Hudson's golfing buddies. Sex trumps friendship any day. At least it trumps golf. He's honest, though," Sarah added. "If you sleep with him, you get your divorce quickly, quid pro quo."

"I did wonder how that happened," Zoe said, remembering the speed of that case, although it was handled by another attorney. It had set some sort of unofficial record with Hudson.

"Now you know. Thanks a bunch, Zoe. I gotta go. Soccer practice waits for no one."

"Bye," Zoe said to a dead phone. She was walking back to the office when she realized it was the end of the day. She called Jimmy's office phone, but he'd already left. She'd wanted to share the latest gossip about Hudson. It was probably not news to him, though. God, she thought, as she started her car and drove out of the parking garage, sometimes I can be so naïve.

6

Nick had awakened early in his hotel room Saturday, in Millbred, NY. He wasn't great at traveling because he liked to sleep in his own bed. Even when he stayed overnight at Zoe's he'd get up early because the room would be unfamiliar, or the bed didn't feel right. He'd wrapped up his business here early but had one more day before he needed to fly back home. Changing his plane reservations would cost him more than the hotel room. The flight was short, about an hour, and he could have driven or taken the train, but flying was the most convenient. It was a pleasant enough hotel in the heart of town, although not much of a town. The place had been really something just after the Civil War, when the latest works of Mark Twain were new, but had long since fallen on tough times. The main street was lined with nineteenth-century Victorians and early twentieth-century Greek revival and neoclassical buildings. There were a few large abandoned factories made of brick. One had been a pocketbook manufacturer, and the pocketbooks had become a rare collector's item. One section of it was in the process of being renovated to become a microbrewery. They had offered free samples of the different beers they were going to feature, and he'd sampled some. He had been polite and smiled at the owners but hoped their brewmaster would get a little more practice before they opened.

This was one of Nick's first really large orders. It was surprising that they still did business this way. He was happy to come in person to visit to take an order and bring them up to speed on the new items scheduled to come out next season. TrendInventions basically sold expensive toys for people with plenty of disposable income. Affluent people from a nearby city had discovered the place and were gradually buying up much of the town and renovating it. This was certainly better than the previous practice that had reigned since the Korean War: slumlords would cut up the large buildings into smaller and smaller apartments, run them into the ground, and then burn the places down for the insurance.

A small country store in the heart of town sold more of his merchandise than some of the online catalogue companies he dealt with.

Nick had met with the owners, two men who had been together since they'd met in the Navy. One was the guy who handled most of the business end of the store, while the other seemed to have a gift for picking out what would sell. One partner pored over the catalogues, making various noises and exclamations while looking at the new merchandise, while the other looked over his shoulder. He chuckled at the remote-controlled rubber ducky that could swim around a pool or hot tub and carry a twenty-ounce drink. They put together an order that made Nick a little dizzy and regretted that he didn't get a commission like he used too. But his salary was more than generous.

He looked at the other merchandise in the store. It was crammed with quality products being a country store in name only. There was a section that had a very high-end artificial Christmas tree decorated with all sorts of elaborate Victorian-style ornaments and the latest in LED Christmas lights. The display was set up year-round. They carried every trendy item that you could read about in any fashion magazine or Sunday supplement including World Wildlife Fund stuffed animals to imported Italian hand-painted porcelain tiles and Venetian glass. Their clientele obviously wanted exclusive, high quality items, and had the disposable income to match their taste.

After finishing the order, Nick walked down the street which had newly opened antique shops and galleries that carried everything someone would need to outfit a weekend home or decorate an urban apartment. He went to a bookstore and looked around, thinking he'd buy something to read later in the hotel room. The store had many of the popular bestsellers and a collection of books written by local writers. He chose a crime/mystery novel thick enough to promise a good afternoon of reading.

When he'd first realized he'd had a whole day in front of him without any plans, he thought of calling Zoe, but then thought better of it. With her moodiness and her outright hostility the week before, he wasn't sure where their relationship was going, but he knew that she wasn't up for a call and chat conversation. She might never be that kind of person, which, in a way, was fine with him. He liked her hard-headed approach to life; he'd had enough of the romantic and spacey with his previous companion. They'd lived together for about three years until she decided that she needed to become more spiritual after reading a popular book on mysticism written by a self-styled stock-broker-turned-guru. When he told her he thought the book was a load of bullshit, she moved out, telling him he was too materialistic. He later found out she had moved only a few blocks away and was living with an ex-prizefighter who had snake tattoos coiling around his neck. Apparently, according to his friends, she had been seeing the guy off and on for the last year of their relationship. Nick was quite sure that the new boyfriend wasn't altogether that into mysticism, he seemed to be much more of a pragmatist: into booze, fights, and sex, probably in that order. He hadn't been that surprised when she had left. The last year had been rocky, and now he knew why. He was just surprised at where she went.

Nick picked up a crime novel after reading the blurbs on the back and paid the used paperback price for it marked in pencil on the inside cover. Although he knew to take the overly excited blurbs full of exclamation points with a grain of salt, he also knew that no one would put a blurb like "Trite, stale, and boring! With a predictable plot and wooden two-dimensional characters! Pass up this piece of crap!" on the back of any book, no matter how true. He bought a cup of coffee and a donut, and then walked to the park to sit and read. This was the nice thing about this small city. He felt safe in the park. At home he'd always have his radar on, even during the day, making sure that no one was approaching too closely, and of course he'd never dream of going out to the park after dark. In this place he was sure that the park was safe no matter what the time.

The novel was the usual crime novel, too much plot; it would make a great action movie. It was amazing how many things could happen to one guy in the course of a day. Nick wondered when the poor protagonist had time to eat, or sleep, or even take a shower without getting shot at or beaten up, although he did seem to have plenty of time for the random, opportunistic sexual encounter.

***

The day was warm, and he sat reading and sipping coffee. A soft blue ball about the size of a soccer ball knocked the book out of his hands, banged into his coffee cup, and landed in his lap. For a moment he had no idea what had just happened, and then he looked up. A boy of about four was staring at him. He looked anxious and a woman about Nick's age with long wavy hair was running toward the boy and angling in their direction. He could see she was concerned. She met up with the boy and grabbed his hand and then dragged him over to where Nick was sitting.

"You pick up that book and apologize to this man. I told you not to kick the ball like that!"

The little boy picked up the book that had fallen on the ground. A page had torn out of it, and it was damp with coffee; he looked as if he desperately wanted to disappear.

"What do you say?" the woman asked the boy.

"Sorry about your book, Mister."

"It's okay," Nick said, taking the book from the little boy and sticking the page back in. "I just bought it for something to read. It's not really that good." He was talking more to the woman than the little boy.

"Sorry. He just won't listen. He got that ball about a week ago, and now he's obsessed with it. I can't tell you how many times I told him to watch out before he kicked it. His older brother taught him how to drop kick."

"It's okay, really." Nick handed the boy back his ball.

"Now Bobby, you be careful with that."

"Okay, Mom," he said as he booted the ball toward some bushes and tore off at top speed.

"It will tire him out enough for a nap. I can't wait until school starts."

"Preschool?"

"Kindergarten. He's small for his age."

"Has one hell of a kick, though."

"That he does." She stood for a minute. "Melissa," she said.

"Nick. Why don't you sit down?"

"Bobby will be out of sight in a minute."

"He seems to be going in one big circle." Nick pointed to the little boy who had reached the ball and kicked it again. She looked across the park and saw he was working his way back in her direction.

"More like a boomerang," she said, and sat down next to Nick. "What do you do?"

"I'm the director of marketing and sales for TrendInventions."

"I get their catalogue. Cool stuff. A little pricey, though."

"Yeah. I can't afford any of it either." Nick smiled. She laughed.

"I work at home. It's the fashionable thing to do today. I design and maintain websites for small mail-order companies."

"So that's why you've got our catalogue?"

"Yeah. I also like to look at it." The blue plastic ball landed next to them. Bobby was back. Nick took a chance.

"You free tonight? I'm at the Stewart House."

"That's such a cool place," Melissa said. "It was falling apart when someone bought it and put a ton of money into it. It's been the backdrop for a couple of movies."

"I thought I recognized it." He gave her his business card. "Here's my cell number. Come by for a drink … or dinner. I'm here until tomorrow morning when I have to head for the airport."

"I have him, and his brother," she pointed to Bobby, "but I'll see what I can do about a sitter."

***

Nick was sitting at the mahogany and green marble bar. The previous owner liked to tell everyone the story that the marble had come from the mountains of Carrara, Italy. However, it had only come from as far away as the mountains of Vermont, although it did have half of an Italian name, "Vermont Verde." The guy had made a steady living with the place but hadn't put a dime into it for fifty years. When he retired, he had almost sold off the marble but instead sold the whole building. After a year of renovation, it had reopened as a cultural landmark. On the wall were photos of famous directors and actors who had used the hotel for scenes from their movies. There was also an oil painting of the hotel from the nineteenth century. The current owner had used it as a model for the renovations. Nick was sipping his drink and wondering if he should ask for a table when Melissa walked in. She was dressed in dark slacks and a cream-colored silk blouse that showed off her figure and her summer-tanned skin. Nick was a little astonished but recovered quickly.

"Hi. I was just thinking of getting a table."

"I thought I was nervous until I saw the look on *your* face," Melissa said.

"That obvious?"

"Yep. I almost turned back, twice."

"I had no idea I had that effect on women. It explains a lot." They sat at a table and ordered drinks. During the meal they got to know each other. She had two boys from two previous lovers, one she almost married, Bobby's dad. He broke it off at the last minute, and she moved out to this place where she could afford a nice house on the money she made and send the boys to a good school. For what it would cost for a very small apartment in the city where she used to work, she got a mortgage on a nice house, and the high-speed Internet connection took care of the rest. She did miss the nightlife and the convenience of a large city, although this place was getting better each year. Nick told her about his previous lover and her eccentricities, leaving off with the bouncer with the tattoos, but held off on telling her about Zoe. He felt she was holding back a bit, too. He walked her home and found that the boys were both asleep. He sat on the couch, and she made some coffee. They spoke in low voices so as not to wake the kids. She looked at him, placed the cup on the end table, and took his face in her hands and kissed him. The couch was small and a little awkward, but that didn't slow them down. He woke her when he got up and kissed her goodbye.

"Hmm, good morning?"

"It's 5:30. I have to pack and catch a 7 a.m. flight."

"Okay ... I usually don't. In fact, I never—"

"Neither do I. No need to explain."

"You want coffee before you go?"

"No thanks. Look. I'll be back in town in another six weeks or so. I'll call you when I know for sure?"

"Really?" She feigned surprise. "You're not going to be a cliché and just leave?"

"Do you want me to?" He asked. She said nothing.

As Nick left, he saw a man's London Fog raincoat hanging on a peg in the hallway. He ignored all the possible innocent explanations and took it as an opportunity to feel better about not mentioning Zoe. After all, she almost broke up with him just last week.

7

Denton Pike was looking across the desk at Zoe. She was working on a divorce between a computer programmer, Marta, a Polish national who had moved to the US and become a citizen, and her husband, who had elected to go back to Poland. She'd been in the US for several years with her husband, but they'd been originally married in Warsaw. Zoe had sent for the original marriage papers and needed to become familiar with aspects of Polish matrimonial law. She had received all the information she'd asked for, but, of course, it was all in Polish. She couldn't have Marta translate it as she was someone who had a vested interest in the outcomes. Since she had moved to the US as a little girl, her knowledge of Polish wasn't nearly good enough to translate complex legal documents, so Jimmy found a guy who had a reputation for languages. He'd apparently translated some hot Nobel Prize–winning novelist.

International divorces could be tricky, as European matrimonial laws could be idiosyncratic, not to mention European judges sometimes had bad attitudes toward Americans. The husband seemed to be angling for something, money probably. She was making about a quarter million dollars a year working as a top programmer and project director for a major software company. Zoe needed to know the nuts and bolts of alimony laws in Poland. She had heard of alimony running as high as 25 percent of pretax income in some European countries, although it usually was paid by the man to the woman; she wasn't sure how often it went the other way. Such a percentage was almost unheard of in her state. In fact, there was no such thing as mandatory spousal support at all, only mandatory child support.

"Jimmy says you're fluent in Polish."

"Yes, but not legal language. I've mostly translated literary works."

"This is boring, dry, literal legalese. I need to know the rules for spousal support in an international divorce. Usually it goes by the country who files first, but it's not set law in any way, shape, or form. I've run into problems with a child custody case for an Iraqi War veteran who was stationed in Germany and married to a German citizen. She sued for divorce while he was on a tour of duty in Iraq, and the poor guy lost everything. Their laws didn't consider that he had a right to see his kids." She paused. "I might have to have you fly to Poland if we need to appear in court there."

"That's no problem. I've done a lot of traveling. As far as legalese goes, I'm sure it's better reading than some poems I've translated."

Zoe laughed, "I'm not sure about that. This stuff can be pretty dry."

"Well, you have my rates. I'm charging a little above the standard per word rate, especially since this is going to require some research on my part. If you're more comfortable with a translator specializing in legal language, I'll look around."

"No. I need to move quickly here. I want to get US jurisdiction if I can. Or at least let them know this will not be a pushover."

"Okay. I also know a good Spanish translator if you ever need one. She's out of state, but that shouldn't be a problem. She's excellent."

"I'll keep that in mind. We have had a few Spanish-speaking clients, not too many yet."

"It's probably that Catholic thing."

"Right. No divorce. That's old hat, though. Catholics keep up their share of the statistics." Zoe smiled, and handed him a thick file. "Here are the papers they sent to me. Let me know if we need to request anything else from them."

Denton took the folder and hefted it; he'd be doing well. His contract to translate Serge Krakow's work, the Nobel Prize winner from a few years ago, had run out. He had plenty of money saved but was getting a little bored with the usual fare, and his girlfriend, Judy, was getting tired of him hanging around the house with nothing to do. He left, and Zoe turned her attention to another case. She had court this afternoon and was still hoping that the opposing counsel would keep his word about the agreement they'd hammered out. She didn't trust him. She started to review the case when her phone rang.

"Hello, Anne, what can I do for you?"

"Just called to let you know I told him last night. He seemed to already know. I did mention it to him last month, but he was avoiding me, so I simply shut off his computer so he had no choice but to look at me, and I told him outright. I know that the papers will be served soon and didn't want him to find out like that."

"Do you know if he's gotten an attorney yet?"

"He might have, but I don't think so. I told him that he needed one. He leaves all that stuff up to me."

"You can't get him an attorney. I can't even recommend one. It's unethical."

"I know. It's just that he's so lost right now."

"That's not your problem, Anne. We'll have enough on our plate without taking on his issues, too. Isn't that why you want the divorce? To get rid of his problems?"

"Right," she said, after a too-long pause.

"Look. The summons is out and will be served sometime this week. If you're having second thoughts, you need to let me know now. Once the summons is served, we must move forward. His attorney will be pushing for his interests, and I will be pushing for yours. It can get ugly. That's how it works."

"You're right. It's taken me years to get to this point."

"Do you have any friends you can talk to? Someone who knows both of you? Preferably someone who isn't involved with work?"

"Yeah. My sister."

"Well, my advice is for you to get her on the phone, and maybe pay her a visit. Get away for a while. You could also get an apartment. "

"Well, won't I lose the house if I leave?"

"Who told you that?"

"My girlfriends."

"Are they lawyers?"

"No."

"In this state we operate under equitable distribution, usually half of everything, no matter what. You can move to Katmandu and still get your share of all marital property. Your friends need to catch up, or maybe they should spring for law school before giving out advice. Of course there are states that still have primitive divorce laws, where everything follows the title, and your spouse can get everything that doesn't have your name on it, but not here. What we need to do is to make sure he doesn't try anything funny, like max out your joint credit cards on toys or empty any joint bank accounts. As far as your business goes, we will hire our own forensic accountants to determine the value."

"Right," Anne said, but seemed remote.

"You gonna be okay?"

"I'll be fine."

"Good. Call your sister. Better yet, visit her for a few days. And think about getting an apartment or having him get one."

"I actually have one already," Anne said. Zoe looked at the telephone like it was something she'd never seen before, an object from another planet. And then put it back to her ear.

"You have an apartment?" She said, trying to not sound as surprised as she was.

"Yes. I have it for when I work late and don't feel like driving home," Anne explained.

"Okay. So there isn't a problem then at all? Right? Pack your bags tonight. Move into your apartment. Don't even think about it, just do it."

"Right. Thanks, Zoe, I'll see you. I'll move in right after work."

"Bye, Anne." She hung up the phone, suddenly relieved. She had been worried about Anne backing out. An apartment she uses for *working late*, she said to herself, right. "I believe that. Maybe I'll tell her the one about a bridge for sale in New York City." She finished reading the brief in front of her and headed off to court.

8

John Raymond, Esq., was in the courtroom across from the judge. He didn't look happy. The original judge's caseload had been very heavy, so the case had been handed off to a new guy who had just been appointed to the bench to help with the county's overburdened caseload. The judge Raymond had been counting on was incompetent and a hopeless alcoholic. As such, he was completely intolerant of any faults on the part of others. Raymond had slipped in the picture of Susan smoking a joint at a party even though he'd said he wouldn't, and Zoe had threatened she would call the husband out on it and make a case of child endangerment against him for not reporting it to the police. It would be like using a nuclear bomb to kill an ant, but with the original judge it would have been her only defense. Since he was as lazy as he was incompetent, it would have forced his hand and made him ignore the issue because of all the work involved with the new charges. Although, there would have been some fallout in the decision, which was what Raymond was counting on, especially with the financial settlement.

Zoe tried to size up the new judge. He was younger than most, and seemed to be attentive and intelligent, but his face was impassive, and he was difficult to read. She noticed that he smiled at his clerk; this was a good sign. Many judges tend to feel far too important to smile at anyone. He hadn't developed *the attitude,* at least not yet. Zoe was probably overreading the judge, but this was what she was usually rather good at, dealing with the people in charge so she could get what she wanted for her clients. She had a knack for reading people and figuring out the best way to handle them and doing it very quickly. The judge called up her case first. She stood next to Susan, and Raymond stood next to Frank. The judge was looking through some papers. Zoe noticed he had taken some notes on the case and she was impressed. At one time she had wondered if certain judges she appeared before were even literate.

"The agreement you are offering is to have a percentage of the salary of the Respondent as defined by law going to the Plaintiff for child support and that the house will be sold when the youngest child reaches the age of twenty-one? Am I right?"

"That's right, Judge," Raymond said.

"Not quite," Zoe responded. "The agreement we are seeking is the percentage is to be based on the income from the business, not on the salary drawn by Mr. Amato. His salary is very low, and he can always decrease it at his whim. Furthermore, we had already asked that the plaintiff get to keep the house, as she spent ten years of her life helping to grow and improve the business."

"She was actually a burden on the business as her postpartum depression caused my client to have to leave on numerous occasions to attend to her as she was incapacitated by her illness," Raymond said, quickly. The judge held up his hand and read from his notes.

"The record indicates Susan was treated for postpartum depression for a period of a little more than a year. Was a caregiver hired to look after the children?"

"No, your honor," Zoe said.

"So she was functional enough to watch her infant children while she was being treated. You claim a salary of $30,000 a year from your business Mr. Amato?"

"I have a lot of overhead, Sir," Frank whined.

"Indeed. The forensic accountant said your gross revenues are about a half million. You have $470,000 in expenses? Does that include the new Corvette?" He looked at Frank, who shrugged and looked at Raymond.

"He needed to buy equipment and hire someone to take over for his wife," Raymond said.

"It costs him that much to replace his wife? Almost half a million dollars? Are you sure you want to go down that road, counselor?" The judged smiled. He wrote a few notes on his pad. "Susan Amato is entitled by the rules of equitable distribution to half the profits from the business and the child support will also be based on that figure. If Mr. Amato wishes to buy out his wife's half of the business that can be worked out later. The Court must approve of the accountant who will determine the profit figure that this will be based on, and/or the value of the business should a buyout be decided upon. Mrs. Amato will be allowed to stay in the house until she sees fit to leave, regardless of the age of the children, whereupon the net proceeds from the sale of the house will be evenly divided between Mr. and Mrs. Amato. The mortgage payments and escrow will continue to come from the restaurant. Child custody will be as previously agreed and specified by Family Court."

"Thank you, Your Honor," Zoe said as she tried to suppress a grin. Raymond was stoic, but Frank looked confused.

"I wasn't sure what this was doing in your folder," the judge said to Raymond. It was the picture of Susan he had agreed to get rid of. "There was no documentation, so I assumed it was some sort of mistake. I hope it wasn't put there to prejudice me in any way."

"No, Your Honor." Raymond took the photo from the judge.

Zoe and Susan went out to the oak-paneled hallway. The courthouse was a Depression-era project and had been built by the local unemployed, mostly Italian, Irish, and Polish immigrants, who were excellent craftsmen. It was a massive yellow brick structure, and the hallways had hand-carved oak panels. There was a mural on the wall across from the entrance that showed farmers and factory workers busy doing their jobs. It was as if they had painted a talisman and were using magical thinking to get people back to work. As if they believed that if they made an image of workers at work, then it would become a reality. Zoe looked at the mural. It was a good painting by a talented artist, back when artists practiced the craft and hard work of painting, and it helped her calm down after court. No matter how well prepared she was, or how things turned out, she always left the courtroom with her heart pounding and perspiration trickling down her back. She stood for a while waiting for the adrenaline to work out of her system. She saw Frank and Raymond down the hall. It was starting to dawn on Frank what had just happened, and he was not looking very happy. Susan, who stood across from Zoe, was very pale.

"Are you okay?" Zoe asked.

"I'm all right. I just didn't sleep at all last night. Can't believe that it's over. We got everything we asked for. I was so worried I'd need to sell the house, or worse, move out."

"I wasn't sure, either. Although, I knew you wouldn't have to move. I thought the judge might change the custody arrangements. He didn't seem worried about those at all. Next time you're at a party, be sure no one is taking photos. Our firm had a client who went to jail because of his social networking page. Someone had posted a photo of him drinking at a bar just before he drove away and had a very bad accident. He had been pinned in the car, and it had taken a few hours before they could draw blood, so the results weren't enough to charge him with DWI, but the picture was all that the judge needed. Nice friend." Zoe had had mixed feelings about the result.

She knew that the guy did drive after drinking and had caused a serious accident, but no one had been hurt but him, and his car was the only one that had been totaled. The accident itself had been one of those things that could happen to someone who was sober. A deer had jumped out in front of the car and he'd swerved into the left lane. He couldn't get back in time to avoid sideswiping a car coming in the opposite direction. That oncoming driver had done nothing to get out of the way, though, and had probably been going well above the speed limit judging by the length of the skid marks. Her client had gone off the road, hit a tree, and flipped over. The other car had some damage, but no one had been seriously hurt. Jail time seemed a little harsh and inappropriate, not to mention the people in the other car sued him for thousands of dollars, money he didn't have that his insurance company refused to pay. Another judge might have had a different idea of fair punishment, which is what bothered her so much, how arbitrary things could actually get. She had no illusions about what had just happened, and knew that the result today had come about, at least in part, because they had landed on the "right" judge, someone who had actually read through the briefs, had called Raymond on his bullshit, and seen through Frank's little scams. Another might have missed those altogether, cut Susan out of the business, taken away any custody of the kids, and thrown her out of her house.

"Thanks, Zoe. Maybe I can get started again. I feel like my whole world has been on hold," Susan said.

"You should go home and take a long nap."

"At least until the school bus drops the kids off." Susan smiled, shook Zoe's hand, and left. Zoe looked at the mural for a while. She suddenly felt a kinship with the hard-working, smiling people, the struggling men and woman tirelessly trying to rebuild a world destroyed by the rich, the greedy, and the stupid. She went back to her office. It was Friday afternoon, so she looked at a brief for a case next week, closed it, and started to drive home. Halfway there, she remembered that she had promised Nick she'd meet him for dinner.

Zoe and Nick were at his apartment. They had met for dinner, and she had gone to his place after. They sat in his living room drinking wine. They'd thought of seeing a movie but didn't like any of the selections in the nearby Cineplex. They were all action-adventure movies that seemed to be more like video games than movies.

"Man, this was a busy week," she said.

"Did you talk to Anne?"

"Only once this week. I've gotten underway with her case; the summons was served, and we are waiting for his response. The accountants and paralegals are getting all the pertinent information together. It'll take a few weeks at least to determine the value of the business and the joint property." She paused and sipped her wine. "They make a weird couple."

"Yeah," Nick agreed.

"Like she's his mother or something."

"Exactly, takes all kinds, I guess. She seems to fiercely defend him, and then pokes fun at him all at the same time. I've listened to an earful of his faults over lunch with her." He paused. "Some people might think we make a weird couple, two workaholics who see each other once a week or so, no commitment," Nick said.

"You complaining?"

"Nope. It works for me."

"Sure?"

"Yeah. Why?"

"Nothing really." Zoe paused, "I wonder if they have sex."

"Anne and Michael?"

"Yes."

"It could happen. Creepy when you think about it. He seems to be one of those people who doesn't have a big sex drive; he almost seems to be asexual. Maybe that's not the right word." Nick poured another glass of wine.

"I know what you mean. There is something odd about him."

"Well, he invents stuff that people love to pay good money for. Bizarre gadgets that people never even realize they want until he invents it. He has to be some sort of genius."

"Did your business trip go well last week?" Zoe asked. Nick hesitated a minute.

"Yep." He paused, "I can't believe those two guys sell so much from that little store. It can't be more than 5,000 square feet. You should see it, packed with stuff. They even have a year-round Christmas display. People come from all over the area to buy from them. I even saw some out-of-state plates on expensive SUVs in the parking lot."

"Personalities, maybe?"

"Yes. More, though. It's almost like they're both born salesmen. Like the genes that put them together are coded to make them charming and obliging so that you really *want* to buy something from them, like you'd feel bad if you left the store without buying anything. I don't know. They've been a couple since they met in the Navy. Over the years I've visited them, I got their whole story, basically a couple of nice gay guys who work 24/7. They vote Republican, too. Got an earful about that one time when we talked about taxes."

"I had an uncle like that. He was always easy to talk to. He sold cars his whole life. He never got married but had a couple of male friends he hung out with. My guess is that he was gay, but no one talked about it back then."

"You think maybe the inborn charm skipped a generation?" Nick said.

"What? You mean I'm not easy to get along with?"

"I'd never say that."

"You'd just think it?"

"Right. More wine?"

"No." She stood up. "I've got to get going." Zoe looked around for her jacket.

"You don't want to stay?"

"I have to get up early," she said.

"It's the weekend."

"Have to go to see my brother tomorrow, and I want to be on the road early. I promised him a visit."

"Chris, the contractor? How's he doing?"

"Not bad, considering the economy. He keeps busy."

"Good. I'd tell you to say hi, but I've yet to meet him."

"Stop." She bristled.

"I just said."

"I know. We're friends, just that. That's the agreement. If I bring you up there, they will have us married off, and we'd both need to answer a bunch of questions. I love him to pieces, but I'm also his little sister. I need some time to relax and to think. I just had one hell of a case and I'm right in the middle of another."

"You're right," Nick said, and poured himself some more wine.

Zoe put on her coat, kissed him quickly, and left.

9

Zoe pulled into her brother's driveway. It was a semicircle that went to the side of the front of his multistory frame house, a contractor's house, huge for a bachelor. It would have fit a large family comfortably; he used it to show potential clients his work. He came out to greet her. They shared the same hair, chin, and eyes, although his hair was cut short and receding a little, a light touch of grey on the edges. "I see you have some new plants on your deck. Are you spending more time at home?"

"I've not been too busy this year. Everyone is holding back right now," Chris said, noticing his sister looking around.

"Are you okay with money?" This wasn't her just being polite. Chris had financed her last year of law school and hadn't asked for a penny back.

"I'm okay. Things are a little tight now, but I've put some away over the past couple of years, but I wasn't planning on such a long dry spell," he paused, "can't complain though, plenty of guys are out of the business altogether or moved to better places. At least they hope they're better. I think this recession is pretty much all over the country. I've had some steady work subcontracting small jobs, replaced a bunch of roofs and ceilings after that big storm, and had to gut a lot of finished basements. Everyone was flooded out, and the power going out for a week didn't help. It knocked out the sump pumps, so some people had three or four feet of water in their basements. I don't think anyone in the county has a finished basement anymore—they're a bad idea anyway in this area."

He opened the door and said, "You remember there's a spare key under that flowerpot just in case you get here before I get home." He pointed to a pot full of light blue flowers. Zoe would have no idea what they were, but Chris probably even knew their scientific name. He let his sister in ahead of him and carried her suitcase up to the spare room while she looked around. It was his usual place. It wasn't quite ready for a Good Housekeeping photoshoot, but it would take little effort to have it ready. Zoe smiled. The two of them were both meticulous about their places, another thing that bothered her about Nick. He was a slob. No, she thought. That was unfair. He just had a looser idea of how neat things should be kept than she did. Chris returned from the spare room. "A lot of insurance companies bailed and stuck FEMA with the damages," he continued. He expected you to remember where he left off. "They didn't pay too well though, and people were caught with about half the money they really needed to repair their homes. Now there's law you could practice, sue the bastards, probably a lot of money in that."

"That's true, but you can't sue the government. There are many laws against that. Personal injury law makes you a little crazy. You don't get a dime until the case is settled, and you could lose the case after spending a lot of time and money and end up with nothing. All you ever hear about are the super large settlements. Even those could take years and run up a lot of costs."

"I can see where that might drive you a little batty."

"Family law can be tricky, too."

"I'm sure. People are not at their best?"

Chris took her on a tour of his house, showing her all the work he'd finished since her last visit. The workmanship was up to his fanatical standards. One reason why he worked with only a few others was the fact that he had no toleration for sloppy efforts. Once, he'd gotten into a fight with a carpenter who worked for him because a wall was framed in a couple of degrees out of true. It wasn't so much that the wall was not perfectly straight, but that the guy had the attitude that he didn't care if it was straight or not and refused to true it up. Chris trued the wall by himself so that it was straight and square, after bodily throwing the guy off the project. He'd learned to control his temper since then, but his standards were the same.

Zoe helped Chris make dinner. "I've been getting into Indian cooking," he said as he blended the various yellow, orange, red, black, and golden colored powders. When they hit the hot oil, the room was filled with a powerful aroma. Zoe retreated to the living room as she let Chris work in the kitchen. Over the years she had learned that at this point, she would just be in his way.

After dinner, they sat in the spacious living room. Compared to her apartment, his house was a castle. She relaxed and he turned on the TV. They both liked science and nature specials, and one was on. It was the middle of a special on the rain forest in Brazil. She liked being with him because he could make her look at things in her life she couldn't see. She did the same for him. Helped him with problems he had that he was too myopic to get a handle on. They'd discussed his latest girlfriend, Lily. She had a lot less baggage than his previous girlfriend, who liked to play psychodrama games. Chris may have had enough of the drama queens, but she was surprised his taste had suddenly run in such an opposite direction. All his girlfriends had had a sense of the histrionic. Lily, however, was normal and had a steady job, something none of his previous girlfriends seemed to manage. Although no man in the world had ever been good enough for his little sister, including her ex-husband, he had always been especially hostile about Nick and advised her to send him packing as soon as he'd heard of him and their arrangement. She told Chris she was just about ready to break things off with him. Chris seemed relived, although Zoe felt there had been nothing to worry about. She never would have gotten serious with someone like Nick. A fact that seemed to escape Chris.

A special came on the Discovery Channel on the Big Bang, and it was pretty up to date on the latest theories about how the universe began. Chris loved it and sat transfixed.

"That is so cool," Chris said when the show was over.

"What is?"

"There was this giant explosion fourteen billion years ago, and it made a lot of dust. That's what we are, all the dust that was left over after the creation of the universe. Just combining and recombining in different forms, all kinds of stardust."

"Then here's to the dust after creation," Zoe said, and raised her glass; they clinked their wine glasses.

10

Zoe and Nick finished their lunch, and it was well past time for her to go back to work. Zoe was already thinking of the case sitting on her desk and arranging the phone calls she'd have to make that afternoon.

Nick wasn't ready to leave, though.

She had told him as clearly as she could that this wasn't working out and that she was not seeing him anymore, not as a friend-with-benefits anyway. As cliché as it sounded, she needed more space, more room. Nick had been very good as far as leaving her to herself, but she wanted no commitments for a while. It was like paying off a car and not having any payments. She wanted to go for a while without any payments, without anyone who might have an emotional attachment to her or someone she felt obligated to. She didn't want to have to explain herself to anyone, not unless it was her idea in the first place. It was her issue more than his and she recognized that, but Nick had been someone she knew she'd never get serious about. He'd been safe, but now she just wanted total autonomy.

"So that's that?" He said for about the fourth time.

"Yes."

"Sorry if I took up too much of your time."

"It's not that."

"Chris? Your brother? He never liked me."

"It has nothing to do with Chris. He never liked any of my boyfriends, including the one I married." She paused. "He was right about that one, though."

"You think he's right about me?"

"It's not about what Chris thinks, or even you. It's about me. I've thought about this for a while now. I've never had much time on my own. I got married out of college and then worked a shitty job while my ex went to graduate school. After I left him, I worked like crazy at law school and at another crappy job to help pay for it, and since then I've been an attorney trying to make partner and competing with people ten years younger, so I want some downtime to be by myself now. That's all there is to it."

"Okay."

Again with the "okay," she thought to herself. He always has to approve. Fuck him. She got up.

"I'm late. I have to get back to the office." He didn't respond. She picked up her purse, put on her jacket, and left. He sat at the table and said nothing, looked at his watch, and then left to get back to work.

When she got to the office, there were pink telephone message notes for her, and her email inbox was overflowing. However, much of it was from the same person—Marta, her international client who wanted a divorce from her husband who had returned to Poland to live. He was suing for some sort of spousal support, something that was not allowed in this state and rare in the US. She left a message with the translator, Denton, to see how far along he was on the court papers. She'd so far not had a lot of luck with international divorces. One of her clients had lost all rights to his kids because he had been a US soldier stationed in Germany who rotated tours of duty in Iraq; the military had him sign papers giving his wife sole custody of their children. This was standard procedure for anyone going into a battle zone. Unfortunately, it had given his wife all she needed to take the kids from him. The wife met someone new who was not busy fighting a war, and the German courts were hostile to the idea of international joint custody. In fact, one justice remarked in writing that the children would be much better off raised in Germany with good German values than in the US. The court remained unpersuaded by any of Zoe's briefs, she suspected they didn't even read them, and awarded sole custody to the ex-wife.

Another case was from a woman who was a U.S. citizen who had married an Israeli she'd met while spending a year working on a kibbutz. After the divorce, she was sent back to the US. She'd no rights at all to her children. After a little research, Zoe had found out that Israeli marriage laws were controlled exclusively by the Rabbinical Court, and usually they gave almost no rights at all to women who got divorced, especially women who were citizens of other countries. She filed briefs and motions, but they were ignored. There was nothing she could do. Short of flying to Israel and kidnapping her kids, the woman had no recourse. Because of these experiences, Zoe had not wanted to take on this case, or any other international case, and this one looked as if it might not go any

Intimate Disconnect

better than the last two. The thought made Zoe's chest tighten. The phone rang. The caller ID showed it was Denton calling her back.

"Hi Denton."

"Hi Zoe."

"Have you finished?"

"Yes." He paused and she heard papers rustling. "Their marriage was pretty straightforward, and according to their laws that are from the mid-sixties, he can have maintenance of one of two types. They call one *narrow* and the other *broad*. The narrow one is confined to supporting the spouse, but not necessarily in the way of the marriage. It's only to cover the basic needs of the spouse who doesn't have an income and is invoked when neither party is fully to blame for the divorce. The broad one is when one spouse is an innocent party and the other is a guilty party and is sort of like when a business is broken up by one partner; usually he has to pay off the other one for the expenses of breaking up. It's not supposed to be some kind of retribution for breaking up a marriage, but a way of making financial restitution for breaking up a partnership."

"Hmm, so there is no real no-fault divorce?"

"Not that I can see. There is less-fault or more-fault. One party is usually the innocent one and the other is guilty to some degree of what they call the 'complete and irretrievable disintegration of matrimonial life.' In the cases where one spouse can be shown to be the sole cause of the divorce, the other spouse is entitled to the broad support."

"That's really quaint, isn't it?"

"Yes. Their laws haven't been updated in fifty years."

"Okay. Will you be available to draw up some papers?"

"For the rest of the month, then I'm going to New Mexico to visit an old friend and her daughter, although I could overnight them to you. Judy and I are thinking of moving there if she can find a job. I can really live anywhere."

"Judy's your wife?"

"No. My girlfriend. Significant other. You know."

"Yeah. I got it. Sorry to pry."

"No problem. It took us a year to figure it out ourselves."

"I completely understand," Zoe said. The husband was looking for almost half of his wife's gross income and was painting her as the sole source of the complete disintegration of the marriage. Zoe was sure she could bring a few facts to the court's attention to show how that wasn't quite true. She had to muddy the waters as to who was really responsible for the breakup of the marriage, and she remembered there was a possible girlfriend. The thought cheered her up and made her forget about the anxiety she felt after the lunch with Nick. She had made a pledge to herself when she moved out on her own to not let anyone "guilt" her. It was a tough promise to keep, but so far, she'd managed to not let others lay a guilt trip on her, or at least not for very long. She thought of all the things she had done that she'd regretted because someone had guilted her into doing it. It had taken her some time, but she felt that she was changing, and she wanted to make sure she stayed that way.

11

Michael had been impossible. He'd whined and carried on like a four-year-old because Anne insisted that he come to the TrendInventions Board of Directors meeting. He usually blew them off and let Anne deal with the board and the investors. She wanted him there because rumors of their divorce had shaken the company up, and she wanted a show of solidarity. Michael, however, was being such a spoiled ass that she was beginning to have second thoughts about having him attend. He was dressed in a shirt and tie, but it was abundantly clear that he'd rather be anyplace but there. He was on a video game on his smartphone and was deeply engrossed playing multiple games simultaneously when Anne grabbed the device out of his hand and shut it off. He went into a deep sulk.

Louis Amory was there early. His tailored suit hugged his body and gave him a predatory look. He sat calmly in his usual chair, directly across from Anne. The others filed in, carrying cups of coffee, munching on bagels and snacks from the buffet table in the adjacent room. Anne met them and made small talk. Michael sat in his chair, drawing on the tablet in front of him. He was working on an idea for a mini battery-operated fan for pets, a way to cool Fido off on a hot day, when he wasn't in his air-conditioned doghouse, of course. The meeting came to order and the general conversations trailed off. After they reviewed the minutes of the last meeting, Anne started with the financial reports, which were solid but not remarkable. They had profits but were short of where they had wanted to be at this time, and far short of the profits they were making at the same time last year. However, considering the poor economy, and the fact that they specialized in toys for people with lots of disposable income, they were doing well. When the last chart was finished and she reviewed the final slide and shut down her PowerPoint, she opened the floor for new business. Louis Amory pounced.

"It has come to the board's attention ..." he started. He always liked to refer to himself as "the Board," or at least in the third person. Anne wondered if this was some form of psychological disorder and if he would someday start referring to himself in the plural, like Queen

Victoria or Margaret Thatcher, the royal "we." She listened as he made comments about the fact that she had filed for divorce from Michael and how she should have informed the board.

"Why?" She cut him off in mid-pontification. It stopped him cold. Like most doctors, he was not used to being interrupted or ever being asked to justify his opinion, unless there was a malpractice suit.

"Because you're the CEO and he's the head of Design and Development for God's sake."

"We both know that don't we, Michael?" Anne said. Michael looked up from his drawings, not sure why anyone called his name. "Still, I ask, why? Whether we get a divorce or not doesn't affect the business one bit. Michael will still dream up new products, and I will still be the CEO and the CFO, unless, of course, you have someone else in mind? Our private lives are just that—our private lives."

"I'm not so sure," Amory said, but not with the same conviction. No one in the room had jumped on his bandwagon. He was too much of a coward to ever go it alone. Anne knew that he had a very good point. The two people who genuinely made the company work were splitting up. It could be a catastrophe; plenty of businesses had collapsed for far less serious reasons. Anne was determined to keep him from going down that road. If the investors got skittish, it could be a self-fulfilling prophecy.

"We need some assurance," he said trying to control the conversation again. "After all, we represent the bulk of your investors. We need to know that this divorce will not impact the performance of the business."

"Lou, for goodness sake, we're investors, too. Michael and I own most of the company. This is our baby. We started the whole thing in the garage of our house. This has been what we've done for almost twenty years. We wouldn't do anything to jeopardize it." She hoped she sounded more convincing than she felt at this moment. Michael had been impossible since she'd served him with papers. He'd refused at first to get an attorney, and now that he had one, he wasn't cooperating with him. Michael had set up about a dozen appointments but had "forgotten" to go. Anne hired a driver to make sure he finally made an appointment. She had just about had enough of him, and she was afraid that his attorney might be feeling the same way. The fact that they were millionaires was probably the only thing keeping him from dropping

Michael as a client. She was counting on the lawyer's need for a wealthy client, but Michael could be exasperating. Amory wasn't mollified, though.

"That sounds fine, Anne, but you know that no one but you can handle Michael and that everything that happens here depends on him. I've a lot of money invested here, and I need some assurances."

"Well. All I can say is what I've already said. If that's not enough, then I suggest you look for another place to invest your money." This made a few board members draw in a breath, but Anne wasn't as reckless as she seemed. She knew that Louis Amory had invested heavily in a deluxe apartment complex just before the economy tanked, and real estate around town was at its lowest in decades. Most of the apartments were vacant, and those that were rented were rented out well below market value. The tennis courts were unfinished, and they hadn't even opened the pool last summer after they failed their health department inspection because they'd cut corners on the filtration equipment. She knew that TrendInventions was his only investment that wasn't losing money.

"There's no need to be that extreme," he said. "I was just voicing some legitimate concerns."

"I agree. They are legitimate. But all I can say is that you have to trust us to do the right thing."

"Okay," he said, and sat back in his chair, not entirely convinced, but unwilling to push any further at this time. They moved on to other new business. A famous international online retailer was interested in carrying their line, but only if they offered a deeper discount than they usually did. The debate was whether or not it would pay to offer their products at such a discount and how that contract might affect the other more traditional high-end merchandisers they worked with. Part of the allure of their products was simple snob appeal. It was decided to offer the giant retailer a limited selection of their older products that were already popular and had been copied by several knock-off factories in China in flagrant violation of patent law. They could afford to sell them at a discount while still keeping an exclusive line with their other retailers. This would cut into the sales of the knockoffs because people would be able to get the real thing for a few dollars more, not to mention the free shipping that the retailer was known for. They moved on to the new holiday advertising campaign and decided to use the same advertising outfit who had a new version of last year's campaign with some updated and new products. The "Santa in Aviator Sunglasses" was becoming an icon, and they were going to use him this season, too. The only difference was that the ads would start to run right after Halloween instead of the week before Thanksgiving. The holiday shopping season was starting earlier every year. As the meeting wore on, Michael, who was completely oblivious to the discussions going on around him, finished the drawings he had been working on, got out of his chair, and left the room. Anne smiled a thin and quick smile and Louis Amory shook his head.

Michael had left the meeting with the intention of going to his workroom at home. Instead, he paid a visit to the development lab at work. These were the people who helped him make his ideas into prototypes. They were looking at the drawings of his doggie fan and coming up with ideas for various models. They could make the fan in several sizes to accommodate different types of dogs, something Michael hadn't thought of, and one of the people had asked if dogs even like to have wind blowing against their faces. Someone else pointed out that dogs always stick their heads out of car windows. This prompted some more sketches and more ideas. Michael's phone rang, and he answered it absentmindedly without looking at the ID. He immediately left the room when he heard the voice on the other end.

"What's up, Michael?"

"Had a very boring meeting. I left."

"You okay? You sound funny."

"I'm fine. I'm with the development guys. Those board meetings are just such a waste of time. They waste Anne's time, too. It makes her crazy."

"I can imagine. Are any of them going to pull out because of the divorce?"

"Amory threatened, but Anne was right about him. He doesn't have the balls."

"Not yet. He can get a few members on his side, and then he'll suddenly be a lot braver."

Intimate Disconnect

"You know him?"

"Not personally, but I deal every day with people just like him."

"Oh, right."

"Look, you want to meet me for a drink tonight?"

"Yeah. Where?"

"Emilio's."

"Good. Maybe we'll get something to eat, too?" Michael said.

"If I ate as much as you do, I'd be 300 pounds."

"I burn it off."

"It must be that brain of yours. I've got to get back to the office. See you tonight. I'll probably get there about seven."

"Okay. Bye."

Michael went back to work. He wasn't really worried about the directors, but he knew that they worried Anne, a lot, and that was something he wished he could help with, but he simply wasn't built that way. He sat down with the fabrication team and spent the rest of the afternoon on his latest project. He did some quick research on the Internet and found that there were over seventy-eight million pet dogs in the US alone. If only ten percent of those owners had the means and desire to buy his latest gadget, sales could be fairly good for the "doggie chiller." He wondered if cats would like a cool breeze, too.

Emilio's was packed, and Michael had a tough time finding a parking place for his Porsche. He didn't want to leave it too far from the main road near the entrance. He remembered vividly when it had been broken into. Lucky for him, whoever had broken in couldn't figure out how to bypass the security and hadn't been able to start it. The car alarm drove him off and someone had called 911. Eventually the police arrived and filled out a report. They took a few notes, looking very bored, and then they mentioned that he had insurance for this sort of thing and drove off, leaving him with a pink, illegible, carbon copy of the report that he was supposed to fax to his insurance company. He found a place about a block up from the front door of the club. There was loud music playing from a DJ who stood in front of giant speakers, and everyone had already had plenty to drink. He knew he was about an hour late and looked around. His friend was at the bar and smiled at him. He moved past the dancers on the very retro, disco-style lighted floor and up to the crowded bar. Jimmy was still in his work clothes, white shirt and tie, but his tie was loose, and the knot was hanging around his throat.

"I just got here a few minutes ago myself. Zoe had me working like a slave all day, mostly on your divorce." He looked around at the midweek insanity playing out all over the club. "We've got some catching up to do." And he handed Michael a double bourbon and soda already wet with condensation.

12

When he woke up, Nick wasn't sure where he was. He'd remembered starting out in the evening at his favorite club, but wasn't entirely sure how he'd gotten here, although the bedroom looked somewhat familiar. He'd seen these silk sheets before, and the perfume was familiar. He made the connection just as Anne came into the bedroom. They were in her downtown apartment. He now remembered running into her last night. She had been upset about Michael, the meeting, the divorce, and everything seemed to be closing in on her. He'd spent the evening listening and drinking. Anne told him that she'd been happy to help build the business; it had been the most exciting thing she'd ever done in her life, but now it was becoming a constant series of problems. While she was good at troubleshooting and putting out fires, she didn't thrive on it, and that's all she ever seemed to do nowadays, usually putting out fires set by Michael or Lou Amory. Even today, she'd had to smooth over ruffled feathers after Michael had gotten up and left the meeting when they were halfway through.

For Nick it was a song that was stuck on "repeat" and reminded him of when they'd been lovers two years back. She seemed stuck in time, stuck in a place where she went in smaller and smaller circles, but never seemed to move on, except now there was the divorce, so perhaps she was breaking out of the cycle. What was different now and made Nick a little wary was her ex-lover Eric. He was getting possessive, and was even getting jealous of Michael, or any other person she spoke with. She'd caught him following her more than a couple of times when she'd left the office at night. He trailed her all the way to her gate, and she had recorded him on her security cameras sitting in his car near the gate to her house. She'd called him on it, and he'd, at first, denied following her, but then admitted it, and said he was sorry. Anne wasn't sure what to make of it, and he hadn't done it again as far as she knew. For Nick, the night had been one of nonstop revelations mixed with old news. He'd gotten into her car, not so much because he wanted to go home with her, but because he was far too drunk to drive himself home. If she had dropped him off at his condo, he wouldn't have minded or felt slighted, they were old friends. She hadn't dropped him off but took him home to make sure he'd be okay. Anne was wearing a green silk robe and was carrying two cups of coffee in large mugs.

"You like it with a lot of sugar as I remember." She handed him one of the cups.

"Wow. I think I was a bit high last night."

"Yes. I was going to drop you off at your place, but I was afraid you wouldn't find your way out of the parking lot. I figured you'd sleep on the couch, but you shucked off all of your clothes and insisted on the bed." She smiled. "Then you passed out. God, you can snore like an old bear. I don't remember that from two years ago."

"Only when I'm really drunk. Usually I don't."

"It's okay. I had to go sleep on the couch, though; you kept me awake."

Nick moved to get up and put a hand on his head. "Ouch."

"I'll get you something for that."

"Morphine? Heroin?"

"You'll have to settle for Tylenol."

"Okay." He said still holding his head with his free hand. "Jesus, you'd think I'd know better than that. Why did I drink so much?"

"You mentioned last night that you're not with Zoe anymore," Anne said, after handing him two white tablets. She looked at him over her coffee. "Maybe it bothers you more than you think? You were together for a while. You can't just drop a relationship like that without feeling something. Anyone would be upset, or hurt, or angry. Maybe all three?"

"We were always just friends, friends with benefits, no commitment." It sounded formulaic when he said it, as if he were reading from a card. He took the pills with coffee. She looked at him, not quite believing his nonchalance. "Besides, she has a bit of baggage herself and was getting to be a pain in the ass. I couldn't do anything right, and she jumped on whatever I said. She even got pissed off when I said 'okay.' I mean she got mad when I agreed with her. What can you do about that?" He paused, "Zoe seems to need to prove to herself that she's tough, free, and independent. She's one of the toughest people I know; just try to get close to her and she'll pound you into the ground."

"I see," Anne said, and sipped her coffee. "You're attracted to strong women, and I fall for needy men."

"Thanks."

"Not you. For a lover I've always gone to the smart, good listener."

"You should date a therapist."

"It would probably save me a lot of money." She laughed. "I seem to separate the men I fall in love with from the men I have sex with. That's a little odd, don't you think?"

"A bit schizophrenic, yeah. Maybe a little." He held his index finger and thumb close together. They sat for a few minutes in silence. They were used to each other and had long since gone past the stage where people talk to just get to know each other. Silence was fine with them.

"How's your headache?" She asked, leaning forward, her robe falling open.

"It's better." He touched his head. "You know something? I'm smart," he smiled.

"And a good listener," she said as she kissed him.

13

Marta was in Zoe's office. She was touching a small pin on the lapel of her jacket. It was a high-quality pearl in a fine white gold setting. She'd had it made from a pearl that had come from her mother's earring. The other earring had been lost after her death. By the time Marta had gotten back to Poland to settle her mother's estate, it looked as if every government official and neighbor in town had been through the house. She was grateful that they'd left one of the pearl earrings, but this might have been due to the fact that it had found its way into the folds of the thick velvet in her mother's jewelry box, and someone looking in haste would not have seen it. Her mother's collection of paintings and sketches had also disappeared, as had much of her furniture and her silver. She had argued with the police, but they had been unwilling to help her very much, other than to file an official report. They took a dim view of Polish nationals who'd emigrated.

"Sorry to have kept you waiting, Marta." Zoe shook her hand.

"No problem."

"I've done a bit of research. Your husband wants to sue for divorce under Polish law. He also claims that you're the sole reason for the divorce. If it goes through this way, you could be liable for a large monthly support payment to him. Now, we've done some checking on the information you gave, and we think we can get convincing evidence that he had a girlfriend here before he left for Poland. He might have a girlfriend there, too. We can use this to offer the court evidence that there was some responsibility on his part for the breakup. In that case, you might have to still pay support, but not nearly as much."

Marta looked up at Zoe. Her blue eyes were clouded and looked wounded. She was trying to grasp what Zoe had said, and it seemed to now be sinking in. Until then she seemed remote; now there was a lot of hurt and disbelief in her voice.

"I don't know this guy at all, I guess. I thought I did, but I don't know him, not at all. I met him when I went back to settle my mother's estate. It had been a mess, literally. Her house had been ransacked, and the police were no help. My guess is that they had a part in ransacking in the first place. He was so nice and helpful, showing me where to go, helping me fill out forms because my Polish is terrible. He helped so much. It was a very fast romance, and we were married before my visa ran out." She took a long pause. "Do you think he had this in mind all the time?"

This wasn't the first time Zoe had heard this question, or something similar. She hadn't ever found a good way to answer it. Some breakups are just a natural change between people, sometimes though, there is a lot more to it. A young woman marries a wealthy older man after his wife dies, has a kid, and then files for divorce. A manipulative man latches onto a rich woman and charms her when she is vulnerable, then leaves and files for as much as he can get. She, however, knew that this meant that Marta would go forward, and that her client had finally reached a decision or, at least, had the blinders removed. There were many people who were in such denial that they never really saw that their relationship, whatever it might have been at one time, was over, or in some cases never existed. Marta seemed to be having a serious reality check and Zoe was happy about it, although sad that it had to happen to her, and she just hoped that the inevitable backlash wouldn't end up in a destructive rage.

"Sometimes people really can't adjust to a new environment," Zoe said, as an image of Nick quickly flashed into her mind's eye. She pushed it out, a little annoyed with herself. "Whatever he had in mind when he married you makes no difference now. This is what he wants now. These are his demands. Do you want to take it to the next level? We need to show how the breakup wasn't your fault. Otherwise, he'll be entitled to a larger amount than you seem to be willing to give him, and frankly, I don't think he deserves. He's focusing on the fact that you won't move to Poland with him and that this action broke up the marriage."

"I came here with my father when I was seven. My mother joined us but went back after Dad died. She never liked it here. I became a citizen of the US as soon as I could and hardly speak the language anymore. Besides, I would make less than a quarter of what I make now. It wouldn't make any sense for me to move there. They don't pay programmers, or anyone else, anywhere close to what I can get here. Plus, I'd have to start all over again with a new company. I have no intention of doing that."

"Nor should you have to," Zoe said. "I'll prepare a response. We'll try to show that there was mutual dissatisfaction here and see what they say. It seems to me that much of the power there is up to the judge. That can be good, or it can be bad. It depends on the whim of the person wearing the robes."

"Thanks so much, Zoe." Marta got up to leave. "I guess this shows me to not be so stupid?"

"You were vulnerable." Zoe rose and shook her hand. "You shouldn't worry. We'll work this out." Marta left. Zoe worked on some of the papers in her folder, making a few notes, and then called Fred Fields, the firm's private investigator.

"Hi, Fred. Zoe."

"Hi. How are you today?" He was big, and his voice boomed out of the phone and spilled onto the desk.

"Fine," she said, pulling the phone away from her ear. "You?"

"Couldn't be better. What's up?"

"I've got a case here, but it might be a bit cold. A guy who left the country six months ago, and I'm 99 percent sure he had a girlfriend at the place he worked. I need some evidence."

"Okay. Do you have her name? Even just a first name would help."

"Yes. I can give you all the details I know." Zoe ran through the facts that Marta could remember. Her husband had usually come home late from the only job he ever had the two years he was in the States, a part-time bartender at a local nightclub. He had always claimed that he had to go out to unwind and get something to eat after work, but he usually didn't get home until well after daybreak. Fred took all the details and asked a few questions. He would see what he could find out. When he hung up, she pushed the button to disconnect and saw a list of text messages, e-mails, and missed calls pop up on her phone screen.

"I guess I'll never be bored with this job," she said, as she scrolled through her notices.

14

Anne left her apartment and drove across town to home. She noticed that Michael's car wasn't in the garage and was a little surprised that he wasn't home. Michael rarely went anywhere and never stayed overnight unless he absolutely had to. He was always a total pain about sleeping in a strange bed. Since it was Saturday, she only checked her notices to see if there was anything that really needed her attention. It was quiet, and there was nothing that couldn't wait until Monday. She sighed a little and tried some yoga to take away some of her stress. She did a few sun salutations, and then some positions that helped relieve the stiffness in her lower back that had built up from sitting far too much. Michael still hadn't arrived when she had finished, so she changed into a swimsuit and took a dip in their indoor pool. The room was decorated in a contemporary style, plenty of aluminum, stainless steel, and glass with a polished granite floor. The water reflected the silver walls and dark stone floor and always looked cold to her. It was invariably a surprise when she dove into the water to discover it was comfortably warm.

While her mind knew that the pool was heated, the color and starkness of the room made her expect it to be cold, emotional cues always seem to surpass rationality. While she was doing some laps, she heard the loud thrum of the Porsche come up the driveway. She swam for another half hour and got out of the pool. The house was certainly big enough for two people to not be in the same room, and if one person wanted to make sure that he didn't see the other, it was very easy to ensure that paths never crossed. For the past two weeks Michael had been especially good at being unavailable; he was either in his shop in the lower floor, or busy in some remote corner of the house. But today she found him right away. He was in the kitchen getting himself something to eat, both were rare occurrences. Under normal circumstances, he seemed to not know where the kitchen was, and if Anne or the housekeeper didn't make him something to eat, he would either skip a meal or order take out. He looked up from the sandwich he was making.

"Hi." He smiled at her and went back to spreading mayo on a slice of bread.

"Hi." She paused. "Just took a swim. The water's nice."

"I turned it up a little."

"It's nice and warm."

"Been home a while?" he asked. She knew enough not to lie to him. He probably already saw the security recording of her driving up the driveway a couple of hours ago.

"Long enough to do my exercises and take a swim," she purposely didn't ask him where he'd been. She knew he'd tell her sooner or later. If she pushed, he'd pout and then sulk, which was never any fun to deal with.

"I was out with a friend," he blurted, just before he took a bite of his sandwich.

"Anyone I know?" she asked, moving the towel up around her shoulders.

"I don't think so," he said finishing the bite of sandwich in his mouth. "You're not the only one with friends you know. I have friends, too, lots of them. He was acting like a little kid who knows something he's not supposed to. "I know you were out with one of your friends."

"What makes you think I was out with a friend last night?"

"Where else would you be?" he snorted.

"I might have been working late, fixing the mess you left after the meeting."

"Well, I'd have to say that staying out all night is working pretty late. Except that we saw you in Emilio's. You were with that guy you used to sleep with a couple of years ago, Nick? I think his name is Nick. Right? Big guy? Handsome like a football player?" He took a bite of sandwich. Anne was taken off guard. "You two certainly looked like you were working hard," he continued, "probably bitching about me, right?"

"Believe it or not, it's not always about you, Michael!" She lost her temper. "Sometimes it's about me, just me!" His smugness was always intolerable, but this was over the top even for him.

"I guess that hit a nerve."

"Maybe ...." She took a breath and changed direction in the conversation. "Well I'm genuinely glad you found someone to sleep with; maybe she'll be able to put up with your moody bullshit and be your 'new' mom. Maybe she can make sure you've eaten and everything is just right so that you're in a good mood so you can invent stuff, and run around after you to clean up your messes. I've certainly had enough," she said calmly, and finished drying herself off with the towel, although she was long since perfectly dry except for her bathing suit, and she wasn't about to take it off in front of him.

"Shows what you know," he said, and sauntered out of the kitchen, smiling, with his sandwich, a bag of chips, and a soda. Anne looked puzzled, and then went up to her bedroom to change out of her wet swimsuit.

Nick had taken a shower before he'd left Anne's apartment. His car was still in the parking lot behind the restaurant, and since Emilio's wasn't that far, he decided to walk the mile or so to the parking lot, cutting through lots and across town. As he walked away from the apartment, he never noticed Eric sitting in his silver Toyota Corolla across the street. Eric's car was littered with empty paper coffee cups and fast food containers. He looked as if he hadn't slept in days. Eric watched Nick until he was out of sight around the corner. He made some notes on his tablet, started up his car, and drove away.

15

Zoe went home early. She needed to take an afternoon for herself. Her apartment was inviting her to sit back and relax, and she relished the idea that no one would stop over. It had reached the point where she always felt that she'd needed to be on guard for when Nick dropped by. Now she felt free to relax and not worry if someone was going to pop in. She knew that this was a little selfish. Nick had actually been pretty good about respecting her privacy; maybe it was the ongoing need she had to feel that she controlled her life, a reaction to the years where she hadn't. Anne's divorce had been quiet so far. Michael's attorney still had a few more days to respond, but the quiet made her uneasy. She sat on the couch and turned on her TV. She selected a movie she'd been meaning to watch. It had gotten good reviews, but she was suspicious, as it had gone to DVD and streaming video in less than a month after its release. Either it was so bad no one bothered to go see it, or it was too complex for the pubescent, sexually fixated fifteen-year-olds who made up most movie audiences today and who seem to need a lot of action, and at least one exceptionally good looking sexual predator in any given movie. This movie was of the second variety: it had a sophisticated plot, and the main characters were difficult to like because they both had far too many flaws. It was a romance, but not insipid, perhaps a bit too real. What Zoe liked was that it absorbed her attention for a couple of hours and didn't disappoint. The end was bittersweet and all too believable, with no supernatural intercession whatsoever. It must have lost a ton of money, she thought, as she went to the kitchen and rummaged through the refrigerator for something to eat. She was watching the news when her phone rang. The caller ID showed a blocked number. She answered it, hesitating a little, because she hated blocked numbers.

"Zoe?"

"Yes."

"Anne here, sorry to bother you. I called your office, but they said you were at home. I remembered you put your cell number on the back of your business card."

"Yes. It's fine. I always have time for clients."

"I just found out that Michael is going to fight this tooth and nail, at least that's what I hear. He fired his attorney and hired Tim Cargil to represent him." Zoe caught her breath.

"Why in the world did he hire him? It's going to cost you a fortune now. He'll be sure of that."

"I know. Michael won't talk to me. I've moved as of today into my apartment. I only go back home to have a swim. And now only when I'm sure he's not home."

"I already know that Cargil plays dirty. Be sure to pull half the money out of any joint accounts and get printouts of all your credit card transactions to date. You might want to open a new account with only your name on it. Also, you need new savings and checking accounts in your name only. Do it today."

"Already done. I started getting suspicious when he was so chipper. I took my name off all the credit cards, and I already have my own. I've got all new accounts."

"Good. They still have time to respond. My guess is he'll wait to the last minute and hit us with a bunch of discovery motions, anything he can think of, and anything else he can do to run up his bill. I'll try to keep our expenses down, but I'll have to respond to each one of his motions. I'm legally obligated."

"I know. Not much we can do about it," She paused, "They might bring up my affairs, which would be stupiMichael certainly knew all about them. I told him."

"Okay, that might work out in our favor. He can't pretend they were a shock or anything. I think we can try to head off some of the damage here. We did file first. So that helps a lot," Zoe said.

"I just don't want it to become a huge deal, or we'll certainly lose some of the partners." Anne's voice, already altered by the cell phone, seemed to strain even more.

"If he hurts the business, he hurts himself. Doesn't he get that?" Zoe asked.

"Sure, but emotionally he's about twelve. He might not care," Anne replied, and Zoe knew this was true. She'd had more mature clients than Michael destroy their family fortunes simply to prove a point.

"Let's not borrow any new trouble. Just hang in there, and we'll see what they ask for." They talked a little longer, and after Anne hung up, Zoe looked at her watch and called Jimmy. He didn't pick up. The thought of dealing with Cargil wasn't something she relished, but she'd dealt with him before, and would be ready for his games, or hoped so.

16

Fred Fields was returning to his car. He'd just had a long conversation with Marta's husband's ex-girlfriend who was only too happy to tell him all he needed to know. He'd never told his girlfriend that has was married, nor did he bother telling her that the money he'd talked her into borrowing was going to be used for a plane ticket for him to go to Poland along with some spending money. He was not coming back anytime soon, or at all. Apparently, he had proposed to her, and she was under the assumption they were engaged. She'd borrowed fifteen thousand dollars to help pay for the wedding she was planning with him as a cosigner for the loan. They had even booked a reception hall and picked a menu from a caterer. The day after the money landed in their joint account, he had taken all the fifteen thousand and disappeared. He simply vanished. She had tried to find his apartment, but he had given her and the bank a bogus address, and his mailing address was a private P.O. Box from a mail service.

When Fred had told her that her boyfriend was a Polish national married to a naturalized American citizen and that he was suing his wife for divorce for estrangement of affection, Fred wasn't sure if the girl was going to laugh, cry, or throw something. She picked up a heavy glass beer pitcher and polished it repeatedly with a bar towel as she told him her story. She would have no problem swearing out an affidavit about the affair, the engagement, and the money, which would show his intention of leaving, not to mention his character. In his papers for divorce, he'd claimed that he left Marta because his wife made his life miserable and wouldn't go back to Europe with him. His girlfriend's story was a little different. Fred knew that it would show the guy to be little more than a cold calculating con artist

Fred sent a text to Zoe asking her if she'd want supporting evidence from any of the girl's friends and coworkers. They could come to her office and swear out affidavits. The owner of the bar had been a little reserved about talking to Fred because he'd hired the bastard off the books and didn't want any trouble with the IRS or Immigration. Fred had to give the husband credit for having brass balls if nothing else. He covered his tracks well and seemed to have played everyone for a sucker. The bar where the girlfriend worked was popular with the cocktail set. And the place was just opening for early dinner and happy hour when he was leaving.

He had written up his report on his notebook, e-mailed it to Zoe, and sent another text message to Zoe's phone. He started his car and looked in his side mirror to check for traffic; he noticed a guy walking into the bar that was another one of Zoe's cases. Michael Mali's face was well known because of the numerous articles written about him and his wife, Anne. He was a local celebrity. Fred decided this was something he should be checking out and shut off the car. He got out and looked up the street. Michael's car wasn't far away. He sauntered over to the Porsche and quickly had the door open. He rummaged through the glove box and looked at the various receipts scattered all over the car among the debris of countless fast-food meals. The car hadn't been cleaned since the day it left the showroom. He was amazed at how poorly someone could treat a car that cost about what he made in a good year. He wasn't looking for anything in particular but for something that might interest Zoe. The car was such a mess inside that he had almost given up when he saw a cheap digital photo of Michael with his arm around someone. He picked up the picture and looked closely. The two were in a tropical place where there were plenty of palm trees. He looked closely at the photo and recognized Jimmy, Zoe's paralegal, looking suntanned and happy. Fred tucked the photo into his breast pocket, locked the car, and reset the alarm. He walked into the bar, the girlfriend recognized him, and gave him a puzzled look.

"I'm on a different case now."

"Okay. I just wondered. If you have any more questions, I'm working now, and I can't talk." She was serious. Her tray was loaded with drinks and food, and the background uproar went up a notch.

"I need a seat where I can keep an eye on that guy." He pointed to Michael. She looked around the room and sat him at a small table near a pillar where he could see Michael, but was hidden from direct view. He handed her a fifty.

"I'll take a Coke when you get a chance," he said. She smiled when she took the money, but then frowned.

"Do you think I can sue the jerk?" she said, shifting her tray. Fred was always amazed at how much weight the average waitress could carry at one time.

"I'm not sure. I think he has to be back in the States for that, but I'm no attorney. You can ask Zoe when you swear out your affidavit." His voice was more hopeful than he was, though. Fifteen thousand was a lot of money for anyone and it was certainly a lot for someone in her income bracket. She had been taken by a real pro.

Fred kept an eye on Michael and the rest of the crowd. They were mostly professionals coming out for some midweek relaxation. Couples hung together around the edges of the room, while the singles congregated at the bar or moved to the center of the room sitting in large groups at big tables. A deejay was setting up, but most people were eating, and there was a low level of noise that competed with the sound system. Michael was sitting at a table near the bar sipping a light green cocktail. After about an hour Jimmy appeared. He and Michael greeted each other affectionately, and Fred took some candid pictures. When the deejay started to crank up the music, Fred left, but waited in his car. He gambled that it would be an early night for the couple, and he was right. Jimmy and Michael left within the hour. Fred followed the Porsche to Jimmy's apartment house. He snapped a few choice photos of them going into the lobby arm in arm. After a while, when it was clear they were settled in for the night, Fred called it a day and drove to his home in the suburbs. He was tired and didn't notice that a silver Corolla followed him for a few blocks but then turned off.

17

Kristen O'Hare was sitting across from her estranged husband, Ken. Zoe was sitting next to him; Kristen's attorney was looking through his notes. They'd had a very long deposition, and Kristen had spent the better part of it as the "injured spouse," making a huge case out of her husband's credit card receipts for a motel room and his obvious affair. While Ken should have been smarter than that, she'd been a complete idiot the whole morning, dragging out a simple deposition for the better part of a day, and her attorney, at $300 an hour, was glad to encourage her to take all the time she wanted. Zoe was losing patience with both of them.

"You agreed to these terms a month ago and said that you'd sign them. Is there any reason why you won't agree with them now?" Zoe asked.

"I've changed my mind."

"Is that why you've been shutting off the power to your husband's office when he's trying to work, to pay the bills for both of you, by the way?"

"I don't do that. That's a lie." She set her face like a stubborn spoiled child.

"So, this journal kept by your husband recording every time you shut the power off to his office over the course of the last month is not true?"

"He made it up." Zoe reached into a folder and pulled out a piece of paper. It was a report log printed out from Ken's uninterrupted power supply that he'd bought after Kristen had started her games. It showed each time there was a power failure.

"This is an electronic record of each and every time you killed the power to his office computer." Kristen looked nonplussed but remained stubborn.

"He could have made that up, too."

"Right, he sat there and pulled the plug on his own equipment over and over again just to get back at you?"

"Maybe." She looked like a four-year-old holding out for an ice cream. Zoe half expected her to hold her breath until she turned blue.

"Why would he do that?" Zoe asked. "Would there have been any reason at all? Not that he would do something that foolish, especially since this caused him to move out before he really could afford to. Why would he do that when he was willing to sign a mutually beneficial agreement just one month ago, and so were you, as I remember?"

"To get back at me."

"For what?"

"Oh. Who knows?" She hesitated. Kristen was beginning to not like the direction of the conversation. Zoe slowly and deliberately took out a package of photos. She had hoped to not have to use them. She didn't like to do business this way, but Kristen O'Hare left her no choice. They were some of Fred Field's best work, night-vision photography through Kristen's bedroom window. It was a part of Zoe's plan. Ken had moved out to clear the way. The photos were very strong and explicit in showing Kristen with her neighbor, a married man who'd been her lover since before the divorce proceeding began. They were very high definition, real quality photos. You could almost count the freckles on her enraptured face. She needed to give this woman a harsh reality check. As she placed the photos on the table, Kristen slowly turned white, and then translucent. Zoe thought she was going to faint. It's amazing, she thought, how stupid this woman thought everyone else was. The fact that her husband had been kind enough not to mention her ongoing affair she mistook as simple weakness on his part, or stupidity, or maybe evidence that she was really clever, which she wasn't. Zoe thought that we all like to think we're above average in intelligence, no matter how much evidence is shown to the contrary. Kristen tried to brush the pictures off the table, but Zoe grabbed most of them before they landed on the floor. Kristen's attorney picked up one of the more graphic photos and studied it. His client was a very pretty woman.

"Well no one sues for divorce for adultery in this state," he mumbled.

"Of course not, I know that. I just wondered if you did. Why have we been playing these games for the past six hours? You've been giving us holy hell because my client has a girlfriend, one he has the discretion to see at a motel room, far from their neighborhood and far from their children, discretion that Mrs. O'Hare seems to feel is unnecessary in her case." Zoe paused for a long time, and then changed her voice to be soft and clear. "There is a perfectly fine and fair agreement on the table; the same one that was there last month. Is your client going to sign it this time, or are we going to dance around some more? I can include these photos as evidence of irreconcilable differences. I'm sure the judge will have fun looking at them."

"You bitch," Kristen screamed.

"Yes. I am when I have to be. When people like you force me to be," Zoe paused. "Look, Kristen, you're not quite as smart as you think you are, and the rest of us aren't nearly as dumb as you'd like us to be. Sometimes people are just polite or nice. It doesn't mean they're stupid or weak. Ken has known about you and the neighborhood Don Juan for a long time. He's just been polite about it. By the way, you're like the fifth notch on his belt in your neighborhood alone, according to my private investigator, but that's your issue. Now, do we settle this with or without these pictures? And are you going to grow up, act like an adult, and sign the papers so you can both move on? I bill by the hour, so does your attorney, so make up your mind. The next stop is court and we can leave it up to the judge. My firm will be happy to take more of your money. Court costs usually double my hourly rates, more if I need to bring my paralegal along." Kristen's attorney sat straight up, like he'd just gotten a wonderful idea.

"Okay, I agree." She was almost in tears, and Zoe had a moment when she felt a little guilty but knew this was the best way to play this out.

"I'll have my paralegal draft the agreement with the new changes, and *you will sign it before you leave*. No offence, but we've been here before." She stood up. Her legs hurt from sitting so long. Ken looked shocked, and Kristen and her attorney left the room.

"Wow. Thanks. I didn't think she'd budge on anything," Ken said.

"She was a bit hardheaded."

"I almost feel sorry for her."

"Don't"

"I won't. I said 'almost,' remember?"

"Keep it that way. You don't need to waste any more of your money. Get on with your life." She stuck out her hand. At this point in the process, her job was pretty much finished. All they needed to do was file the final papers and wait for the judge to sign them. "Bye, Ken. Jimmy will have your papers ready soon, and then we file them in court. When the judge signs them, you're divorced."

"Wow. I can't believe it, not yet. It's over." He paused. "Bye, Zoe. Thanks." He shook her hand.

18

"They're being difficult in the way they're writing, even for legalese. They probably think you have no idea what they're trying to do, and that you'll just sign off on their demands, thinking that this is normal," Denton Pike said as he handed Zoe the latest translation of Marta's divorce papers. The lawyers in Poland had responded, insisting that Marta was the sole cause for the breakup of the marriage and their client was the innocent party, and encouraged Zoe to simply have her client sign off as a matter of formality. She had Denton draft a response, and they'd been working on it the better part of the morning. He was attentive and had helped her frame some of the more subtle legal points dealing with joint property and bank accounts. He also translated the affidavits that she had gotten from the waitress at the bar who had thought she was engaged to Marta's husband just before he absconded with the "wedding" money.

When they were finished, Zoe made copies and called in Jimmy to get the package ready to go in certified international mail. She had responded with the whole story about the husband, right down to copies of the loan, with his signature as a joint signer, and the contracts for the reception hall. She couldn't see a way out for the husband at this point, but she knew he was slick and wondered what bogus con-artist explanation he'd come up with to worm out of this one. If the divorce went through with him as an "innocent party" he could demand to be supported in the way Marta had supported him here, and she had a very good income.

"We have other international clients. I spoke to the partners about putting you on contract," Zoe said to Denton.

"That would be fine. We might have to continue this at long distance, though."

"I know, you said before that you might relocate."

"How is you high profile case going?"

"You mean the Mali's?"

"TrendInventions is a huge company in this area. Thousands of people depend on it."

"Yes. You know I can't discuss a case with you," Zoe said.

"Of course not, but it's made the newspapers more than once."

"Yes. About half of what they print is actually true."

"I'm sure. Hope they work things out," Denton said.

"Me, too. Believe me. I hate it when clients do this the hard way."

"That makes you a rare one in this business."

"Maybe, but a collaborative divorce helps everyone, especially if kids are involved," Zoe said.

"There were no kids involved with my divorce, but it still wasn't too collaborative. I gave her a lot to get rid of her," Denton replied.

"Sorry to hear that."

"It was a long time ago. Judy's divorce was worse. Her fundamentalist relatives made sure of that. She had to get a restraining order to stop them from calling her and telling her Jesus wanted her to be with her husband. Apparently, they'd spoken to him personally. Her ex even flew back here and showed up on her doorstep demanding for her to come home with him and be his wife."

"Wow."

"They justified it by saying they were trying to prevent her from becoming a fallen woman; they were saving her soul, fighting Satan. It was either return to the marriage bed with him or go to hell for eternity," Denton said.

"It was for her own good, I see."

"Right. Just doing the Lord's work."

"Not too self-righteous," Zoe said, rubbing her eyes.

"No. Not when it comes to saving someone. You can never be too self-righteous I guess," Denton smiled. Zoe smiled back.

"Looks like she's gotten over it. You, too, I see?"

"It was a long time ago for both of us."

"That's what usually happens, but sometimes people don't get over it. They don't move on or let go. It's sad when that happens. One of my first cases, she still calls me about once a month and carries on like it was yesterday. She still follows him and checks out his girlfriends. He's recently become engaged again, and she's beside herself. The odd thing is that she initiated the action. She wanted the divorce, and she got what she wanted. Very weird. I was a little worried about her and had our private investigator check her out to make sure she wasn't planning on doing anything stupid, but she's not crazy or potentially violent, or anything like that, just won't let go. I try to vet people a lot more now before I take their case. I have that luxury now, though, not when I started."

"You've got quite a reputation."

"It's all true," Zoe smiled, "especially what you read in the papers. They make me out like I'm some whiz, at least for now. If anything goes wrong with this case, I'll be the idiot who blew it." She smiled again and then stood up. It was early afternoon, and she had had enough already. The morning had been productive but exhausting, and she had the feeling that this case she and Denton were working was not going to get solved very quickly. The husband had time on his side, and knew he would wear down Marta, and that she would give in eventually, even if his demands were ridiculous. Zoe knew this, too. Marta liked harmony in her life. She wasn't a fighter. Zoe knew she'd have to come up with an alternative plan before her client reached the end of her patience.

19

Anne and Eric – The previous winter

Eric had gotten up earlier than Anne. He made coffee and then went out for some pastry. The morning was cold, but her apartment wasn't far from a local bakery.

"Hi. Coffee is a little old, but I can make a fresh pot," he said as she walked into the kitchen.

"That's fine. I usually never have a hot coffee anyway, too busy. She sat down and ate one of the pastries and sipped the coffee. She and Eric had been together for a month or two, but she wasn't sure if she wanted to keep this thing going. Her husband was one of those people who seemed to be able to live without sex, she wasn't; it was simple as that, and the lovers she usually slept with understood that. It was only for the sex, but she might have made a mistake with Eric. He seemed to feel there was a lot more going on than there was.

"I got you something." Eric said. Anne felt the pastry stick in her throat.

"Really? Eric, you know that this is just a causal thing, right?"

"Sure," he said quickly as he gave her a wrapped box. She hesitated, and then opened it. It was a gold name bracelet inscribed with "Anne" with several small diamonds around her name.

"It's so sweet of you, but you know I can't wear it. Michael is not an idiot."

"Maybe you should face the fact that you need to leave him."

"Then what would he do? He'd be lost."

"Not your problem."

"Yes, it is, Eric," he happens to dream up all the stuff we sell," she paused, "we all happen to make a good living from his ideas. Don't forget it."

"Yes, but at what cost?" Eric said.

"Look, Eric. You're sweet, but I don't think you understand. Even if I left Michael, and yes, I've been thinking about it, it wouldn't be for you. Not for anyone. It would be for me, for myself, for my own life. Get it?"

"Not even for Nick?" Eric said, his face red, and anger rising.

"Nick?" What has he got to do with it?" Anne said, genuinely confused.

"You went out with him. Don't deny it."

"Why would I? Everyone knows we were together for a while."

"He doesn't love you."

"Of course, he doesn't. That's the point, Eric!"

"Isn't that why you broke up?"

"No. We broke up by mutual consent. When he got his new job, we simply drifted apart. We didn't have time for each other. It was too much to try to meet up when we both had a few free minutes. It seemed silly to maintain a relationship like that."

"You're lying!" He was almost hysterical. "You know that I love you more than Nick or Michael ever could. You have to know that."

"I know no such thing, Eric. Sorry if you think it was more than it was." She reached out to him. He pulled away and snatched the id bracelet from her. He hastily gathered his things from the night before and went for the door. "Look, Eric, let's cool this thing now. We're both adults. We had fun, but let's just call it quits now."

"Sure," he said. "Anything for you, Anne." He smiled and gently closed the door. Somehow Anne thought that she would have felt a lot better had he yelled at her and slammed the door behind him.

20

Eric had been shadowing Anne for a few days. It had been hot in his car, but he never missed a moment. He'd seen Nick leaving her apartment in the early morning hours more often. He was at his desk at TrendInventions and he'd gotten very little sleep over the past few days. Between tailing Anne and Michael, and with his unfocused rage, sleep was out of the question. Anne had been in a meeting all morning and was just getting ready to go get lunch. He'd sent her an e-mail asking her out to lunch, with a handful of emoticons, mostly smiley faces, at the end of the message. She'd not responded. He came over to her as she was going in her office.

"Hi, Eric."

"What's up, Anne? Are you ignoring my e-mails?"

"No. I don't think so. I haven't checked my messages yet today."

"I was wondering about lunch."

"Today? No. I'm really busy."

"Maybe tomorrow?"

"Look, Eric, I'm not sure if that's wise."

"It's just lunch, for goodness sake."

"No. Not really. Not with you. You always seem to make a lot more out of it than what's there."

"I apologized for following you that day," he said.

"I know." She paused. "Look, with the divorce and all I need to be very careful. Maybe some other time. Okay?" She pushed past him into her office.

"I'm sure you have time for Nick though, right?" She looked at him, and then closed her door. Eric had been well over the top lately with his behavior. She'd almost fired him more than once. She'd realized too late that he was not the kind of guy who would simply have some fun with her and then move on. He was obsessing, and that was getting annoying, and now it was a little scary. Obviously, he'd been following her again, otherwise how would he have known about Nick, although he could have seen them together while they were out having dinner. She thought that this was probably not how he knew, not by accident. He was probably stalking her again, only doing it more carefully. She needed to keep an eye out for him to make sure. Anne noticed her hand was shaking and grabbed it with her other hand. She called her secretary, April, to order a sandwich and told her to hold all nonemergency calls. When the sandwich arrived, she took a few bites, but had no appetite. Her stomach was queasy, and she thought that she'd vomit. She called Nick on his cell. He was out of town for a few days. She never called him, and he never bothered her during her long workday. He answered on the third ring with a puzzled tone.

"Anne?" he asked, not sure if she would be on the phone even though her name came up on the caller ID. She told him about Eric's comment.

"He's just an asshole," Nick said. "Don't pay any attention to him."

"But what if he starts talking?"

"About what? Us? We're just friends."

"Well, maybe a little more?"

"So what? It's not the nineteenth century, and we don't live in one of those bizarre countries where they stone you to death for having extramarital sex, at least not yet. Give the conservatives a few more years."

"He's just gotten really creepy."

"Then fire him."

"No grounds. The union would have a fit," Anne said. "And I'd feel guilty about him losing his job. I should never have slept with him. He seems normal when you first meet him, but then you find out there is something weird about him, nothing you can put your finger on, but he seems to live a little too much in his own mind. I think he thought that we would get married for god's sake. He might even think that I am divorcing Michael to marry him."

"Sounds like a candidate for the Twilight Zone. Just give him time. I'm sure he'll give you grounds to fire him."

"In a way, I'm worried about that, too. He might just go to the press and make up a lot of nonsense. The scandal would be enough to have some of the investors jump ship. We'd never be able to recover."

"Don't worry. Look. I'll be back the day after tomorrow, we'll have some fun. You've been too serious lately. Don't let the asshole get to you. Just give him enough rope, and when he screws up, get rid of him. And he will screw up. Don't you have a court order for him to stay away after work hours?"

"Not quite. I didn't want any public record. After I had him arrested for stalking me, he promised he'd behave."

"But you can get Zoe on it and get an order. She can be discreet. You're too worried about image. If he steps out of line in the least, you have to fire him. Even if he files a grievance, you can postpone the hearing until he decides to not be a jerk. After he runs out of money, he might listen to reason."

"Makes sense." Anne was feeling better, but then felt a little guilty about feeling good about possibly firing someone. She still blamed herself for having an affair with Eric. Then she stopped herself, how was she supposed to know he was a psycho? If he had been a woman, or a secretary instead of a top-notch budget analyst, he'd have been fired a long time ago for just half of the crap he pulled. She finished up the work she had from the morning's meetings and went to her afternoon meeting with some of the development guys. There was a glitch in one of the new products that might delay shipment. They needed her advice. She perused the notes while walking down the hall. Apparently the specs had been off on one minor component, but it made it impossible for the final assembly to take place without it, so the development guys had come up with a few ideas to work around the problem, some cost a few cents a unit, other solutions cost more, but were a higher quality fix. She was fully absorbed in the problem and working out costs in her head when a loud voice cut through her thoughts.

"So, you'd rather have lunch by yourself than with me?" Eric ambushed her in the hall.

"No. I have a lot of work to do."

"Bullshit."

"I beg your pardon?"

"You heard me."

"Look, Eric, I'm your boss. Your behavior is offensive and way out of line. You need to get hold of yourself and stop acting like a sixteen-year-old boy with hormonal issues."

"You're the one who needs to get over yourself. You own this company and you think you own everyone in it. You think that you can do anything you want because you're God's gift to the world." He was getting louder. Several people had stopped to look. "You're just a Goddamn slut. You and that faggot husband of yours. The two of you would sleep with anyone who'll have you." A security guard appeared and made a move toward Eric. Anne waved him back.

"You're obviously upset. You need to get ahold of yourself," Anne said, as quietly and calmly as she could under the circumstances. Eric looked at her for a minute, started to turn away, and then spun around and launched himself at Anne, grabbing her by the throat and knocking her down on the floor. She hit the back of her head against a table. Anne blacked out. When she came to, she saw her secretary, April, hovering over her.

"We've called an ambulance," April said. "You shouldn't move."

"I'm okay," Anne said, and sat up, but she was dizzy and wobbled. She noticed the blood on her blouse and realized it was hers. Her first thought was that she would need to get changed before her next meeting. She couldn't go to a meeting with blood on her blouse. Then she saw Eric. The security guard had obviously tackled and restrained him. He had a large bruise on his forehead, and the start of a black eye.

"I've called the police, Mrs. Mali. They're on the way. I can give them a statement. You want to press charges?" the security guard asked.

"No. Just get him out of here," she said, holding a cloth to the back of her head. The guard looked a little confused. "Have him pack up his things and leave. Tell the police we've got it under control." She turned to Eric. "Eric, you're so fucking fired. What the hell is wrong with you?" Eric looked at the floor. The guard shook his head, but got on his radio, and marched Eric down the hall to his office. He looked as if he contemplated another "accident" for him on the way out the door. Anne met the paramedics in her office. A small, wiry, woman cleaned and dressed the cut on the back of her head and explained to her that she needed an x-ray to find out if she had a concussion. She promised she'd go and see her doctor and signed the release form the women handed her. The paramedic looked at her with some concern.

"You can't mess around with a head injury. You definitely need to make sure you haven't got a concussion or any other problem."

"I will take care of it," Anne said. The paramedics left after giving Anne her copy of the release form. April walked her back to the office and insisted on helping Anne out of her bloody blouse. She got a robe from the closet in her private dressing room.

"I'm going to stay here in case you need me," April said.

"No. I'll be fine, really."

"I'll just be on the other side of the door. I was going to leave early today because my son is home from school for the week, but I can stay if you want me to."

"No, April, please go home." After April left, she was alone in her office. She sat back in her chair, noticing the dried blood that ruined her expensive silk blouse which was neatly folded in a pile on the table next to her desk. Anne rinsed it in the sink in her private bathroom. There was a complete change of clothes in her closet. She showered, being careful not to get the back of her head wet. It was still very sore, although the painkillers that the paramedic gave her were just kicking in. While she dressed in fresh clothes, her mind wandered. Eric, what an asshole, she thought, and then, I wonder what he meant by calling Michael a faggot?

21

Tim Cargil and Michael sat across from Zoe and Anne. They had answered the summons at the very end of the time limit and had demanded a hearing, which was normal procedure, but Cargil had already filed several nuisance motions so he could cause problems. Zoe had held him off for a while so she could go over the responses. They demanded that Anne give most of the company to Michael, and that she stays on for a period of one year as CEO/CFO until they could find a replacement her. The reasoning was that while Anne was an important part of their business, Michael was the inventor, and his name was on most of the patents. Therefore, he deserved the lion's share of the business. Zoe essentially countered with the argument that the business had been built by mutual effort. Michael designed and built the unique items that they produced, and Anne did everything else, from supervising marketing and development, to securing funds, to running the everyday chores of the company. Without her, there would be no company, so she was entitled to half in accordance with state law.

"We have evidence that she is not necessarily that beneficial to the company," Cargil said.

"She built it, while your client fiddled around in his garage." Zoe responded.

"Not the way I hear it. According to some of the board members, she has been less than effective as a CEO/CFO, and recently there was an incident at work where she had a physical altercation with one of her employees. I wouldn't call that the behavior of someone who is building a company."

"The incident at work was from a disgruntled employee. That sort of thing happens. It's neither here nor there. I read some of the depositions from the board that you have. They're whining, just plain and simple. The main complaint is that she doesn't take their advice like they're some sort of financial oracles. They need to read the fine print they signed when they agreed to the limited partnership. Her record speaks for itself. In this recession she's kept the company comfortably profitable while introducing new products." Zoe paused.

"Products that were developed by Michael," Cargil said.

"No one has ever contested that. Michael is the idea man of TrendInventions. Anne is the person who's made the company work and brought it to where it is today, a profitable company that is one of the best of its kind in the country," Zoe answered.

"Actually, TrendInventions has underperformed in the last two quarters," Cargil countered.

"The whole economy has underperformed in the last two quarters." Zoe was losing patience. The entire economy had been in the toilet for the last five years. TrendInventions had made a profit! Just keeping out of bankruptcy court had been a major feat for many smaller companies. She signaled an end to the conversation. The meeting was supposed to have a fact-finding, question-and-answer format. "Now we're here to establish the facts of the case. What questions do you have for my client?"

Cargil purposely asked questions designed to fluster Anne, but she kept her cool. Years of dealing with morons in tediously long meetings had helped her develop patience. It was clear where Tim Cargil was going. He had researched every minor and major mistake she'd made since the company began. Zoe could only imagine what his billed hours already were. He'd interviewed pretty much every disgruntled employee from the day the business opened. His strategy was to try to show how Anne had been riding Michael's coattails, and in some cases holding him back over the years, while doing a mediocre job of running the company. If he could make the argument that she was just an employee, and not necessarily the best person for the job, that she had been a burden to the business, he might be able to get a reduction in the division of marriage property even though she and Michael were cofounders of the business. Zoe was well aware of this, as was Anne, who was good at heading off his line of questions, and he ended up getting tedious and repetitive, but he was tenacious and seemed well aware of every mistake that Anne had made, no matter how small or unimportant. Zoe was at once impressed with his research and wondered where he'd gotten his information. Since Michael had almost no clue as to how the business was run, he must have interviewed just about everyone who had any contact with Anne since the start of the business, or someone who had been there since the beginning. But there was obviously a source here, someone who was in

Intimate Disconnect

on the most privileged information of TrendInventions, someone in a position who obviously had a grudge against Anne. Zoe made a note to ask her about this. She then began to question Michael.

"Do you remember the first gadget you invented for the company?"

"Yeah."

"Could you please elaborate?"

"A super-insulated coffee cup that has a battery operated warmer. You can charge it with your car's USB port."

"Do you remember what you called it?"

"Anne named it the Coffee-2-Go mug."

"So, Anne named it and it was your first patent. You must have been proud," Zoe said.

"Yes. And I invented it by myself in my garage. She had nothing to do with it."

"What job did you have at the time?"

"None," Michael said, a little peeved. "I was inventing."

"How much was your mortgage on that house? The first one you bought right after your marriage?" Zoe asked.

"Don't know." Michael shrugged.

"Monthly utilities? Cable? Internet? Do you know how much any of these were?"

Michael shrugged.

"Do you know how much the materials cost for you to make the prototype of the Coffee-2-Go mug?"

"No."

"Is that because Anne paid all the bills with her salary as an advertising executive? Isn't it true you never had to work a steady job at all from the moment you married her?"

"She latched on to me."

"And you certainly are a prize, aren't you?" Zoe said under her breath, and then changed tactics. "The Coffee-2-Go mug, how much did it cost per unit to make the first run?"

Silence.

"Okay, that might be an unfair question, how about something simple like how large was your first production run?"

Silence.

"Which company made the first consignment of mugs for you?" Zoe asked the rest without pause. "How did you pay for them? Did you take out a small business loan? A thirty-day note? Where did you advertise? What large catalog company placed the very first order with you? Who designed the packaging?"

Silence.

"Okay, let's move on. How many patents do you actually hold?"

"All of them. They're all my ideas."

"How many exactly?"

"I don't know."

"How do you apply for a patent on one of your inventions? What is the procedure to file with the U.S. Patent Office?"

Again, Michael lapsed into silence.

All her questions along these lines were met with mute silence, and as she went on, thoroughly making her point, Michael started getting red in the face and angry. He began to sputter, and he pouted like a child. She persisted with the questions, pushing him, hoping he would lose his temper.

"How the hell should I know?" he finally bellowed. "That's *her* job. Anne takes care of all that!"

"Well I'm glad you realize that." Zoe sat back and smiled. "Anne took care of all of those little things that made the company actually run and kept people from stealing your ideas. Is that true?"

Michael sat in stubborn silence.

"That's okay, it's on the record." Zoe smiled. Tim Cargil showed no emotion. He was too professional for that, but for one brief moment he looked across the desk with an expression of rage that immediately switched to cunning. Never one to stay mad, he was known for always getting even. Zoe finished her questions and had strongly established that Anne was the main driving force behind the company, not quite the incompetent and replaceable cog that Cargil was trying to paint her, which is when he shifted tactics, going back on the offensive.

"I will let you know that we're getting a restraining order," Cargil said, causally.

"What?" Zoe asked, and Anne tensed. "On what grounds?"

"Stalking. On several occasions my client went home to find her in the house."

"It's her house. too, for God's sake, she was swimming."

"That's her claim. That and the violent incident at work are enough."

"She was attacked at work."

"We don't know that for sure. The police were never called. In fact, they were told specifically to not come. All we have is hearsay from people who work for her, who owe their jobs to her. We have no idea who started the altercation. We do know she'd had an affair with the guy." Cargil looked through his notes, more for a dramatic pause. "Eric. He actually swore out an affidavit saying she started the altercation by pushing him."

Zoe looked at the affidavit. It was so chock full of legalese that it was obvious Cargil had written it and Eric had signed it. Jilted lovers can always be a problem, especially the stalking, slightly unhinged variety.

"We have an investigator's report that shows this man stalking Anne over a month ago," Zoe said.

"Was it reported to the police?"

"No. He was warned. It's in the employee records."

"How convenient for you," Cargil replied. He got up to leave and tapped Michael on the shoulder. They started to go when Cargil turned around, as if by afterthought, but there was no such thing as an afterthought with him.

"I almost forgot to show you some photos that our investigator gave us." He dropped an envelope on the desk. Zoe picked it up and opened it. There were photos of Jimmy and Michael in an embrace in front of Michael's house, coming out of a bar, and of Jimmy leaving Michael's house obviously early in the morning. There were no intimate photos, probably because of Michael's high-tech security system. The investigator couldn't get close enough to point a camera in through a window.

"Two friends out for an evening?" Zoe said, recovering from the shock.

"Perhaps, but I do believe one of them works for you." Cargil was cool.

"He has little to do with this case," Zoe said, which happened to be at least partly true. She'd had assigned him to work most of her caseload with a newly hired attorney while she focused mostly on this case alone.

"I think he's your paralegal. He must have something to do with the case."

"I'll take care of it."

"I just want to say that this could be a conflict—"

"I said that I will take care of it." Zoe raised her voice and locked eyes with Cargil, a man not used to looking anyone in the eye. He backed down and closed his briefcase as if it were a mousetrap, smiled his broad, most political smile, and left.

***

Jimmy was standing in front of Zoe's desk. Her eyes flashed every now and then as she dressed him down. He, of all people should have known better. He should have told her about his relationship with Michael instead of letting her find out as a surprise. He was tall and thin, and although he was standing, he looked smaller and smaller. Jimmy expected to be fired, and Zoe had expected to fire him right after the meeting with Cargil. However, she allowed herself to cool off and had talked with a couple of the partners. It was decided that they'd build a firewall between Jimmy and the Mali case. He'd also have to agree to not see Michael until the case was resolved. He would be moved to another office and would be required to leave the room if the Mali case came up for discussion. The consensus among the partners was that Jimmy was too valuable an asset to fire. One partner who handled all of their civil rights and workers' comp cases pointed out that they were doing far more to separate Jimmy from a case where there might be a conflict of interest than some Supreme Court Justices felt was necessary or ethical in the decisions they handed down. If it is acceptable for those justices to rule on cases involving a close friend, or to rule on a case where one side was a cause publicly championed by a politically active spouse, then an employee involved with a client's husband would certainly be fine, especially when that person wasn't even officially involved with the case. In fact, that was the argument Zoe would make if questioned. The ethical bar concerning conflict of interest was far higher in her firm than at the Supreme Court of the United States.

After scolding him, she told Jimmy to leave. She couldn't help but feel disappointed in him, but she also knew he was excellent at what he did, and she would rather have him work for her firm than anyone else's in the city. The move to retain him was strategic. But it was a good thing that she didn't find him right after the hearing. With her temper, she would have fired him on the spot.

She turned her attention to one other case she was still handling. Marta's husband's attorney was the Polish equivalent of Tim Cargil and was going for the jugular. He had upped the requested amount for support because of the emotional strain caused by the "delaying tactics" of Marta and her attorney. They claimed that the story about the young woman from work and her marriage plans was an outright lie. Her affidavits were the product of the fevered imagination of a young woman, possibly in love with an older man. Zoe chuckled a few times while reading Denton's translation. What he also managed to translate, though, was the distinct tone of anxiety that formed a strong subtext. They were trying too hard. It was a bluff. Zoe immediately thought that the husband must have just about burned through the fifteen thousand he scammed. She took a gamble and called Denton who was visiting his friend in New Mexico. She spoke about an idea she had, and he agreed. She gave him a few details, and then called Marta. In about an hour Marta was in her office, and the letter, with translation, was in Zoe's email box.

My Dearest,

I am so sorry for all the trouble I've caused you. You must understand that I was very frightened of moving to a place where I know no one and am clumsy with the language. But it occurred to me that I'd expected exactly that from you, and I am deeply sorry that you were unhappy here in America. Can you forgive me?

I realize that this divorce is only your lashing out because you feel hurt, and I don't blame you. To show my love for you I've decided to turn in my resignation. It will take me a few weeks to get a work visa, but I will be moving to Poland to be with you my love. I already have a job offer from a company near your hometown, but the pay is less than a quarter of what I can make here. That won't be a problem will it? Our love will survive, and that's the important thing.

With all my love,
   Marta

"I think that should do it. Don't you?" Zoe said to Marta.

"Do you think he will take me up on it?" Marta said.

"What do you think? But you will have to send him *some* support, not that he deserves it, but it will cost you more to fight it than to just pay him off," she paused. "Now I have two beautiful types of stationery here," Zoe said, holding up two sheets of fine linen paper. "Both are nice and thick with a pretty watermark. Do you want the cream or the blue? Do you have any perfume on you? We could sprinkle a little on the letter."

That evening, Zoe sat in front of her TV. She found it distracting enough to keep her from thinking about work. While the story line was a little thin and the characters somewhat simple, the special effects were first rate. The phone rang. It was Chris. She paused the movie and answered the phone.

"Hi."

"Zoe, you were supposed to call?"

"I know. Just tired, I guess. Sorry I forgot. Got home late today."

"I thought you'd be out dancing and partying."

"Me?"

"With your buddy, Nick."

"I haven't seen him for a couple of weeks. I guess he's got a new girlfriend. You can just come out and ask, Chris. No need to try to be coy about it."

"Busted. You know how I worry about my sister. Can you come up this weekend?"

"Let me think about it. I have this case that's not going well right now."

"You always have a case that's not going well, and then you win it."

"Maybe not this one. I'm hoping for a draw."

"Sounds serious."

"I'm also being dramatic."

"Surprise," he said. "Well, if you change your mind, I'm having some friends over for dinner, and you know that you like to get away, need to get away, once in a while." He paused. "And I love to show off my little sister the lawyer."

"You haven't set me up with one of your friends, have you?"

"Would I do that?"

"Yes, of course you would."

"He's very nice," Chris said, like a little boy who's just been caught.

"I'm not interested. All I want at the most is a friend with benefits right now. Just someone to have sex with and then send him home."

"Too much information, Zoe."

"You asked for it."

"You're right. The party is on Friday about seven."

"I might just take you up on the offer. Maybe I'll leave early on Friday and we can catch up."

"Great! You can help me set up."

"Now the real motive comes out."

"Just kidding. See you if you can make it. If not, then that's okay, too."

"If I can get caught up, I'll be there. I'll call you Friday morning."

"Okay. Bye, Zoe."

"Bye, Chris."

She hung up, and then shut off her phone. Maybe Chris was right. She needed to get away. And maybe it wouldn't be a bad idea to meet someone new.

22

Eric was sitting in front of his PC looking at a new group of videos. If he got caught doing what he was doing, he'd certainly go to jail. Right now, his finances were fragile. He certainly couldn't possibly cover a check to a criminal attorney with the funds he'd had left in his bank account. He'd already cut back on the medication his doctor had given him to help level off his mood swings. Eric was looking at a new group of photos that he'd just started to collect that week. They were almost entirely of Anne in her apartment. He now had cameras in every room on motion detectors. It hadn't been hard to explain to the doorman that he was supposed to check on her security system, especially when he had a very convincing-looking work order on the same letterhead used by the maintenance contractor for the apartment house. It was a surprisingly good forgery, including a signature from the guy who signed the doorman's paycheck. Eric spent a quiet afternoon in Anne's apartment setting up the cameras, proud of himself for the forgery, and for doing his research. He knew she'd be working very late that day because she had a dinner meeting. She wouldn't possibly be home before nine at the earliest. He also knew her new boyfriend, Nick, would be out of the picture. He was away on one of his business trips. Eric's stomach tightened when he thought of Nick, and his jaw clenched. The arrogant piece of shit was probably banging someone he picked up in a hotel bar. The guy had the sexual fidelity of a rabbit. He had no idea what women saw in him, especially Anne. She should know better; how could she fall for that jerk?

Eric noticed movement on his screen, and as if on cue, Nick's image appeared in the living room camera. Anne wasn't home yet, which meant that she had given him a key. Eric's face flushed at the thought. He picked up the plastic one-liter bottle of vodka he'd bought on his way home that afternoon. It was half empty. He took one of his anti-anxiety pills and followed it with a healthy shot of vodka. It burned his throat, and then released some of the pent-up frustration in his back muscles. After a few minutes, the pill started to take effect and he felt it level off his mood. Looking at the screen he noticed that Nick had changed into his robe and was heading for the shower. While this gave him a pang of anger, it was insulated, subdued, and he poured himself vodka in the water tumbler next to his keyboard. He listened to Nick take his shower. Nick watched the TV news, and then turned to a station that rebroadcast old cop shows. Eric watched Nick watching TV and sipped from the glass of vodka. It was a while before Anne showed up. She looked surprised to see Nick and asked him how his trip went. Nick gave her a glass of wine and rubbed her shoulders. Eric knew there had been a lot of blowback for her from his leaving and from her divorce.

Eric felt bad that he'd caused her any problems, but he knew that she knew deep down that it wasn't really his fault. If anything, it was that bastard Nick's fault. He had stepped in just as their relationship was about to take off again.

He was watching as Nick started to kiss her. Anne's eyes were pointed at one of Eric's cameras. Eric hit the zoom and got a close up of her eyes. She knew he was really looking at him. He smiled at her, knowing that she was really thinking about him, otherwise why would she be staring right at his hidden camera? She loved him. Eric knew it. It was that simple. He finished his vodka while watching the monitor.

23

Zoe pulled up the long circular driveway to her brother's house. Chris had worked on some of the landscaping since the time of her last visit, and there was a new cedar gazebo sitting behind the house near the woods. She could see that he'd moved his Buddha sculpture into the gazebo. He had been enamored of Buddhism for quite some time and had visited Pondicherry when he was fresh out of graduate school after earning an advanced degree in religious studies. Zoe had wondered if that's what had influenced his taste in women. Except for his latest girlfriend, he'd invariably fallen in love with someone who was on a journey, needed to "find herself," and had a tendency to be dramatic.

One in particular had suddenly left to study with a spiritual guru somewhere in Oregon. While Chris was upset by her sudden departure and was hurt that she hadn't let him in on her plans, he really resented the fact that the fairly steep fees for the course of study with the guru had been charged to his Visa card. As one of her first cases as a new attorney, Zoe wrote a few letters to the guru, and Chris had to close all his accounts because the guru kept putting charges on his card. Each charge on the credit card corresponded to the various stages of enlightenment his ex-girlfriend was achieving, and she was making record progress. Eventually, the guy was arrested for fraud and embezzlement, but it took a while to clear up the financial mess. The girlfriend suddenly appeared on his doorstep about two years ago. Chris had immediately sent her on her way. She accused him of harming her soul and harassed him for a while for money. Zoe figured that she probably wanted the money to apply to her soul as a sort of healing balm, but then the young woman moved on when he adamantly refused to support her. Being very pretty, she probably had little trouble finding another sponsor for her continual spiritual quest.

Chris had remained alone for quite some time, and then started seeing Lily, who worked at the local high school as a school psychologist. Zoe had found out about Lily the last time she visited Chris. The local school was ranked in the bottom third of the state, and Lily was one of the few people who worked there who wasn't related to anyone in the small town. The story that Zoe got from Chris was that Lily was offered the job after it was found that the daughter of the owner of the local Chevy dealership had lied so completely on her application that to keep her on as the school psychologist would have exposed them to a lawsuit—actually *another* lawsuit. It had been hard to ignore the private sessions the woman had had with many of the very good-looking male students and even harder to not notice that she almost never had any meetings with young women who sought her advice. She'd also insisted on going to away sporting events to offer psychological counsel to the football team. None of this was enough to get her fired, of course, due to her family connections. The final straw was when she totally ignored a young boy who was incessantly bullied for being gay. One day, after a half dozen macho morons spent the entire day bullying him while the faculty and administration pretended not to notice, he went home and attempted suicide. She claimed he never told her he was having problems. However, his mother had recorded several calls with her in which they discussed the bullying her son was getting and had recorded her saying that the boy should simply "man up and grow a set of balls." There was a multimillion-dollar lawsuit that now working through the courts. It was only then that someone thought that maybe they should check the woman's credentials and found out that not only had she lied about graduating college with a degree in psychology, but she had never been enrolled in any college at all. Then it came out that several members of the search committee had suddenly acquired brand new cars, all Chevys, about the same time they were interviewing her for the job. Even the most corrupt of small-town school systems couldn't sweep that much dirt under the carpet. She was fired, and the next person on the list who had been interviewed for the job had been Lily.

Lily bought a small house near the school. She hired Chris to renovate a kitchen that had been a victim of the 1980s, a curious time when no one seemed to have the slightest clue about interior design or anything else regarding taste. A time when people wore lime green leisure suits, danced to disco music, thought that the Gremlin was a nice car, and that big hair was cool. He met Lily at her house just before she moved in, first noticing her curly black hair, and when she turned around, he saw her blue eyes before he saw anything else. Chris pulled out pink countertops,

Intimate Disconnect

tore down tacky print wallpaper, mirrored tile, and removed almond appliances. The cabinets, which were off-white melamine trimmed with fake oak were in good shape, so he donated them to a local charity. Her electric bill dropped noticeably after he replaced the double-wide monster refrigerator-freezer with a modern energy-efficient version.

Chris was usually at the house, cleaning up, when Lily got home from work. Neither could remember when their talk moved from the professional, about cabinets, flooring materials, and colors, to the personal.

They quickly found that they both liked to travel. Like Chris, Lily loved to meet new people and see new places. She'd not only seen the Taj Mahal, the Uffizi, the Louvre, and Machu Picchu, as he had, but, like Chris, she also noticed the crushing poverty, ubiquitous racism, and class disputes that kept her from overly romanticizing the places she'd been to. No matter how exotic the place, Lily realized, like he did, they were still inhabited by people—not better people or worse people, just normal everyday human beings. No one had any secret formula that would make everything suddenly clear or answer every question about the meaning of life. People in the East were just as clueless about the big questions as the people in the West; they just sometimes had a different attitude about it. He told her how a friend of his from Japan put it: "You eat, you shit, and you die."

"You're kidding," Lily said. "He really said that?"

"Yeah. There is little that I can add to that."

"I've heard of people who are very Zen, but that's a bit extreme."

"He's an extreme kind of guy."

"I'll bet."

"Anyway. I'll be putting in the new quartz counter next week. The cabinets are finished now."

"Thanks for getting such a great deal on them for me. I just love the fact that the pink and almond are gone, not my favorite colors."

"Well, that will be it," Chris said hesitantly. "The new counter will be here, and after that's in I'll put in the new sink. You already have the new fridge, stove, stove hood, and dishwasher, the painting is done." He counted on his fingers. "The tile floor is finished, and I finished the rest of the tile work today." He pointed to the glass tile behind the stove. She nodded approval. "I can grout the tile after the counter gets installed, so I should be done by the middle of next week. We can leave the backsplash painted for now and tile it later when you have the money."

"That's great," she said.

"Yes. I should be done by next week," he said again.

"Great," she said again.

"You won't owe me any more money. I got a good deal on the counter. Someone had ordered it, but never picked it up."

"That's nice." She smiled. He had told her this before about a half-dozen times. "So," she added, "will you be asking me out pretty soon? I'm getting tired of rushing home so I can see you before you leave."

***

Zoe parked her car where it would be out of the way and climbed the steps to Chris's house. He wasn't there yet, so she let herself in with the spare key. She wheeled her suitcase to the extra room and changed into more comfortable clothes. She'd left right from work and didn't want to stop back to her apartment for fear of finding more work that might keep her there. It was hard enough to get out of the office on time, even on a Friday. She promised Chris that she'd shut off her cell phone, so she made a few quick calls before he got there, shut the phone off, and then plugged it in to recharge. When she went downstairs, she saw him drive up. He was in the house in a few minutes. She had made a pot of coffee and filled one of his giant hand-made ceramic coffee cups.

"That coffee smells good," he said, and kissed her on the cheek. She could smell sawdust and sweat. "It's nice to see you. How's everything?"

"Busy." She sipped from her cup. "You know, always something going on. This divorce with Anne is starting to get a little wilder than I'd hoped for. It looks like they're getting ready to do things the hard way. I just hope it doesn't mess up their business."

"Yeah. You told me. He's got a real nasty lawyer?"

"I have no idea why Michael hired him. He's the one who's going to be making the most out of this thing."

"And your office, too, I imagine."

"We aren't shy about billing, that's true," Zoe said.

"How's that guy you were seeing?"

"Nick?" She smiled.

"Yeah."

"Well, you needn't worry about Nick anymore. He's out of the picture. I already told you, more than once."

"I wasn't worried."

"Really? You could have fooled me. I never had any intention of getting serious with him," she smiled.

"Oh."

"He is one of those guys who's just for fun. Now he's having fun with someone else. Rumor has it he's going out with Anne."

"Really?"

"Yes. And you will never guess who Michael is going out with." Zoe felt free to discuss the case with her brother. He had never met any of the people involved and with a case like this you had to vent on someone, if only just to keep from exploding. He could be trusted to be discreet. He shook his head when she got to the part about Jimmy.

"I thought he had more sense than that," he said.

"What was it that you told me when I first started dating?" she smiled. "'A stiff dick has no conscience.' Isn't that what you told your little sister?"

"God, yeah. Was I a jerk or what?"

"Actually, you were right about that. Gay or straight, it's the same thing. The hormones take over."

"It's amazing he didn't get fired."

"We need him too much." She drank some more coffee. "It could cause some problems down the road, though. I'll have to think of something to neutralize it." She was thoughtful. Chris stopped her from thinking about work by insisting that she see the new landscaping he'd just finished. He showed off the cedar gazebo and all the new plantings. The gazebo had been fitted together with raw cedar branches and split cedar logs, and he had shingled the roof with hand-split shingles. He'd also built comfortable benches into the sides. It was quiet and peaceful sitting at the edge of the woods. Zoe began to relax. She hadn't realized how tense she'd gotten over the past few weeks with the cases she'd been working on, not just Michael and Anne's, but it seemed every case she had at the moment was a tough one. While she had gone to law school with the intention of helping people during a trying time like a divorce, she hadn't quite counted on so many of her clients being completely unreasonable and selfish. That's what made things the most difficult. The work itself was filling out forms, calculating net-worth costs, and other issues. But that simple mechanical process was screwed up repeatedly by people just being stupid and vindictive, with a little help from their friends sometimes.

"You with us?" Chris asked, waving a hand in front of her face.

"Sorry, just lost in thought."

"I can see that," he said. She noticed that she'd finished her coffee. She looked at the Buddha, and then out to the woods.

"You have a nice place here, Chris. You should be proud of it. I know you've worked hard on it."

"Thanks." He got up from his bench and started to walk back to the house. "You can stay there as long as you want. I like to sit and read here, or just sit and try not to think of anything." He finished his coffee and dumped the dregs on the ground. "I need to get a shower," he said, as he went to the house. She sat for a while, just looking into space. As the sun went behind the mountain, the air cooled off very quickly. She felt a chill and got up to go to the house. As she turned her head, she noticed movement in the woods. She looked hard, but all she saw were some branches waving back and forth, as if something big had moved very quickly. She shuddered and headed back to the house. Chris was making something in the kitchen, and she joined him.

"What can I do?" she asked.

"Chop up some celery." He handed her two stalks. "Lily is coming over for dinner. She wants to meet you. She might be bringing a ... friend."

"What?"

"Just someone she thought you might like to meet."

"I don't need to be fixed up, Chris," she bristled, even though Chris had told her to expect someone to be at the dinner. She was surprised, maybe she was too sensitive about feeling manipulated, but she knew she could trust Chris.

"It's just dinner, and I have a movie for later, so you won't even have to talk to him much."

"I know. You did warn me. So, who's the lucky guy?"

"Someone she went to graduate school with. He's a psychologist and has a weekend home not far from here."

"Just what I need. Maybe I could get a deal? Maybe we could get a twofer? We could both use the help," she smiled sweetly.

"Be nice." He pointed the large steel spoon in his hand at her.

"I'm always nice. Besides, you might have a spoon, but I have a knife," Zoe said as she attacked the celery with a French chef's knife. "Hell," she smiled, "if I don't like him, I can always tell him I'm gay and make a play for Lily."

Chris and Zoe made dinner, and Lily arrived about an hour later. Although they'd never met before, both seemed to feel they already knew each other, although Lily was taller than Zoe expected, and athletic, which made her a good match for Chris. While he finished making dinner, the two went into the living room.

"Did he show you the new gazebo?" Lily asked.

"Yes. I was there until it started to get dark. Very peaceful."

"I like it, too. After a stressful day at work, I sometimes come here first before I go home. It's on the way," Lily added quickly.

"I like it. And it's nice to see him building things for himself again," Zoe said, and smiled. "Wish I had a quiet place at home to go to. I just seem to end up at my apartment after the day is over, when there's no place else to go and nothing else to do. I just pour some wine, turn on TV, and crash."

"I know what you mean." Lily sat on the couch, and Zoe sat across from her. They spoke for a while about Chris, their jobs, and things in general. It was quick for Zoe to see that Lily was what she had expected. She wondered if it was Chris who had changed or was it more Lily's idea. Maybe he'd just gotten tired of high-maintenance women and psychodrama. Perhaps he wanted an equal partner instead of being someone's nurse. She wondered where he could have developed that taste. Their parents had been almost boring in that they had never indulged in dramatics and were very much equal. Even their fights were quiet and held behind closed doors. Maybe the conflict and drama in his other relationships were part of his need for adventure, perhaps a form of rebellion. There was a knock at the door. No one had heard the car drive up. Lily went to the door and ushered in Jeff. He was tall with curly red hair.

"Jeff, this is Zoe." Jeff smiled, and shook Zoe's hand.

"Hi, Jeff," Chris called from the kitchen. Lily took the bottle of wine from him and headed to the kitchen to open it, leaving Zoe alone with Jeff.

"Chris tells me you're a psychologist," Zoe said.

"Yes. I try to wait a while before I tell that to anyone. It sometimes changes conversations completely. I like to have people get to know me first, and then spring it on them. I hear you're a divorce attorney?"

"I like to wait to reveal that, too, for the same reasons. Either people get funny, or they want free advice. Looks like Chris has been busy."

"He told me about you in great detail. He's very proud of his little sister."

"Did he show you my resume? I can fax it to you if you like."

"E-mail will be fine," Jeff said, not missing a beat. "I can send you mine if you want."

"That and your last three years' tax returns will be acceptable," Zoe smiled.

"I can see that you definitely have spent a lot of time around divorced people. After you're finished with them, they come to me," Jeff grinned. Lily came into the room and handed out wine. The three chatted for a while, and then Chris called them all in for dinner. He was a good cook, but almost never cooked for himself, so having a few guests over brought out his talents. He'd kept it simple with a whole chicken for each person and plenty of sides. He had a big appetite and cooked as if everyone else ate like him. Zoe cut her chicken in half and put the larger half back on the serving platter.

"Sorry, Chris. I can't eat that much in a day, let alone one meal."

"Sure, you can," he smiled, and made as if he was going to put it back on her plate.

"Plenty of food," Lily said, and reached over and pulled his hand away from the serving platter, "and it smells great."

"Just a little rosemary and lemon," Chris smiled at Lily.

"Wow," Jeff said, trying to talk politely with a mouthful of food. "This is great. I basically can boil water and sometimes I fry an egg."

"Me, too," Zoe said. "Chris is the one with the patience. I just try to cook everything instantly and mess it all up."

"That's because you wait so long that you're starving. You have to start cooking just before you feel hungry," Chris said.

"My sister's the cook," Lily volunteered, "not me. She'll think nothing of inviting eight or ten people over and making them dinner. I'd have a nervous breakdown." They ate and had the sort of conversation that people have who don't really know each other that well, running up test subjects, avoiding confrontation, keeping the conversation moving. Jeff was obviously the listener of the group and kept quiet for the most part. Lily was a bit more talkative, but Chris seemed to have the most to say. Zoe liked listening to him and wondered if he was so talkative because his job involved so little conversation. He usually worked alone these days and many of his conversations lately were pretty much all about business. Even Zoe was able to have the occasional lunch where she could gossip and catch up with her friends. She was listening to him and could see that his Ph.D. in religious studies was getting put to good use. Then he was talking about one of his pet issues, fossil fuels.

"You know that gas and diesel are basically distilled essences of living creatures," he said, picking up Zoe's half chicken from the serving platter after finishing his own. "The wood I use almost every day in my work, for instance, if it had been around three hundred million years ago, it could now be coal and could be burned for energy. I wonder if we're releasing the spirits of dead beings when we burn their essences. Maybe the world is getting crowded with spirits from the Carboniferous period?" Chris finished his observation and cut up the rest of Zoe's chicken on his plate. Lily looked at Zoe inquiringly.

"Has he always been like this?" Lily asked.

"Yes, as far as I can remember. Dad used to call him 'the professor' when we were kids," Zoe replied.

Chris said, "I taught college for a while, but there were no full-time jobs available, only part-time ones, paying about minimum wage. The last time I taught I made more money in a month as a carpenter than I was making in a year teaching. So, I eventually gave up. I needed to make money to survive. I also majored in a field not known for employment."

"You could have become a preacher," Jeff said. "The money isn't great, but the work is steady, unless you become a televangelist."

"I'd actually have to believe all that stuff, though. I'm more of a religious smorgasbord guy. I take a little bit of this and a little bit of that from all the belief systems that I've read about. I couldn't be exclusive enough to be a minister. I'd probably stop in the middle of a sermon on Original Sin, for instance, and say something like, 'While this is all well and good, some people believe that you're born in a perfect and pure state and that living on the Earth is what corrupts you, and that's kind of cool, too.' Might not go over too well with the suburban crowd. They want their reality neat and tidy."

"I find that my clients are the same," Jeff said. "They want everything in a neat and tidy package. They've spent their whole lives screwing themselves up, or getting screwed up by relatives and loved ones, and they expect me to get them all straightened out in a couple of sessions and with a script for antidepressants. The pop psychologists make it even harder because they oversimplify people's problems to fit them into a short TV segment, or to make their incredibly reductionist worldview fit neatly into a best-selling trade paperback. Sometimes they propose therapies that are even dangerous for the disorder they're supposed to be treating or propose something that misses the real problem altogether. It's not that easy. The same mental problems in different people can have many different causes. Some are nurture, some are organic. It can take a long time sorting out the difference." Jeff sipped some wine.

"I wish my clients would want things neat and tidy. They just seem to want to make things more and more difficult," Zoe said.

"But they're not all like that, right?" Chris smiled.

"Yes. You're right. Some of them are great, and I like helping them out," Zoe said. "It's a great feeling when a case ends up well, and everyone is at least mollified if not happy."

"To being 'mollified if not happy,' that's a goal I can live with," Chris raised his glass, and they all toasted. He got up, ushered everyone into the living room, and took out a movie he'd rented that had been out for a couple of months. It was one that everyone had meant to see, but no one had gotten a chance to go to before it was out of the theaters. Before he switched the TV to the proper mode, there was static on the screen and over the speakers.

"Big Bang noise," he said.

"What?" asked Lily.

"The static on TV; it's the noise left over from the Big Bang. It's fourteen-billion-year-old noise. Like the Universe is making one long birthing scream, like it thought that it just made one huge mistake."

24

Zoe picked up the folder on her desk. She wasn't supposed to take new cases for the time being, but it was a case that had come as a referral from a friend who was a realtor. A client of hers was buying a condo and had mentioned that she had been in the market for an attorney. Her husband had left her some ten years back, and she met someone and wanted to remarry. They were looking for a home to buy together. This should have been a straightforward abandonment, but they'd had bad luck in drawing Judge Barnum. He had made her take out a series of ads in local papers covering several states. Now, he was stonewalling the divorce. There seemed to be no reason for this, but the old bastard simply wanted to draw it out as long as possible. Everything had been done as the judge had ordered. The ads alone had cost the woman thousands of dollars. The estranged husband had not responded. It was a clear-cut case of abandonment, but the judge, for some reason, was insisting on waiting. Barnum tended to drag out proceedings, and then lecture the plaintiffs, especially the women, about the sanctity of marriage. He could go on for twenty minutes, all of it going into the record, his sanctimonious ramblings costing the clients extra, as they must pay by the page for the recording of the transcripts, the official divorce record. Zoe wasn't surprised that he was doing this. She read through the file; everything was done. There was no reason why this shouldn't have been signed, sealed, and delivered.

She made a few phone calls and was just finishing up when the client arrived. The woman wasn't young, but a little older than Zoe had expected. She sat down and told her story. Joan had married when she was in her early twenties and everything seemed fine for four years or so. Then her husband started to act strangely. One night, he simply didn't come home at all. She checked with his friends, and with his mother, his only living family, but no one knew where he was or what happened. He never showed up to work, just took off in his car and never came back. She alerted the police and filed a report, but they weren't much help. That was over ten years ago. She'd spent a few thousand dollars on useless newspaper ads trying to find his whereabouts. Joan simply wanted to get married to the man she'd been living with for the past five years, but now everything was messed up. The wedding had been scheduled a few months ago when she had thought this divorce would be a no-brainer. Now, time was running out because the wedding was in less than two weeks and there was no way that the paperwork would be done before then. She would have to cancel her wedding, which would cost her even more money. That's when she burst into tears.

"When is your wedding?" Zoe asked, while handing her a box of tissues.

"Next Saturday. It's not a big affair, just some friends at a restaurant where my maid of honor works as a waitress. "They're shutting the place down for me for the whole night. Why is he doing this to me?"

"It's nothing personal; really, he's just a terminal jackass. You have to look at it this way, most attorneys around here make well into the six figures. A few of them might be part-time justices, but that's usually because they're community oriented, and the pay they get is just a little extra. They usually have a practice outside of the courtroom. He's a full-time judge making maybe two-thirds of what a mediocre attorney makes. Maybe there's a reason?"

"Oh," Joan said.

"Now, who was going to give you your vows?"

"Mary Robinson."

"Excellent." Zoe allowed herself to breathe. She was a Justice of the Peace who Zoe knew well because she also had a law practice and taught at the local college. She called her.

"Hi, Mary. Zoe here."

"How's it going, Zoe?"

"Fine. And you?"

"Well I'm okay, but Abigail thinks she's pregnant." Abigail was her five-year-old Labrador retriever.

"What?"

"She's been moping around the house and not eating, and I even took her to the office with me thinking she might be a bit lonely, but that's not it. The vet said she's having a false pregnancy."

"You're kidding."

Intimate Disconnect

"Nope. Can you believe it? He also said that I wasn't making matters any better by codling her. When she started moping around, I made her all of her favorite meals, fried liver, chopped meat, the vet said I had to stop, but she just looks at me with those eyes, and she breaks my heart. I dropped her off at my mother's. She's making her run around and act like a dog."

"She'll get Abigail in line if anyone can." Zoe had met Mary's mom, a woman who owned a small farm outside of a small town. She also owned a good deal of the town, having bought up properties over the past fifty years.

"That's for sure. What's up, Zoe?" Zoe quickly explained, and Mary agreed instantly. They promised to meet for coffee soon, and Zoe hung up. She talked to Joan. "She's agreed that you can take your vows in front of your friends. Then you can have the party of your life. You won't really be married, but you've been living together for some time now, so that isn't the issue. I'll push this through as fast as I can, and then when the divorce is final, you can meet with her and she'll give you the vows, Las Vegas style. Just be sure to bring two witnesses, and then you'll be legally married. No one at the wedding need know that you won't really be married. How's that?"

Joan looked at her and thought about it. "You're right. That's a great idea! If I cancel the wedding that son of a bitch Barnum wins. People like him should never win."

"People like him should be taken out and shot, but there are laws against that," Zoe said. They shook hands and the woman left, much happier. Zoe called a clerk she knew at the Courthouse. She knew that Barnum would be on vacation soon. She called in a favor, and the clerk scheduled the final decree for the time that he'd be away. She hated to judge-shop but made an exception in this case. She'd seen Barnum sandbag cases arbitrarily for months. He simply had landed on this poor woman and made her life a misery for no reason other than he could. Zoe had found that there were a lot of people like that in the justice system.

"I wish all my cases were that easy to fix," she said to herself as she turned to the mail. She opened a large envelope that she assumed was full of legal papers but found a handful of photos. They were grainy and graphic pictures of Nick and Anne in a bedroom, probably Anne's. Zoe was surprised at the sudden surge of anger she had. Even though she had broken up with Nick, she couldn't help but feel angry and betrayed. She'd heard the rumors, but now here was graphic proof. He didn't waste any time, she thought. Then she wondered who had taken the pictures. She certainly hadn't hired her PI, Fred, to do this. There was only a P.O. Box listed as the return address. She wondered if this was one of Cargil's little tricks he liked to play, but this wasn't his style. He'd have put pictures like this on the record as soon as he could. It gave her a shudder to think that someone, some creep, sent these to her. Why? she wondered. They wouldn't help her case at all. She had no misconceptions about Anne, or Nick for that matter. It was as if someone was simply sending these to her out of pure spite. She shoved the photos back into the envelope, and then put them in her drawer.

25

Anne was busier than usual this morning. On the desk next to her was a takeout egg and cheese sandwich with a few bites missing and a cold cup of coffee. Nick had been at her apartment when she got home the previous evening. She wasn't sure that she liked his moving in like that, and she remembered why she'd cooled their affair a couple of years ago. While he was charming, fun, and a great lover, he could also be very presumptive, even a little arrogant about their relationship. She really couldn't spare the time to think of Nick or what she planned on doing about him. There was a thick folder of notes and spreadsheets she needed to finish reading before the meeting. The business was still doing well, but sales were certainly down from the previous two years, and the dividends for the investors were not going to be nearly what they had gotten used to. She knew that Louis Amory would take this as an opportunity to blow off some steam and make noises about having more control over the business, or even replacing her. It was a move that she might have welcomed if not for all the other issues. She was getting a little tired of the continual fight with Amory and had seriously contemplated buying out his shares. She simply didn't have the liquid assets to do it at this point. All her available money was tied up in the company or in other investments.

April, her personal assistant, walked in with more papers for her to glance through before the meeting. They were the most up-to-date figures, and she found no comfort there, either. While sales usually dropped off this time of year, this was the worst slump they'd ever had. She might have to hold off on some of the orders and delay shipments because there would be no room to store the goods in their warehouse. The only bright spot was that they had made a large shipment to an online retailer, and the sales were good. However, the deep discounts the retailer had insisted on had cut their profit margin to the bare bone. Despite all of this, TrendInventions had posted a profit for the month and would finish off the quarter stronger than most businesses. April had brought her a fresh hot coffee. Anne brought the coffee with her to the meeting so she would have something to hold on to. April came along to take the official minutes.

The meeting came to order, and the previous minutes were approved with a few changes. Anne started her presentation. She spoke quickly and didn't try to obscure any part of what needed to be said. Business was off, but not as bad as other sectors of the same market. They had a backlog of goods in the warehouse, and shipments had been far less than normal to their usual distributors, one of whom had just filed for Chapter 11. This would keep them from paying any outstanding bills with TrendInventions, and they would have to carry them on the books at a loss until the Chapter 11 issues were resolved, and then they'd probably get pennies on the dollar. She recommended cutting back on some of their orders and delaying the shipment of completed orders because it was cheaper to keep them at the factory for now than to rent more warehouse space here. However, that might change soon because a large local business that shares some warehouse space with them just announced major cutbacks. TrendInventions might be able to sublease their space cheaply if they cut back enough.

"Are we cutting back?" Amory asked, while Anne was in midsentence.

"What?"

"Are we cutting back, too?"

"Why would we? We've turned a profit this month, and sales are steady."

"Yes. But they're down, way down from even last year."

"Cutting back is a two-edged sword," Anne said with great patience. "Whoever we lay off can file for unemployment, and we also take a charge on each layoff. At this point, it doesn't make sense to lay anyone off. We have a very productive staff. I think that if we hold back on new orders that should be enough."

"With all due respect, it doesn't seem to me that you're getting serious about this situation. We need to cut back now before we end up stuck with a bunch of deadwood," Amory said.

"I don't like referring to my staff as 'deadwood.' This isn't a huge company. We run this place with a small staff. I don't think we can cut out anyone, to be honest. And, furthermore, I don't see the need yet. This is our slack season, and we always perk up during the holiday season, which is not far away. Our products are essentially gifts. Eighty percent of our sales are to people who are buying a gift for someone else. ..." She started to say something about the large online retailer and the increase in online sales, when Amory interrupted her again.

"What if we have a bad holiday season again this year?"

"No one knows how the season will be. We've got some new products and the focus testing went very well." Anne paused and started talking before Amory could interrupt her again. "If this holiday season is bad, we won't be the only manufacturer in trouble."

"That's why I say we should cut back now. Fire some people and save the money now." Spoken like someone who never actually had to worry about having a job, Anne thought. Then she replied, slowly and carefully.

"I don't fire people for the sake of firing them. What if we suddenly need them? What if sales perk up and we're short-staffed? We could end up losing customers because we can't fill their orders. If we lay people off, it's not like they'll be sitting around waiting for us to hire them back. They could find jobs elsewhere, which means that we'd have to train a bunch of new people. You have to trust us that we're doing the right thing."

"We finished the last meeting, Anne, with the same words. However, since then you've had problems with the divorce you assured us would be no problem, and now we're seeing slipping sales. I'm not sure if that's good enough," Amory said.

"So? What do you want? I'm certainly not about to resign for your sake. And I'm not about to start layoffs. That should be the last thing we do in a crisis, not the first thing. And the divorce is my personal business, not the board's."

"You've also had personnel issues. You didn't seem to be troubled about firing someone who worked for you for several years," Amory continued.

"He was way out of line. He attacked me. I could have had him charged."

"Nothing personal, Anne, but it does show a problem with your leadership," Amory said. Something suddenly clicked in Anne's head.

"You're the one, you son-of-a-bitch!" She was furious.

"What?" Amory looked a little worried.

"You got that monster attorney Tim Cargil for Michael."

"Well I didn't want him to get screwed out of what he's owed." Amory turned red.

"Bullshit. You wanted to manipulate him to get to me. What's your next move? Get his approval to vote on his behalf? Do you know what you've done by having Michael hire Cargil? You've turned a simple divorce into something that will surely be protracted, costly, and is already in the papers and on the local news. None of this will be good for this company or any of your investments. The last thing we needed was a drawn-out public display." That last phrase about investments got the attention of the very quiet board of directors, who were now beginning to get on her side. Amory was smart enough to shut up after a few board members gave him dirty looks. After she cooled off, she quietly asked if they could move on, since they had a full agenda. The motion was made to table the present discussion and move to the next agenda item, but she knew that Amory was not finished yet. He would certainly bring this up again.

That afternoon Anne went to her house for a swim. She knew that Michael was having a meeting with the R&D guys about his latest gadget. It was having problems with power consumption, and they were working on changing the software to use the battery more efficiently. She didn't bother with her bathing suit, but simply took off her work clothes and jumped into the pool. She swam multiple laps because she had plenty of nervous energy to burn off. She didn't notice Michael when he came into the pool room.

"You're not supposed to be here," he shouted. She heard his voice, but not what he said, and turned on her back to float.

"What?"

"You heard me. You're not supposed to be here at all."

"That's not true. I moved out to make things easier for you. I made it clear that I was to be able to swim in the pool. I like having a swim once or twice a week. You know that."

"Cargil said you're not to set foot on this property," Michael pouted.

"Your attorney is an asshole. And while we're on the subject, Louis Amory is not your friend, either. Do you want him to take the company from us? That's probably what he has in mind." She got out of the pool and covered herself with a bright blue beach towel.

"You think you know everything, and you can push me around. You don't know anything, anything at all." Michael was getting hysterical. "I can't see my friend Jimmy because of you, and now you want to take the house and push me out of the company."

"What?"

"You heard me. Lou says you're trying to get rid of me."

"Why would I do that?"

"So, you can take over. You always take credit for everything I do."

"That's not true. Who's been feeding you all this bullshit? Let me see. Is it Lou and that asshole attorney, Tim Cargil? They're telling you all of this?" She didn't wait for an answer. "Who got your first idea to market? Who takes care of all the details of running our fucking company while you play around in the basement coming up with ideas? You ungrateful bastard! And your friend Jimmy had a choice between seeing you or keeping his job. He's smart enough to go with his job, something you will never understand because your whole damn life you never had a fucking job or had to worry about money because I worried about it for you."

"Right, it's always about you and all the work you had to do." Michael was going over the top. "Without my ideas you'd have nothing. I could have replaced you years ago, but you just hung on." Anne couldn't quite believe him.

"I'm not going to argue with you anymore," she said quietly. "It's partly my fault. I created you. I let you behave like a spoiled little monster and shouldn't be surprised that you've turned into one. I'll leave, and if I need to go for a swim I'll go to the pool in the condo. I've had enough of you." She turned and started to leave, but he reached out to grab her from behind.

"No you don't," he said, as he grabbed her shoulder and pulled hard, trying to spin her around. His hand slipped and he pulled off her towel. Her instinctive reaction was push back hard with her elbow. She didn't even think, just fired her elbow straight back. Since he was leaning over and off balance because the towel had come off so fast, her elbow caught him full force in his eye.

"Ow! You hit me in the eye!" He burst into tears.

"No. I didn't. You grabbed me! Let me look."

"No. Don't touch me." Michael ran off holding his hand over his eye. Anne got dressed and went looking for Michael. She found him hiding in one of the upstairs bathrooms.

"You need to have someone look at that eye. I'm sorry, but you did grab me. You shouldn't grab hold of people," she said to the door. He sniffled on the other side. "I'm leaving. Do you want me to take you to the emergency room? I can call your doctor. He'll probably want to see you. I can even call an ambulance if you want."

"Just go away," he screamed through the door.

"Fine, Michael, as usual, we do whatever you want." She turned. "You spoiled little prick," she shouted, plenty loud enough for him to hear.

Anne pulled into her space under her condo, went to the elevator, and pushed the call button, but she was too agitated to wait. She took the stairs to the fourth floor. Smelling the pool water on her skin as she jogged up the stairs, she thought of taking a nice hot shower and kicking back with a good stiff drink as she took the stairs two at a time, working up a sweat. When she walked into her living room, she could feel the moisture in the air and smell the hot soapy smell of the shower. Nick came out of the bedroom wearing her robe and toweling off his wavy black hair.

"I thought we agreed that you'd call before you came over," Anne said.

"I just thought I'd surprise you."

"You surprised me on Tuesday. That's when we had the talk, remember?"

"Sorry."

"Get out," she said quietly.

"What?" Nick asked, blinking.

"Get the fuck out."

"Wow, what's wrong with you?"

"Nothing. I want to be alone, and I wanted to take a shower and collapse, alone, by myself. Me! Alone! What part of, 'Call first before you come over' don't you understand, Nick? I've had enough of taking sloppy seconds in my own shower. I want you out of here and leave the key on the table before you go."

"Okay," he said, and threw the towel on the bed. He dressed quickly and left. She had to remind him to leave the key. She cleaned up the bathroom and started a bath. The doorbell rang. She thought it was Nick, and contemplated ignoring it, but answered on the third ring. She was greeted instead by a deputy sheriff.

"Anne Mali?" he said, studying a photograph in his hand.

"Yes."

"I have to serve you with this." He handed her a piece of paper, filled out a form, and gave her a carbon.

Anne read the document in her hand. It was a domestic abuse restraining order forbidding her to be within fifty yards of Michael Mali. Tim Cargil hadn't wasted any time at all.

26

Eric was sitting in his Corolla in the parking lot of the County Fairgrounds. People, mostly men, were drifting into the pavilion. He saw two rough-looking guys with long scraggly beards dressed in camouflage carrying a large ammo box between them. They each had a rifle slung over their shoulders, and one had an assault knife strapped to his leg. They were typical of the customers arriving for the gun show. He wasn't sure of what he wanted but knew this was the place to buy it. He went to the door and paid the five-dollar entrance fee. Inside were tables, from one end of the building to the next, full of rifles, pistols, ammunition, gun accessories, and knives. Some of the weapons were fully automatic machine guns. Eric thought that they were illegal to own. He walked over to a table that had one on display. While he was looking at it a guy came over.

"It's a beautiful weapon."

"I thought they were illegal."

"Not in this state. You can buy a fully automatic machine gun as long as it was made before 1986. This one's a HK 33, and it's fully transferable, all you need to do is pay a $200 transfer tax. Of course, you got to pay for the gun, too," he laughed.

"How much is it?" Eric asked. The guy sized him up, not sure if he was a looker or a buyer. "I can let you have it for fifteen thousand. It's real clean, as you can see." Eric gulped a bit and stood back. The guy realized he was a gun virgin and started to talk.

"What exactly are you lookin' for?"

"I'm not really sure. Something I can shoot on weekends at my club." Eric had rehearsed that part.

"You want a handgun or a rifle? What kind of club?"

"Hunting club."

"Maybe you want one of these?" The guy pulled out a Winchester 30.06 with a wooden stock. "I also have the same model with a synthetic stock, or maybe you'd prefer a twelve-gauge shotgun? Lots of guys hunt with them, and you can change the load depending on what you're hunting: birds, small game, deer, whatever. I've got all kinds of shotguns, wood stock, synthetic stock, auto load, pump action, twenty-four-inch, twenty-six-inch, you name it." He gestured to an assortment of shotguns on the table, showing them to Eric, who wasn't keen on any of them.

"I have a picture I cut out of a magazine," he said, holding up the wrinkled photo, an advertisement from an action movie starring an overbuilt actor who usually played a caricature of himself. The guy looked at it and smiled.

"That's some hunting club you belong to. Yep. I got a couple of those *hunting* rifles too." He went to the other end of his table and came back with a Rock River LAR-15 Hunter, which, in spite of its name, is really an assault rifle; some people refer to them as sport-hunting rifles. "This what you're lookin' for?"

Eric nodded. "Yep."

The guy continued as Eric gazed at the rifle, mesmerized, "That's one totally cool weapon. It's got an anodized camo finish that looks like real antelope hide. Anodized right into the finish, not a decal or appliqué that's gonna come off, and the finish won't show fingerprints. This one's practically new."

"This is great," Eric said, holding the rifle, examining the finish. It was surprisingly light. He sighted down the barrel. The guy took the weapon and showed Eric how to hold it and how to take off the magazine, load, and replace it. "It's chambered for .233 caliber. I don't have any ammo, but I'm sure someone here has a box or two. You can always get all the ammo you want online." He took the gun and flipped a lever. "This one has a three-position collapsible stock. Makes it easier to carry." He showed Eric how to push the stock in to make it smaller. "And you gotta keep these babies clean or they jam up." Eric picked up the rifle again, took off the magazine, put it back on, and collapsed the stock. "You learn fast, my friend," the guy said. "New, that baby goes for over $1,000. I can sell it to you with a couple of extra thirty-round clips for $700 even, and I'll throw in a cleaning kit." It was more than Eric had planned on spending, but he had the cash. They shook hands on the deal. Eric passed the background check, and within an hour he was heading out to the car with his new sport-hunting rifle.

27

Zoe returned from court to find five messages from Tim Cargil and one from Anne. Tim knew she was supposed to be in court today; the call from Anne troubled her. Unlike some of her clients who seemed to need to have her hold their hands at every step of the way, Anne was the opposite. She never called, or only called to return a call. Cargil was playing every trick in the book to run up his bill. He'd sent four revised drafts of the same document, each revision would be a charge, and would make sure to call her when he knew she was in court so he could charge Michael for making the phone call. She returned the call to Anne, sensing there was a problem. Anne was in a meeting, so she called Cargil. His secretary told her that he was out and couldn't give her a firm time when he would be available. "One more charge for Michael and Anne," she said as she hung up the phone. She knew that he was probably in his office and would have been surprised had he picked up but wanted it on the record that she returned his calls. If she ignored his numerous bogus calls, he'd try to paint her as incompetent, uncooperative, and difficult when the case went before a judge.

She was working on some paperwork bearing on the case, and was reviewing the forensic accountant's report on TrendInventions, which showed a strong business in very good shape, something that would play well in her arguments to the court. Her secretary announced that Anne was in the waiting room. She came into her office and handed Zoe the now-wrinkled copy of the restraining order. She briefly told Zoe about the problem from the night before. How Michael had grabbed her, and how she'd simply reacted. They were threatening her with third-degree assault charges because she'd cracked a bone in his face, not to mention the restraining order. Zoe listened impassively, trying hard to have no expression on her face, but knew this could cause some major problems with their case. Restraining orders were the mainstay of nasty divorces. She recommended a good criminal attorney; someone she'd worked with off and on over the years and gave Anne one of his cards. And she reminded her that she had told her to stay away from her house for now.

"You can swim in the condo pool. I told you to stay away from the house and from Michael."

"I know. It was stupid. I thought he said he was going to be busy for the night. I wanted to swim alone, and the condo pool is sometimes crowded, and they use a ton of chlorine." She paused, "He seemed to be out of his mind when he came over, though, like someone had been pushing his buttons."

"He and Cargil might have rehearsed something, or he's probably feeding Michael a line of bullshit that he's beginning to believe, but you certainly gave them plenty of substantiation if they want to paint you as incompetent and volatile. A black eye is hard to argue with."

"You mean like the one he gave me?"

"When?" Zoe sat up.

"About four years ago. He was drunk, and we were at a party. He wanted to leave, I didn't."

"Were the police called?"

"Yeah. The hostess insisted. I didn't want to make a fuss."

"Be sure to tell your attorney. He'll get the police report to show there is a reason why you might have reacted so violently, and make sure he forwards a copy of the report to me. Did you get any photos?" Anne shook her head, "don't worry," Zoe continued, "My guess is that Michael neglected to mention that to Cargil. Also, since he admitted to ripping the towel off you, we could charge him with attempted spousal rape."

"No. Only if we have to."

"Anne, you need to get clear on this. It's now a war. We have to fight like hell, or we might just lose. You need to think of anything we can use against Michael. Any time he was out of line, hit you, or even threatened to hit you, anything. It would be best if we had some witnesses, too."

"I'd be surprised if he even remembers the black eye, but it was in front of plenty of witnesses. He probably never told his lawyer because I'm sure he thinks it was all my fault. Everything that goes wrong in his life is my fault."

"The police report will help because it's part of an official record, not hearsay. Don't give them any more ammunition. You should have gone to the police first and told them that he assaulted you and you defended yourself. While that's basically what happened, it's going to look like tit-for-tat now. If anything happens at work, you need to officially document it with the police. Everything from now on has to be on the record — everything." Then she opened her drawer and pulled out the pictures she'd received a few days before, handing them to Anne. She looked at them and turned bright red.

"My God! Where did these come from?"

"I thought you could help me with that. They were sent right to me from a bogus name and address."

"I'm so sorry. Nick told me you'd broken up."

"We did. I don't give a shit about Nick, but I want to know who could be doing this. This is a sign of someone who is disturbed and could need help." She paused. "Think. Is there anyone who could be maybe just a little disturbed who could have done this?"

"Maybe Eric?"

"The guy who knocked you down? Who you had fired? Why?"

"I went out with him about a year ago. But he's been hung up on me ever since. He was stalking me a few months ago but promised he would stop. Then he attacked me at work."

"You were gonna tell me this? When?" Zoe sat back. "It's time to stop being nice, Anne. They want a war. So far, they're winning."

"It's that bad?"

"Nothing so far has been good. Now these photos look like they were taken through a window. You need to close your bedroom shades. Obviously, there is someone out there who has an unhealthy interest in your private life."

"They must have worked hard for them because I'm on the fourth floor. They must have been on the roof of the parking garage. That's one story below my apartment. My private life has suddenly gotten a lot less exciting. I threw Nick out yesterday when I got home. He was there. I didn't want him there. Sounds funny, doesn't it?"

"No, he does have a tendency to do that," Zoe said. "I have a friend in the police department. I'll give her these photos and have her pay Eric a visit. I don't want to make this official if I don't have to." They talked some more about certain details of the case, and Anne left to go back to her office.

Zoe went back to the files on her desk. There were several motions from Cargil that she had to respond to, but were routine, so she gave it to the small army of paralegals she'd hired just for the case. While most were bogus and calculated to increase his bill, some of them were questions that Anne needed to answer that dealt with minute and specific issues from the very beginnings of TrendInventions, most of them were times when Anne made a wrong move as she was learning how to run and manage a growing business, mistakes anyone in the same position would have been bound to make. They were details she was sure that Michael had no idea of—they were nothing he would ever have concerned himself with. The fact that Cargil hadn't yet asked for another meeting, which would have been an excellent way to bolster his hourly charges, showed Zoe that he wasn't ready to tip his hand yet as to the source of his information. He must have a source that goes back to almost the very start of the business. He certainly would line up a group of people to give evidence against Anne's ability to run the company and Zoe would need to be ready with a list of her own witnesses. She listed the questions and made a note to ask Anne who could have been around at the time who would have known about these mistakes. Cargil was going full ahead with his plan of painting Anne as incompetent, unpredictable, and violent. The latest event wasn't going to help her case at all. Zoe needed solid evidence that Anne was the fundamental force that grew and developed TrendInventions, something that Cargil couldn't take a cheap shot at. Barring that, she needed to find this source, and shut him or her down, if possible.

28

Eric was online on a chat with a group of guys who seemed to work under the assumption that everything but the sunrise each morning was somehow a conspiracy. A conspiracy that was usually perpetuated by a handful of elites who were Jews, Catholics, billionaires, Nazis, Communists, or extraterrestrials, or sometimes all of them, all bent on world domination. There had been a tragic collision between a ferryboat and an oil tanker a couple of weeks ago with a huge loss of life, and the chat room was abuzz with proof that the oil companies had purposely arranged for the collision in order to kill an agent on the ferryboat who was about to expose the dirty secret that they, the oil companies, were behind recent terrorist attacks because they wanted to get NATO to invade the Middle East and take all their oil. A competing theory was that they did it to kill a guy who had developed an engine that would get over hundred mpg on tap water, who happened to be on the ferry. Another told them all that oil didn't come from fossils, it came from Jesus, and there was no shortage of oil, Jesus would always make more. Some were debating the finer points of how this also would give oil companies an excuse to raise the price of gas, when one person uploaded photos of a UFO hovering over the site of the collision just before the ferryboat sank. He wasn't clear on the source of the photos.

Eric was engrossed and busy typing his take on this latest proof that extraterrestrials caused the collision and didn't hear the knock at his door the first couple of times. Detective Pepe had to really bang hard to get his attention. Eric was not used to anyone knocking on his door, so it took him a minute to realize what the noise was all about. He looked pretty much like hell. His sleep patterns were nonexistent, and he had worn the same clothes for several days, long enough for them to develop an aroma. He'd long since run out of the pills to control his mood swings. He had no health insurance since he lost his job, so he had no way of getting any more. He answered the door and saw a woman in a business suit looking at him. At first, Eric thought she might be a bill collector. He thought he'd caught up with the bills with the latest unemployment check and was wondering if he might have missed one. A short woman with dark black hair and brown eyes was standing at the door.

"I just wondered if we could have a little talk, Eric?" Detective Naomi Pepe said while showing her badge. "Can I come in?"

"Okay," Eric said, confused, and opened the door. The detective came into the apartment, and Eric cleaned off a seat that had been covered with empty pizza boxes. The police officer sat down.

"I just wanted to talk to you about Anne Mali."

"Oh man! I didn't mean to hit her. I told the security guy it was an accident."

"I didn't mention anyone hitting her. Tell me about it." Eric explained the altercation he'd had at work and apologized over and over. "Well, there was no complaint, so I really can't do much about it. I'm here about these." She pulled out some of the photos and showed them to Eric. "Would you know anything about these?" Eric looked at them and let out a gasp.

"No," he said softly, and his face started to twitch.

"Mind if I look around your apartment?" she asked Eric, who seemed to be in a fog. "It will only take a minute."

"No way!" Eric found his voice. "You can't look around. I would never take pictures like that. He's pointing the camera through her bedroom window for God's sake. Do you think I'm some sort of pervert?"

"Whoever took these photos broke the law. You can't take pictures if someone has a reasonable expectation of privacy. I think a bedroom qualifies. Don't you?"

"I didn't take them."

"Did I say you did?"

"What are you doing here then if you don't think I took them? Who sent you? Who gave you my name?" Eric was livid, and the police officer took note.

"I really can't tell you that. But I can say that I really hope there are no more pictures. If I had photos like these, I'd destroy them."

"I didn't take them," Eric insisted.

"I heard you the first time. If you know who did, you should tell them it would be a good idea to stop." Naomi stood up and did a quick survey of the room. It was obvious the guy lived in front of his computer, as that was the only surface that was clean. She noticed a lot of electronic gear but wasn't sure what the purpose was. She also noticed that Eric had three monitors hooked up to his PC, and a laptop sitting next to his keyboard. Naomi Pepe had seen a setup like that before when she worked with a drug bust, and the nerds in the van were monitoring several people at once. It was obvious to her that the guy was keeping a close eye on someone. She'd done all she could for now, but she certainly was going to keep this guy on her radar screen.

After she left, Eric had a long drink of vodka, and went to his desk. He pulled out an envelope addressed to him just like the one addressed to Zoe. It had copies of the same photos. He turned on his shredder and shredded each picture. His hands shaking each time he fed one in the shredder, he finished by shredding the envelope. When he was done, he then went to his computer and activated the cameras in Anne's apartment. Anne was sitting in her living room reading a magazine. The TV was on in the background, but she was paying no attention to it.

"You told her about us you little bitch," Eric yelled at the screen. "You think I would take pictures like that? Do you think I'm a damn depraved pervert? You bitch," he yelled and hurled the half empty bottle of vodka at the screen. The thrust threw him over the back of his cheap office chair, he missed the monitor and the bottle hit a stack of old newspapers and magazines he had been clipping and knocked them to the floor. The noise of the papers crashing to the floor made his neighbor in the apartment below knock on the ceiling. Eric ran to his closet, pulled out his assault rifle, pointed it at the floor, and pulled the trigger. Nothing happened because he hadn't taken the safety off. He clicked off the safety and pointed it again at the floor, but now he was more under control and didn't pull the trigger. He sat down on the floor, the rifle in his lap, holding his head in his hands, tears rolling down his face, staring at the monitor, and watching Anne sip a cup of tea and read a magazine.

29

Zoe was talking to Denton Pike in her office. They had been going over the finer points of the settlement between Marta and her soon to be ex-husband. He had agreed to just about everything that they'd stipulated

Denton was putting the finishing touches on the translation of the final offer, and the lawyer in Poland was expecting it sometime tomorrow. If all went well, Marta would have her divorce by the end of the month. The "love" letter had been enough to push the guy to where they wanted him. He, of course, probably knew she was bluffing, but couldn't possibly take the risk. The court would have taken a dim view of his refusal to reconcile, and there was no way he would want Marta to move in with him. If he was true to form, he probably already had a new girlfriend.

It was past lunch time when they got the final papers e-mailed to the attorney, and Zoe didn't feel like having sandwiches in her office again, so she asked Denton if he wanted to go to a late lunch, her treat.

They ended up at a diner near her office. There were very few customers in the place. They were seated near a window that looked out on a busy commercial drive. The place was an exercise in stainless steel and art deco, certainly from the 1950s. The waitress gave them each their drinks and took their orders.

"I can't thank you enough for the help you've been on this case," Zoe said.

"It wasn't for free, you know. I still have to give you my last bill," Denton smiled.

"Of course, but I just wonder what in the world I would have done without a translator. How do you happen to know Jimmy, since you're not—"?

"Since I'm not gay?"

"Right."

"He's a good friend of my companion, Judy. They had worked together at the college before he finished his degree and got the job with your firm."

"That explains it. And he happens to know you."

"Met him at one of those parties I couldn't get out of. Judy wanted me to meet the people she works with. They're certainly an interesting bunch," Denton said.

"You don't like them?"

"Not all of them. But I have an advantage in a way. Judy talks about them all the time. Some of the people she works for can be real jerks with enormous egos, so I sort of know about them already. It's interesting meeting them in person, though. There are a lot of decent people she works with."

"I know what you mean. Ego is a real issue in my profession, too. Sometimes you can use it against them, though."

"You mean like with Tim Cargil."

"You know about him?"

"Just by reputation. If you're guilty, he's your man."

"He's tough to beat, but family law is not his forte. He's more of a criminal attorney, so I'm hoping he'll mess up on a point of procedure, and I can capitalize on it."

"Sounds like wishful thinking."

"I know, but let's not talk about that. I'm feeling rather good about this case. So, let's toast." They clinked their soft drink glasses, and their food arrived.

"It's really fast here when you're the only one in the place," Denton said.

"They can slow right down when it gets crowded."

"I was here once right when a bus pulled up."

"Oh no."

"Yep. I think we had a real business lunch that day, about two hours." They ate for a while in silence.

Zoe continued the conversation. "How did things go on your trip to New Mexico?"

"Judy interviewed for a job, but we still haven't heard anything. We looked at houses, and some of the cool attractions in the area. I was surprised that so few places used solar power or even solar hot water there. You'd think that everyone would have solar collectors. Anyway, it was a nice trip. Our friend, Rita, is doing fine. She was worried about teaching since she has basically been a translator for the past few years, but she seems to be doing well, and her daughter is about a foot taller."

"I guess it depends on where you go. My brother, Chris, spent a couple of years out there in a community that aimed for zero carbon. They had plenty of solar collectors, water recycling, passive solar, you name it, they had it."

"Where was it?" Denton asked.

"I'll have to ask him. I can't remember the name, and I never got a chance to visit him since I was in law school at the time."

"So, this was a while ago?"

"No, just about six years ago."

"Really? I thought—"

"Right," Zoe laughed. "I'm a late bloomer. I was a decade older than most of my fellow students."

"That must have been hard."

"Sometimes, but sometimes I think that my age and absolute lack of any social life helped me out a lot. I had no choice but to study, and fear of failure did the rest."

"I see. That makes sense. Anyway, it's more my plan to move. I can work anywhere, so why stay where the weather gets cold? I think Judy's had enough of where she's working, too, but she wants a sure bet before she packs up."

"I don't blame her. You told me she owned a house; would she sell it?"

"Not yet, but she would rent it. You know anyone interested?"

"Maybe me. My lease is up in a couple of months, and I'm tired of apartment life. The place is too noisy. I have an odd schedule, and I know I'm a workaholic, so I can't expect the whole world to conform to my timetable, but there is usually some activity going on in the apartment building no matter what. So, when I want peace and quiet it's almost impossible to find. When I was at my brother's the other week, I remembered what real quiet was actually like. Where I live now there's always noise somewhere, a TV, an appliance running, people talking. Some people like that and take comfort in having people around them. I'm more of the solitude type. My ex-husband never quite got that."

"I'm the same way. Judy knows when to leave me alone."

"That's good when that happens. My ex thought of my personal time as an excellent opportunity to bug me about something, anything really, the bills, the laundry, food, the car. It drove me crazy. When Nick started to get like him, I told him to move on."

"Nick?"

"Oh, right, you don't know him at all. We were close friends for a while, but it didn't really work out." She sipped her coffee. Denton had ordered a carrot cake and coffee and was working on the cake. She watched him eat and then looked out the window at the constant flow of traffic.

"I hate making a left out of here."

"This time of day I usually turn right and go up to the light at the mini mall and turn around," Denton said.

"Me, too. It would drive my ex-husband nuts when I did that."

"Two types of people in the world," Denton teased Zoe while holding a forkful of cake, "those who have to make a left turn into traffic no matter what, and those who are willing to go right and go around." He finished his carrot cake and sipped some coffee. "You need to meet one of those who go around."

30

"My God, this is a disaster!" Anne said to April, her personal assistant. She had been at work for a short while when the fax came in. "I've got to get hold of legal right now." April had anticipated this, as she anticipated most of Anne's needs, and had them on hold on line two. While Anne spoke on the phone, April quietly closed the door and went back to her desk. There was more than enough to keep her busy without the present crisis. She thought of when she'd first started working for Anne and Michael, back when they rented an old unheated warehouse. The office was a corner of the building where some carpenters had made a small room, just large enough to hold two desks. Anne had put three electric space heaters in the place, and it kept the temperature almost tolerable during the winter. The rest of the warehouse was filled with the gadgets they sold. Their inventory consisted of exactly five different items. Anne was a master of making the business look a lot larger and more established than it really was. Expensive full-color brochures, an expert website, and Anne's confident professionalism all made buyers trust her, and trust that she could deliver.

April remembered when Anne made her first big sale, her first very large order for a big mail order company. After the check for the orders went to the factory, Anne realized they had exactly $10.78 in the company checking account. April had to run to the bank to deposit cash that the two had pooled from their pocketbooks so the monthly bank fee wouldn't bounce the account. Michael would drop in but spent most of his time working out new ideas at their home. Even today, she wasn't sure if he knew her name. She had been with Anne through many crises, but this one could really sink the company.

The disaster was a contract that had just been faxed to them, signed by Michael, and cosigned by Louis Amory for AmeriMart, a big box retailer. The contract had promised delivery of far more items than they had in stock, which in itself wasn't bad, because their factory was tooled-up for these items and they could easily order more of them, the problem was he'd agreed to another thirty percent cut in the wholesale price, which was a common practice with this particular retailer, and one major reason why Anne didn't want to do business with them. The original price that Amory had negotiated that he'd brought to the last board meeting was at their lowest possible margin. The board had told him to wait and had left the decision to pursue a contract to Anne. This new price would cost them ten percent more per unit than what they would make on the sale. She was on the phone with their corporate attorney, a middle-aged man whom they kept on retainer. He was a fastidious and quiet man who always seemed to be preoccupied, but had guided them through more than one crisis, and had set up the limited partnership that brought needed capital into the business, but unfortunately also brought Amory. He listened to the problem, asked her a lot of questions, told her to email the contract to him, and promised to get back to her within the hour. April brought her a cup of coffee. Anne noticed that her hands were shaking as she reached for the cup. She hadn't even had breakfast yet, and now she was so upset that she couldn't eat.

"I can't believe he would do something so stupid!" She drank her coffee, "We need to get rid of him. We have to buy him out before he wrecks the company." Anne was talking to herself but knew that April was in earshot. She would usually bounce ideas off her, or simply let off steam.

"What was the attorney's take on this?" April asked.

"He thinks we have a good chance of getting out of it but needs to review the agreement we signed with Amory, and the fine details of Michael's position as chief of product development." She sipped the coffee. "Amory simply might not have the authority to make the contract. It's a little iffy, since he's a board member. Michael is not usually one to make contracts either, but it depends on the fine points of his job description." She paused. "God, Amory's such a complete asshole." She started to get some of the daily work done, working on the costs of one of their new gadgets. It was going to be significantly more than the estimate, and she was going over the prices of the parts and assembly, trying to find out where the extra costs were coming in. She thought of emailing it to Nick—he was very good at finding problems just like this one, he'd puzzle it out in no time—but she was too preoccupied to really do anything at all.

She'd heard of this problem happening to other small and mid-sized businesses. They'd get a contract with AmeriMart, and not too long after their big celebration would realize that it was a gigantic mistake. The retailer would squeeze them to the point where they made little or no profit, while at the same time becoming their largest customer, giving them even more leverage on the prices. Some would cope by cheapening the product so they could make some money with a slightly better margin, but that would inevitably backfire. She knew of several businesses that ended up in bankruptcy, or worse, because of contracts just like this one. The coffee grew tasteless as she punched at her keyboard. She decided that she needed some air and told April to forward her calls to her cell phone and went for a walk around the building.

April nodded and went back to her screen. Anne didn't notice, but April was messaging her husband, Alfred. April spent many of her morning hours online, networking with her husband or her kids. Her two kids, Andy and Abigail, were away at school, and her husband worked at a nearby software development company. She felt no compunction about gossiping about the latest work drama with Alfred, and he had no problem giving her his opinion about how to handle the situation. She liked that their names all began with the letter "A" and thought there was some significance that Anne's did, too, but lately she wasn't so sure. In fact, the last couple of years had made her very bitter with the company or at least very bitter with Anne. The phone rang and it was the company attorney. April forwarded the call and went back to her conversation. She mentioned how Anne was her usual incompetent and confused self and had fucked everything up. She, April, had spent the morning trying to fix things. If it wasn't for April, TrendInventions would have gone bankrupt years ago, only they didn't appreciate her work, not at all. Alfred agreed, and they commiserated about how long she'd been working for the Malis and how ungrateful they both were. They hadn't any idea of the amount of work that April did or the hours she spent in unpaid overtime just keeping the company together. She ranted about that "pretty boy" Nick who had no brains at all but made more than she did and had been there only a few years. He got where he was because he fucked Anne, that was all there was to it.

Alfred did what he did best, enabled her, and pointed out the many injustices April had suffered at the hands of the Malis. Hell, they'd just been lucky they hired her back when they'd just started. They would both have gone out of business in a year if it hadn't been for her. She'd worked her ass off to make the company what it was today, not that either of them appreciated it. Anne just promoted her boyfriends or got rid of them when she got tired of them, like she did to poor Eric. Eric had been a prince of a fellow, a wonderful guy who always had something nice to say to her. Anne had led him on, and then dumped him. Is it any wonder he smacked her? She deserved it, the bitch, and now there was yet another crisis because Anne was an incompetent fool. April spent the rest of the morning complaining through her social network messenger to her husband about how hard she worked and how she was unappreciated, and how she would quit the moment their youngest graduated from college. He spent the morning in complete agreement, however, neither managed to get much work done.

Anne went for a walk around the atrium. It was an area that had huge skylights and an assortment of subtropical trees and plantings. There were comfortable benches and bistro tables with a sculpted fountain in the center. Basically, it was a miniature indoor park, and many employees took their breaks there or ate lunch together. Some would have lunch with their children, who were at the company day-care center. She had put this mini park in the center of the building so people could gather and talk. Many excellent ideas had come out of this mingling, and people sometimes met each other just to socialize or have a friendly chat. She was preoccupied and barely noticed the people who nodded to her or acknowledged her as she walked by, and she sat on her favorite bench in a remote corner and listened to the fountain. This usually steadied her nerves, but she was still on edge, and the usual calming touch was minimal. The forwarded call came through to her phone and she covered one ear and answered it. Anne listened for a few minutes, and then asked a couple of questions. She nodded a few times, and then hung up. She got up from the bench and walked with great purpose back to her office.

Louis Amory was looking smug sitting in Anne's office. He'd already guessed why she'd called him in. He felt he needed to prod her along so that she would start getting the idea that they needed to make more money with this place. He'd certainly shown her how to sell some products. Amory wondered how she could have possibly managed to run the company without his help. She came into the office and showed him a faxed version of the contract he'd signed with Michael.

"You signed this?" she asked.

"Sure. It's a great deal. Do you see how many units they want us to ship? Michael thought it was a good idea, too."

"Did either of you notice how much they are paying us?"

"Of course, I did."

"You agreed to an additional thirty percent discount?"

"Sure."

"Exactly how are we supposed to deliver these when they cost us more than that to make?"

"You'll just have to cut costs." Amory was full of himself. "That's your job, to figure out how to cut costs."

"There is no way to get these costs lower without cheapening the product. While we happen to sell gadgets that no one needs to people with more money than they will ever need, they do like the fact that what we sell actually works and is built to a high standard of quality. We have a reputation for excellence. Our products are not like the crap they sell in the big-box retail outlets. By just associating with this retailer we put our products under suspicion, not to mention that our high-end retailers would have a fit. For God's sake, even if we could cut our costs that much, we'd still barely break even on this contract."

"So, you say." He looked belligerent. Anne resisted the urge to hit him and spoke in a calm voice like you would speak to a child—or an idiot.

"Here are the facts, something you seem to have trouble with," she started. "We've made these particular products for years, almost since the time the business began. We've already gotten to the point where we can't possibly manufacture them for less than we do right now. When we add in overhead, shipping, product returns, etc., this is the minimum we can sell for, and that's at a quantity discount." She wrote figures very large on a piece of paper. "This is the figure you agreed to." She wrote another number somewhat lower than the other. "So, we would lose about one million dollars on the first shipment from this contract alone." She paused because she could see Amory was being stubborn. He was a man who could never be wrong, no matter how many facts stood in his way. "But this is really an academic exercise, since we're not honoring the contract."

"What?" he yelled.

"If you read your agreement that you signed when you became a limited partner, you will see that any contracts entered into for this company must be cosigned by the CFO. Michael is not the CFO, I am, and his job description specifically states that he has no power to enter into sales contracts. He can only control the research and development end of the business. I'm just giving you this explanation as a courtesy, which is a lot more than you've given me. Now, I will remind you that I have the power to buy out your interest whenever I see fit. You will be hearing from the company attorney on your buyout by the close of business this week. You can leave now, Lou."

"But—"

"No. There is nothing more to say. Now, I need to spend the rest of the day with our attorney who's already been in contact with the retailer you contracted with and has been explaining why we can't honor this contract. I'm sure that I will get to speak to their attorneys, too. They might threaten to sue us, which means even more expense. However, our attorney thinks they'll just let it go since neither of you had the authority to make this contract in the first place. They have no leg to stand on. AmeriMart is a huge company, and they have a lot more to worry about than us, although I'm sure this fiasco just used up our retainer for the rest of the year." She turned around and sat at her desk. "Goodbye, Lou." She went back to her desk and started working.

"I'm not done with this yet," he said, like a spoiled child.

"But you don't understand, Lou," she said, with her last bit of patience, *"I'm done with you."*

***

Nick was working at his desk when he got a call from Anne. He could tell that she was upset. He'd been avoiding her since she threw him out

Intimate Disconnect

of her apartment. He walked over to her office and she motioned him in while she finished up a phone call. She liked Nick's fundamentally pragmatic view of the world and wanted his advice. She sat back, thinking that this wasn't as uncomfortable as she thought it might be. While they had been lovers, and she didn't rule out maybe seeing him again, he was always very professional. Nick felt a little awkward but took his cue from Anne and followed her lead. She briefly outlined what had happened. His face grew taut, and the muscles in his neck twitched a little. When she told him Amory's reaction, he started to grit his teeth. Nick knew the inner workings of TrendInventions enough to know how close this came to a complete disaster, to bankruptcy. He talked with her about the options the attorney laid out. Thank goodness that AmeriMart couldn't really do too much to them, even though they had a reputation for holding their suppliers to backbreaking contracts. They could sue Amory, and, possibly, Michael, but they probably wouldn't since it wouldn't be productive in the long run. The only way to buy out Amory would be to draw in every spare penny, and possibly take out a sixty-day note, which would be paid off with next month's revenues. It would be very tight for a couple of months, but it would also mean getting rid of someone who could cause serious harm to the business.

"I'm sure he's bending Michael's ear telling him how I messed up the deal."

"It's never going to be his fault," Nick said. "He's just built that way, and Michael doesn't have a clue. They're a lot alike when you think about it."

"I need to know what's going on. That restraining order keeps me away from him, so if he's cooking up another stupid idea with his new buddy, I've no way of knowing."

"I'd be happy to help out. I know a lot of people in R&D. I know that they've not been too happy lately. Michael has been impossible."

"I don't want you in the middle of this."

"It's my fight, too. I don't want to have to go out and find a new job right now. If he blows up the company, then I'm out of work, right?" Nick said, placing his hands on the desk.

"You're right." She sat back in her chair and started to go over possible scenarios that they needed to be on guard for. This is where she and Nick worked very well together. He was very practical and could quickly translate a theoretical need into action. While she laid out what had to be done, he could figure out ways to make it happen. They both realized that Anne couldn't be blindsided again. She might not be able to put out a fire next time if it got too big before she could get to it. When they finished working out their general strategy, Nick turned toward the door, but hesitated.

"I'm sorry about the other day. I do tend to crowd people without really knowing it. I'm a little stupid like that. Zoe tried to tell me."

"I'd had a bad day."

"I know all about it. Everyone knows about the restraining order. God, Michael's a fucking wimp." Nick was getting angry, then settled down and smiled. "Hell. I would have punched your lights out," he teased.

"Of course, you would have, but I don't think I'll ever have to resort to giving you a black eye." She laughed for the first time in a long while. Nick left, and she went back to work and was thinking about how things had been working out. They could be far better, but maybe they weren't as bad as she had thought.

The night after Amory and Michael had pulled their stunt, after she'd spent most of the day and part of the evening getting it straightened out, Anne sat in her living room reading magazines. One was full of photographs of impossibly gorgeous homes, the sort of home that no one really lives in. She was relaxed for the first time in a long time, as if all the emotion she'd spent the past two days had used up her capacity to worry for a while. She was in a curious, neutral sort of mood. It occurred to her that her entire adult life had been about caring for Michael and caring for their business. She knew her relationship with him was different than others, but figured it was because he was some sort of genius. He always managed to come up with something that people wanted that no one had even realized they'd needed. There was even a cottage industry that made a good living copying their gadgets. She, however, was tired of the stress, and hadn't realized how great it was to be alone. She could finally stop worrying about whether Michael had eaten, or if he was in a good mood, or if things were going well with his latest project. She didn't have to listen to his daily litany of complaints, and, for the first time, she realized that she didn't have to *care*. His affair with Jimmy explained a lot, too. It wasn't as if Michael was gay or straight, just sexually indecisive. It made her feel a little less guilty about her affairs.

Michael was now on his own, or soon would be. Between the restraining order and the stunt he pulled with Amory, she couldn't care less about any of his problems anymore, even if she wanted to. She couldn't even talk to him, and he couldn't call her with his usual whiny issues. There was a kind of freedom in that. A freedom she was just starting to feel, to understand. It was a little scary at times, but she knew she could cope. She had been working with a lot of numbers, trying to get to the figure that her lawyer had come up with that they were contractually obligated to pay Louis Amory to buy him out in a forced move. There were some penalties, and there was some money in dividends to the current quarter that would have to be paid out to him. Currently, the money was put into a trust and paid out at the end of the year. It was more than she had realized. She simply couldn't figure out a way to pay him without coming up short somewhere else, and she wasn't about to fire employees so she could buy him off but might not have a choice. Her phone rang. It was Nick.

"Hate to make your day, or evening as the case may be, but this can't wait."

"What's the problem?"

"I talked to one of my buddies in R&D. They're ready to kill Michael. It seems his new refrigerated tray is full of bugs, but he wants to put it in production. Rumor has it that he has already ordered a production run."

"What? That's impossible. It would have to come through my office."

"That's what I hear. I'm just the spy here. You're the spymaster, Control, or should I call you *M*?"

"Thanks. I'll check this out tomorrow morning. I owe you one." Damn, she thought as she hung up, she couldn't relax for a minute without Michael fucking it up, even if it was only by proxy.

She called April first thing after she got to her office and asked her to pull all the latest production orders. Sure enough, there was an order for a run of refrigerated hot-tub trays. She called Henry, the production manager.

"Hi Anne," he said, and she couldn't help but hear the urgency in his voice, as if he already knew why she'd called.

"You have an order for some refrigerated trays?"

"Yes. I've been trying to call Michael about that, or anyone in R&D. He hasn't retuned my calls. This is one hell of an expensive item here. I'd have to order a bunch of parts, and we will take weeks to tool up for this. We're in the middle of getting the Christmas orders out."

"So, you haven't made them up?" She asked.

"Hell no. I'm not even sure how he wants them made."

"Great."

"I was wondering what in the world was going on. This thing is a nightmare. It's not even really finished. Half the parts list is missing. The drawings aren't complete. You want me to send it all back to them?" Henry asked.

"No. Send it right to me. And don't make anything at all from an order that doesn't have my signature on it. Nothing."

"Okay. What's going on anyway?"

"Somebody's about to grow up. Maybe just a little. See you, Henry." She hung up and went back to her computer. She'd just found a way to buy out Amory. Other than salaries, she deleted the budget line of the research and development team for the next two months. They would be able to work on what was in the pipeline, but no new items could be developed, including the refrigerated tray, and Michael's monthly expense allowance for research and development was zeroed out for the next two months. "I'm going to take your toys away from you for a while, Michael," she said, as she started to write a memo to the company business office.

31

The phone had been commanding attention all morning from Zoe. It seemed like each of her cases suddenly demanded all her energy, and she had someone sitting in the waiting room who had an appointment fifteen minutes ago. So, when Jeff called, his timing was terrible. She picked up a call on her cell without looking at the number as she hung up the office phone.

"Hello, Zoe speaking."

"Hi, Zoe, this is Jeff." Zoe had no idea who it was, and the silence over the phone was beyond awkward. "You remember? Your brother, Chris? Lily? Jeff? Dinner at your brother's and a movie? I'm the one with the red hair who brought the cheap red wine?"

"Oh. Hi. How are you?"

"Sounds like you're busy. Sorry."

"No problem. It's been unusually wild this morning." She trailed off to another round of silence.

"I just wondered how you were. I thought you said it was okay to call you."

"I did, didn't I?" There was more silence. "Look, Jeff, I'm not—"

"Neither am I—"

"Well. It's just that—"

"I know I'm the same way," Jeff said.

"Good. So, you see since I'm not and you're not then maybe we can just forget it?"

"It doesn't mean we can't just go out."

"I don't go out very much."

"I somehow gathered that," Jeff said. "I work not far from your office. I can swing by on Friday about six. We'll go from there. If nothing works out, at least you won't have to cook dinner."

"Okay," Zoe said, "but I never cook anyway."

"Then we have a date?"

"I hate that word."

"Me, too. We have an 'appointment for dinner?'"

"Much better."

I'll see you at your office on Friday, then." They hung up, and before Zoe could think of anything else, the phone rang. It was Cargil, returning her call.

"I was just returning your many phone calls," Zoe said.

"There's nothing pressing. I just wanted to touch base with you on the material I requested," Cargil said.

"You'll have it by the end of the week. Then we might as well get on the court calendar. I don't see any reason to wait much longer. This is going to take more than one appearance, and we need to get started."

"I agree completely," Tim Cargil said in a very smooth voice.

"Okay then. You agree that we're ready to see a judge?"

"Certainly. There's no need to drag this out too long. There's going to be enough to settle when the accountants finally give me the figures."

"I will have the papers to you by the end of the week," she paused, feeling like something wasn't right with this conversation.

"Okay. I guess I'll see you in court." After Cargil hung up, Zoe couldn't help but feel something was terribly wrong. There was something not at all right about his being so cooperative. She wished that she could have Jimmy on the case. He had a way of finding things out that no one else knew. But there was a firewall between Jimmy and Mali v. Mali. She couldn't ask for his help, at least not officially. She started to dial his number, but sent him a text instead, asking him to meet her for coffee tomorrow before work at the diner off the highway exit.

There was a thick envelope from Anne that had been mailed from TrendInventions. She knew that it was the rest of the material that Zoe had asked for: memos, ad copy, but mostly business plans that Anne had put together over the years to get loans for their start up, and to direct the growth of the company, anything that showed her hands-on approach to the business, and how much she contributed to the sum total of what became TrendInventions. Zoe was going to counter Cargil's charges of incompetence with years of substantial evidence that Anne was the force behind TrendInventions. They would show that Michael would have gotten nowhere with his ideas had she not known how to produce and market them.

Zoe thought that they had built a pretty good case so far. This envelope would be added to the several Bankers Boxes of material that her paralegals had prepared and catalogued for the judge. There was evidence going back to the beginnings of the company that showed Anne making all the major decisions that got the company started and kept it going. She still wasn't satisfied, though. She knew that Cargil was much too glib and far too confident. At least that's how he seemed, but that was the way he played the game. He liked to put up a strong front of confidence to intimidate his opponent. She wondered if this was all that there was to it, or if he really had something he would pull when he got in front of the judge. While she thought, she looked at the front of the envelope and noticed that it was stamped "First Class" in bright red ink. The stamp caught her attention and nagged at her. She saw that the top of the "F" was faded, and the middle horizontal line was almost completely missing. She thought about it for a while and then it came to her. Zoe took the envelope out from her desk that contained the photos of Nick and Anne. The "First Class" stamp was identical. She realized that Eric couldn't have sent it because he had been fired at least a week before the envelope had been mailed. There was no way that security at TrendInventions would have let him on the grounds, let alone near the mailroom with a package. Zoe looked at the package, and looked again at the envelope with the photos, shaking her head.

32

Eric was driving out of town. He had his new rifle in the trunk and was following his GPS to the shooting range. It was a hunting club his friend belonged to, and he had told Eric about the range. He'd ordered a couple of boxes of ammo from the Internet, had loaded his extra thirty-round clips, and had one already in the gun. He drove down a back road where a range of soft, rounded, tree-covered mountains ran parallel to the road. It was a little overcast, but the air was clear. There was a short dirt road that ended up at a parking lot in front of a one-story brick building. The name Ridge Riders Rod and Gun Club was carved into a rustic wooden sign that hung from an inverted L shaped pole. An American flag was flying next to the sign with an MIA flag directly underneath. Eric took his rifle out of the trunk and walked up to the front door. He knocked on the door and a man that was a little paunchy, but also looked very strong, and dressed in jeans and a flannel shirt opened it.

"My friend, Cliff Waters, sent me, said I could do some shooting," Eric said.

"You know Clifford? Hell, I ain't seen him since last hunting season." He looked at Eric's rifle, and his expression tightened, and eyes focused on it like it was exposed cleavage. "You gonna shoot that thing? You expecting an invasion or something?" He chuckled. "Hope you got some headgear, that muzzle brake's gonna throw all the sound right back at you. Them rifles is louder than a son-of-a-bitch as it is." He looked at it admiringly. "Must have set you back a few bucks—for sure." Eric had no headgear and had never heard of needing headgear for shooting. He'd only shot a .22 rifle years ago when he was a kid. "Then come on in. I know I got a couple extra pairs."

"My name's Eric."

"Frank," the man said, and held his hand out while turning to look for a set of headgear. There was a workbench and a shotgun was in a vice. Frank had stripped it down to repair and clean. He shook hands with Eric while walking over to a shelf near the back of the building. There was a large room with a table that took up most of the space covered with stacks of papers and envelopes. "My granddad started this club, but it's got almost no members anymore. Cliff's old school, he keeps up his dues. His daddy belonged until the day he died. I'm just getting the annual mailing out for our potluck game dinner. You like wild game?" he asked, but before Eric could answer he said, "Here they are!" Frank pulled out a couple of pairs of deep blue earmuffs that looked like old-fashioned stereo headphones. Frank and Eric went out to the range, and Frank pointed to a target that was already set up. Eric switched off the safety, pointed the rifle at the target, and pulled the trigger six times. The target didn't have a scratch on it. He felt a tapping on his headgear and took it off.

"You don't know jack shit about shooting a rifle, do you?" Frank said. Eric shook his head. "Hell, I'm surprised you even knew how to load the goddamn thing." Frank took the gun out of his hands and showed him how to stand, how to hold the rifle, and how to squeeze the trigger. Eric listened and watched as Frank sent four rounds in a tight group in the center of the target. "You try it." He handed the rifle back to Eric. He took a proper stance, his left foot in front of his right, his right knee bent a little, and head up straight. He looked through the sight, and carefully squeezed the trigger. He hit the lower right side of the target. Frank clapped him on the back. "There you go," he shouted, and Eric finished the magazine, grouping his shots closer and closer, moving toward the center of the target. While he reloaded, Frank set up several new targets: a bull's-eye, a figure of a man with a gun, and one that looked like a fox. He had Eric shoot six rounds in each, reset new targets, and repeated the lesson over and over again, showing Eric several shooting positions. After shooting for a while, the barrel was hot to the touch, so the two set the rifle down for a while to cool and took off their earmuffs. Frank smiled at him.

"You learn fast. You're getting a nice grouping. You just got to move the whole thing a bit over to the left. You're still shooting off to the right a bit. You might be pulling on that trigger a little still."

"I see," Eric said, and then added, "Someone told me I could make this fully automatic."

"Not in this state you can't! They'd put you in jail for that for sure. They could even give you a hard time about that muzzle brake. Why would you want to do a thing like that anyway?" Frank asked. Eric shrugged. Frank lit a cigarette and walked back to the building. After a few minutes, he came out with a bunch of empty beer bottles which he set up on a ledge a little further downrange from the targets, butting his cigarette out in one of the bottles. "For five cents apiece deposit, you can't find a cheaper target," he smiled. They put on their headgear and Eric resumed shooting. By the end of the day he was consistently hitting three bottles with six rounds. He was no marksman, but he was a lot more accurate than when he started. As the grey Corolla went back out of the dirt driveway, Frank waved to Eric, a fresh hundred dollar bill in his pocket. He made a mental note to talk to Cliff about his odd friend with the fancy rifle the next time he saw him.

Eric drove into town, stopping to pick up a few items at a grocery store. As he was looking at the various loaves of bread, he heard someone call him.

"Eric? Is that you?" It was April, Anne's secretary.

"April? Hi, how are you?" He was awkward. He'd spoken to more people today than he'd had in some time.

"Good. You look like you're doing okay," she said. He looked well compared to what he'd been looking like the past few weeks. The day outside in the fresh air had given him a little color and taken away his sickly pallor.

"How are things at work?" he asked.

"About the same. The divorce has everyone on edge, but we just do our jobs, and everything moves along." She paused. "Anne seems to be doing fine." She winced as he perked up.

"I hope she's okay."

"She knows you didn't mean it. Things just got out of hand," she said. "Look. You want to get a bite to eat? I'm alone for the rest of the week. Alfred's away for work." She and Eric had an affair a few years back when April and her husband had a trial separation. She had decided to go back to her husband, a decision she'd grown to regret, and then Eric had taken up with Anne, another bad idea.

"I was just going to go home and have a sandwich. Kind of tired," Eric said.

"Maybe some other time? We could have lunch or something?"

"Sure, April, that would be nice."

"Take care of yourself, Eric." She kissed him on the cheek and noticed a flash of anger in his eyes. It frightened her, took her by surprise. She pulled away from him quickly. The anger disappeared, and he became remote.

"You, too," he said, as he took a loaf of white bread from the shelf. Without another word he headed in the direction of the canned goods aisle. He didn't notice the expression on April's face. The look someone has who's ready to shriek in frustration, but holding back with every fiber, every effort, where a falling leaf, or the sound of a drop of rain would let loose a pent-up torrent.

"Goddamn that Anne Mali," she said out loud and went toward the other end of the store.

33

Zoe was sitting in front of a cup of coffee when Jimmy walked into the café. They were meeting far from downtown to make sure no one from the office saw them together. She had been waiting a few minutes.

"Over here," she said and waved her hand as he stood scanning the booths. Jimmy came over and sat. The waitress asked what he wanted to drink and gave them both menus. While Jimmy pored over his menu, Zoe said, "How are things in corporate?" Jimmy had been moved far away from the family law division of the practice into the contract law division.

"Boring. It's reading a lot of contracts all day long and trying to play a game of 'gotcha' on behalf of your client. You spend your day asking yourself, 'Is there a way to screw over the other guy legally with this contract? Is there something they forgot? Can I find a loophole?' It's even more fun when something goes wrong and costs a ton of money; everyone tries to stick everyone else with the bill." He paused again. "You're paying for breakfast, right?"

"Of course. I did ask you, right?"

"Yes, you did. What's on your mind?"

"You still have contact with Michael Mali?" Zoe asked.

"Not really." Jimmy made a face. "He's such an asshole. Likes to be gay when no one is looking. He's the kind of guy you want to ask: 'which one of you is gay? You, or your boyfriend?' God do I hate that. Why do I always go for the jerks?"

"You and me both, but I'm not here to gossip about my love life."

"That wouldn't take too much time," Jimmy smiled. Zoe laughed.

"That's true."

"Now my love life, that's another story."

"I'm sure it is." Zoe paused. "I just wondered if you heard anything about Cargil. He's the one I'm interested in."

"Why?"

"He's being really nice, and really cooperative."

"You're screwed!"

"Thanks, Jimmy. I thought you were my friend."

"I am your friend and that's why I won't lie to you. If Cargil's happy, you're screwed, simple as that."

"I thought you might have heard what he has that makes him so confident?" Zoe asked. Jimmy was thoughtful for a moment.

"Who's the judge?"

"Barnum."

"You're doubly screwed. Those two are so close they would be lovers if they were gay." He shrugged, "Who knows? Maybe they are, in secret. There's more of that going around than you might think, even today with everyone out of the closet and getting married and all, although the thought of those two going at it is a little scary. That would be something you couldn't ever unsee," Jimmy shuddered. The waitress arrived with his eggs and bacon and refilled both of their coffee cups. Jimmy continued, "I heard that some people think that Cargil wins an awful lot of cases that he probably shouldn't."

"What do you mean?"

"He sometimes will come to court with a pretty weak case, nothing on his side, no real counterevidence, maybe some bogus hearsay, and then he, you know, blusters and puts on a show." Jimmy imitated Cargil's voice and demeanor: "And Judge you can see that this man is really a good man, and he certainly wouldn't have beaten his wife the way that she accused him. She's a known klutz, and she's run into doors on several occasions, we have the emergency room records to prove it. Now she claims he hit her and that she was lying the other times? Why is she making up stories about my client? What else is she mistaken about? What else does she lie about? He's a loving and kind husband … blah, blah, blah." Jimmy stopped imitating and resumed his own voice. "And the sonofabitch will win! Even if case law is not on his side, even if it's obvious his client is guilty as hell. The judges just seem to like his bullshit, especially Barnum." He paused. "Come to think of it, I don't know if he ever tries many cases in front of a jury. His clients tend to waive jury trial and elect to go in front of a judge, usually Barnum."

"That's weird, but I've seen a lot of weird things since I started to practice," Zoe said. They sat in silence for a while, and then caught up. Jimmy was a never-ending source of gossip from their office, and, it seemed, most every other office in town. As he spoke, she half listened,

Intimate Disconnect

wondering about what he'd said about Cargil and Barnum. Maybe she should have asked for another venue. She'd done it before when it came to Barnum; the man could be impossible. Then Jimmy said something that piqued her interest while explaining the complicated love triangles at TrendInventions.

"Wait a minute. You mean April and Eric, the guy who got fired because he attacked Anne were an item?" She said.

"Yes. A couple of years ago, right after he first got there."

"That's odd. She acted like she hardly knew him when I asked her about the altercation."

"Well, what I heard was they went out for a year or so. She and her husband were at odds, some kind of trial separation where one spouse tells another to 'wait right here while I go get my shit together and fuck a bunch of other people' and she put the moves on just about every guy in the office. She went out with Eric, and then she and her husband made up. She spends most of her day chatting with him on the Internet."

"Now how do you know that?" Zoe was incredulous.

"I know a lot of people, including the guy who gets stuck doing her work while she bitches and complains about Anne to her husband on Internet chat. She acts like she built the company herself and Anne and Michael were along for the ride. Basically, she just answers the phone and brings Anne a cup of coffee occasionally."

"Why doesn't she leave and find another job if she's so unhappy?"

"This is where it gets interesting," Jimmy said leaning forward, "she interviewed for a job at Solarite about a year ago. I have a friend who works there."

"I'm sure you do, Jimmy."

"Now don't get wise, Zoe, or jealous. You could have plenty of friends, you're totally gorgeous, and any guy would love to go out with you. If I were straight, I'd ask you out. I mean Nick Mason, for God's sake, what was that all about? He looks great but he's got the brains of a tuna fish, which is probably why he's in charge of sales. Maybe he's good in bed?"

"That's my business, Jimmy, and Nick's a lot smarter than he looks. Now what about April?"

"That's still a low bar," Jimmy said. Zoe stared at him until he squirmed. "Right. April. She interviews for a management position at Solarite, which goes pretty well at first, and then they take her to lunch. You know, a standard business lunch, nothing special. She basically tells them they were doing everything wrong, and it's a good thing they're going to hire her because she will turn the company around. She has a ton of ideas on how to change everything. Needless to say, they didn't hire her. But it gets weirder. She actually calls up a bunch of times asking about the job and threatens that she will sue them if they didn't hire her."

"Really? On what grounds I wonder?" Zoe asked out loud.

"Temporary insanity?" Jimmy replied. "Anyway, she threatens them, and then she shows up at the boss's house. The guy who started the company—his name is Bill something-or-other. He's a good friend of Senator Steve Sears. Some say that's how he got the business permit in the first place. Plus, they get tons and tons of government contracts, so the business is doing just fine. They don't need anyone to 'straighten it out'. Anyway, one bright Saturday morning this crazy woman is on his front lawn calling him all kinds of names and screaming obscenities. He has no idea who she is. He certainly wasn't part of the interview process. Why would he be? Now this is in Forest Lawn right up near the golf club where the houses start at about a million five? She made a copy of a visitors pass she'd used a couple of months ago. So, she's committed a bunch of crimes just being there. The police come right away and haul her ass to jail where she sits for the whole weekend. This is summertime, so half of the courthouse is on vacation, but the crime is not so bad that they want to keep her locked up. They set the bail at $25,000. Anne Mali, of all people, bails her out, even pulls a few strings, I hear. Bill gets a restraining order, but she promises to be a good girl and the charges get dropped after an Adjudication Pending Dismissal. She got over it, and never bothered them again." Jimmy shrugged.

"Wow," Zoe said.

"Yeah. Certified loony-tunes. Not all of them are locked up."

"Don't I know that." Zoe signaled the waitress for the check. "I had no idea she was that nutty. I've only met with her a couple of times, and she seemed very professional, kind of mousy and quiet, really."

"It's the quiet ones you gotta watch out for."

"So, I guess I'll never have to worry about you?" Zoe said, as she smiled and put her credit card on top of the check.

"Touché," Jimmy said, "and thanks for breakfast. Now when are you gonna rescue me from corporate contracts? I'm going blind from reading the small print."

"You got yourself into that one, Jimmy." She paused. "I'll see what I can do. It's a waste of your talents to bury you like that. I'll see if your punishment is over. You can't work with me on this case, though. You know that, right?" She smiled at him.

"I know, but there's nothing wrong with me filling you in on the rumors and the gossip. What you do with it is your business." He left first, and she followed a short time later.

Zoe went back to her office and worked through the day. They would be meeting on this in a few days, and Cargil would present Michael's proposal. Her cell rang, and as soon as she saw the number, she glanced at the clock on her desktop. "Oh shit!" she said aloud and answered the call.

"Sorry, Jeff, mea culpa! Are you waiting for me at my apartment?"

"It's okay. I'm just out in the hallway of your office, but the door is locked. I figured you'd be in there. Where else would you be at six o'clock on a Friday?"

"You have me pegged. I'll come over and let you in." She went to the main door to the office, unlocked it, and greeted Jeff. "Sorry," she said as she let him in, and then locked the door behind him. He looked at her curiously. "We had a break-in a few weeks ago. We keep the door locked after hours even if someone is here."

"Did they take anything?"

"Some change that people had in their desks, and papers were moved around here and there, but nothing really. Very strange."

"That's odd," he said, and added, "Would you happen to be hungry?"

"I guess so, but I have a lot of work still, maybe we should do this some other time?"

"I'll be right back. Can you hear a knock on this door from your office?"

"Yes."

"Okay. I'll be back in twenty minutes." He left, and Zoe went back to her office. She was skimming a brief when Jeff knocked. She could smell the Chinese food before she opened the door. Jeff came in with a paper bag folded over at the top with a receipt stapled to it, and he had a bottle of sake under his arm. "I hope you have a lunchroom," he said. She pointed down the hallway. He went into the cramped room and placed the bag on the counter next to the small sink, then opened the various boxes and placed them on the table. "Do you like your sake warm or room temperature?"

"Warm," she said.

"Me, too." He poured sake into two demitasse cups he found in the cupboard and put them in the microwave for a few seconds. She could smell the aroma over the pungent smells of the food. "You're supposed to serve this in delicate tiny cups, but this will do." He took the small but heavy ceramic cups and put them on the table.

"I'm impressed," Zoe said. "You get an 'A' for improvisation."

"Thank you. I try."

They sat in silence for a while and ate, and then talked in small bursts.

"I can see becoming an attorney," Zoe said, "but a psychologist? Isn't that a bit masochistic?"

"I agree," Jeff laughed. "I started out with a BS in psychology but had to work right after I graduated—too many loans and my parents were in bad financial shape because my father got sick. I went to work for a hospital and eventually became their mental health coordinator, which was as far as I could go with a BS."

"I see," said Zoe. "And no one else wanted the job?"

"Almost. I was the only contender with the degree and any experience. Later I went for a master's in clinical psych, that's where I met Lily. She was finishing up and specializing in school psychology. Later I went back and got a Ph.D., and now I'm a certified psychologist, but I've only been practicing a few years."

"I took a similar route to my job. Had a bad marriage and then finally got out of it by applying to law schools. It took me a few years to get the courage."

"Really? I would think nothing could scare you."

"Everything scares me."

"You certainly don't show it."

"It's bad for business. Can't tell a client you think you might lose their case." She paused. "I will tell them realistically what they can expect, though. You'd be surprised what some people will anticipate from a divorce settlement."

"Same here. I can't just tell people that I have no real idea why they're screwed up. Usually I can figure it out. Sometimes, though, it's obvious. Usually someone has a bad behavior issue that's been encouraged or at least enabled by someone close to them. Like a wife who stops on the way home every day to get her husband a case of beer. Then she has no idea why he gets drunk and abuses her."

"Really?"

"That's nothing. I had a client who told me with a straight face that his wife drinks a bottle of vodka a day, but she's just fine. The fact that she broke her arm and almost drowned after falling off a boat on a sunset river cruise never really registered with him that she might be out of control. She, however, knew she was in trouble. That's why she came to me. We had to convince *him* that she was an alcoholic and needed treatment." He paused. "And I had a client who scored heroin for her son."

"No!"

"Yeah. She got caught one day buying from a police officer in a sting operation, and the ADA referred her to me. He was a decent guy who didn't want to put her in jail. It turns out that she didn't want her son to have a record, so she went out and got drugs for him."

"Amazing," Zoe said.

"That's not all. The best part is the guy was twenty-eight," Jeff said. "Twenty-eight, living at home, and having your mother go out and get you drugs, and they busted *her*!"

"How'd you deal with her?"

"Mostly talk therapy and cognitive behavior modification. After a few months she seemed to get the idea that she was being stupid. It took the threat of a couple of years in jail, though. He supposedly moved out, but I have my doubts about that. If he moved, he didn't go too far. My guess is that he's waiting for her to get off probation, and then he'll come waltzing back in, and she'll go back to scoring for him. I could be wrong."

"It must be frustrating," Zoe said. "I get the same sometimes. Work like hell getting a fair agreement between two people, get the family court custody issues all set, equitable distribution, everything ready to go to the judge, and then someone gets stupid and the whole deal blows up. Some people never really get it. They will leave here in agreement after working things out, and then. I don't know. Maybe they talk to a friend who is clueless but full of advice? Maybe they have a delayed reaction and get really angry, and then they come back with a deal that no one would agree too, one that would ruin both of them financially. It's just stupid."

"I agree. I think most people are afraid, not of anything in particular, just afraid. I wonder if it's a Darwinian thing. Maybe people who are always anxious tend to survive?" Jeff said.

"Maybe. It could have the opposite effect though—early heart attack, nervous breakdown, etc.," Zoe said.

"You're right, maybe it's just the world of fear and paranoia that we live in." He paused and smiled. "In any case, it's great for business. Without fear and paranoia, I'd be out of a job. Not to mention denial. Denial definitely helps pay my bills." For a couple of hours they traded stories and anecdotes about their jobs. Zoe sat back in her chair, rubbed the back of her neck, and yawned.

"I can be boring," Jeff said.

"No. I'm tired. This case is bothering me. I've let it get under my skin. Have to meet on Monday with the opposing counsel, and he's basically a jerk, but a smart, talented jerk."

"Sorry to hear that."

"Lots of them in this profession. I just can't figure out what his angle is now. Usually I have a better handle on things before the second meeting. We've made a bunch of telephone calls, and we've both made motions, but I still don't know what he's got up his sleeve. I can't tell if he's just really super confident, or if it's an act."

"Maybe you just need to wait until Monday, and then you'll find out?"

Intimate Disconnect

"Don't really have any choice. I'll be meeting him alone. This meeting is where the attorneys usually meet without the clients. It's like making sausage. You don't want to see it done, just want the finished product."

"Maybe I should try that? Have a session without my patients? Might make some real progress that way."

"Psychiatry at a distance? You might have something there," Zoe said. "You could be the greatest therapist in the world; it's the patients that screw everything up."

"I agree," Jeff said. "There might be an ethical issue or two here, but I could make a lot more progress without actually having to meet with the patients, not every time anyway." He smiled and stood up and put the empty food cartons in a bag. "I've held you up enough. You should get back to work," he said.

"I might just call it a day anyway. You're right in that I will find out exactly what he plans on doing on Monday. I'm sure it'll be nasty." She paused. "I wonder if this feeling that I'm just a 'poser' who has no idea what I'm doing will ever go away?"

"Probably not. It's possibly what makes you good at what you do. You don't take anything for granted. You don't get lazy, don't assume."

"I hope you're right. I'd hate to screw up this case," Zoe said. Jeff was smart enough not to say anything. She wasn't looking for encouragement or an empty platitude. She was just talking to get the words out in the open. She felt that when her words go out into the air, they have more form, more substance, than when they stay in her head, even if no one is listening, or no one makes a comment. There's something cathartic in simply saying a word.

He finished clearing up the cartons from their dinner, put the cap back on the bottle of sake, and asked if there was a garbage can. Zoe pointed to under the sink. He threw the bag away and stood in front of her. She looked at him for a minute, and then kissed him. It took him by surprise. He wasn't ready at first, but then kissed her back. "I'd like you to call me," she said. "Maybe next week we could go out?"

"We could try this again. Do you want me to just come here with a pizza and a bottle of Chianti next time?"

"Sorry." She smiled. "I'll remember next time."

"Okay. But if you go hungry it'll be your own fault." He was being funny, but the kiss had distracted him. He remembered it as he walked to his car. Sure, he was attracted to her, but he had not really thought much beyond a nice friendly dinner and some conversation. Thoughts of her occupied him as he negotiated Friday night traffic and drove to the highway taking him out of the city, almost missing the exit to his suburban home.

Zoe wondered if she should have kissed him and wondered why she kissed him. There was no mistake she'd made the first move. After that long talk she had with Chris about being on her own and wanting to be alone for a while, and getting rid of Nick, she goes and makes a play for this guy. She felt a flash of anger, but let it pass, and did what anyone else would do, she rationalized her irrational behavior. He seems nice, she thought, and he's certainly attractive. Not in the football-hero way that Nick is, but more in a subdued, charming way. He was more her type than either Nick or her ex-husband. Then the doubts came back. She wanted her freedom and had promised herself no new relationships and wondered if she should beg off the next time he called her, just let it go and end it before it moves on to another level. She worked for another hour, and then went home.

34

Tim Cargil came into the office on time, neither early nor late, and he met Zoe in the conference room. They were cordial, but as always, he had the attitude of someone who seemed to be in a hurry. Maybe it was just his way, or maybe it was because of arrogance, but it was something that usually annoyed Zoe. He got right to the point.

"Have you read all the material I sent over?"

"Only the relevant stuff. You managed to bury it well, but we found most of it. And you? I believe I answered you point for point."

"Well, yes, but your case isn't very strong if you ask me," Cargil said.

"I'm not sure what you mean. It's obvious that she founded the company and has grown it to this point. Without her there would have been no company, just Michael fiddling around in his garage."

"I'm not so sure about that."

"Well I am, and I've seen nothing that argues against this. She is the main force behind the company, and equitable distribution should split the majority shares they control between the two of them," Zoe said.

"I'm not sure that you have much of a case," Cargil smiled. "She might have been an adequate manager when the business was small, but now it's pretty obvious that your client is in way over her head in trying to run a business like this one. In fact, I have numerous examples of her utter failure to do her job, going back many years."

"When she was fresh out of college? When she had no experience? She even took night classes and hired consultants to help her along the way."

"All the more evidence of her incompetence."

"You can't possibly believe that?"

"I don't have to, it's what the judge believes. All those consultants and classes could be seen as a sign of ineptitude. She constantly needed advice to do her job," Cargil said.

"Or maybe it could be a sign that she isn't a macho idiot and is willing to ask for advice?"

"Maybe." He shuffled through some papers, and they went over several points. He certainly had an inside source regarding the history of the company, someone who was working very closely with him. His arguments were simple. He pointed out the times that things went wrong at TrendInventions—many of them were normal problems that could be expected from any company just starting and especially one that had grown as fast as this one had. He, however, managed to take even the positive efforts on Anne's part and put all of them in a negative light. Borrowing money to pay for an unexpectedly large order was "poor planning." Paying people more than the going rate, which for some of her competitors was minimum wage, was called being "fiscally irresponsible." Refusing to release a product that had already been marketed and missing the holiday season because it still had some bugs that needed to be worked out was "foolishly timid." However, spending a large sum of money to position the company so it could enter the European and other global luxury markets was "being foolishly aggressive." In other words, no matter what Anne did, Cargil twisted it to its most negative possible interpretation. This was a point of view that no one who really knew TrendInventions would share, with the possible exception of Michael, and the person informing on Anne.

"This is absolutely ridiculous," Zoe said, holding up the restraining order. "Your own client has a history of violence. If you bring this up, we will bring up the charges against him."

"That's just tit-for-tat."

"Maybe, but do you really want his assault charge in the record?" Zoe asked. "You pull your restraining order, and I'll put the assault record. Nothing is going to come of that order, and you know it. Besides, I have other witnesses to Michael's fits of temper and his outbursts. We could play this game all day long if you want. The main focus is that the business has always been split between Michael and Anne, and that's all there is to it. This case requires a simple equitable distribution. Anne has done nothing but make that company grow, and now she's managing to keep it profitable in the middle of a worldwide recession."

"Maybe, but is that why she put the kibosh on a multimillion-dollar contract?"

"I don't know anything about that."

"One of the board members had negotiated a contract with AmeriMart, and your client, the financial genius, killed it. Shut it down cold." He pulled out some papers. "This only happened a week ago, so I hadn't had time to include it."

"I believe that," Zoe said. "I'm sure that there is no way would you try to blindside me."

"She had her business attorney break the contract on the grounds that Michael and this other guy, Amory, had no authority to make the contract in the first place. It sounds like she's a bit jealous to me. Like she wants to be in charge, and no one else can do anything without her okay." Cargil paused. "Not only that, she immediately bought out the guy's limited partnership and threw him overboard. Now that's a real bitch if you ask me." Cargil handed over some more paperwork.

"That could be true, or maybe she just plays hardball," Zoe said quietly. "Sounds to me like he was insubordinate, and she fired him, like any CEO would in any other business. If she were a man, you'd say he was a 'tough boss with brass balls, and no one to mess around with.' But she's a woman, so she's a jealous bitch. You want it both ways here. When she isn't aggressive enough, she's being too soft. When she's aggressive she's being a bitch. What will you say next? That it was 'that time of month' and that's why she broke the contract?" Zoe had seen this double standard in more than one divorce case. The problem was that it sometimes worked. Some judges liked their women placid, obedient, and meek, like the mom vacuuming the floors in high heels on a fifty's TV sitcom. Any evidence of strength would go against their case—any deviation from the stereotype would be used as an argument against them.

"So, your argument then is that Anne has always acted for the good of the company, and that Michael's only role is to make new things for them to sell?" Cargil asked.

"Yes. That's pretty much it. Michael is R&D, and Anne takes care of everything else. She even put together the limited partnership so they could capitalize and expand their business. I doubt if Michael has a clue how that all went together. My understanding is that he spends his time in development, nothing else."

"That is most likely true. He does all the development that makes the products that the company sells, but do you know how she got the money to buy out the offending board member?" Cargil loved the dramatic pause. "She gutted the R&D budget and used the money to buy out Amory's contract, buying him out at a pretty high dividend plus penalty fees." He paused. "Does that sound like a smart thing to do? Not to me. Shut down a multimillion-dollar contract, and then gutted her R&D budget. Sounds like a recipe for disaster."

"I'm sure she had her reasons," Zoe said.

"Oh yes. I'm sure she did, too. She wanted to get even with her husband for filing an Order of Protection, maybe?" Cargil said. He leafed through some more paperwork. "Like I said before, you'd better reconsider your case. My client is willing to overlook Anne's incompetence and let her stay on for a full year as CEO/CFO. After a new CEO is found she can stay as CFO if she chooses, on salary, but she must give up her majority stake in the company to my client. Those are our terms. If she doesn't agree, we'll ask for even more from the judge. And we'll get it," he smiled.

"She won't go for this deal. I'm sure of it."

"Well you are loyal to your client, but you're not being realistic."

"I don't agree. Anne is no fool. Whatever she did was done for the good of the company. She wouldn't purposely sabotage TrendInventions."

"Not according to the evidence I have, not to mention the violent altercation she got into with one of her ex-lovers."

"That man needs psychiatric help. He started the altercation with her. They hadn't been lovers for over a year. Like I said, I don't think your evidence is as conclusive as you'd like to believe. I can think of alternative explanations for everything you present."

"Of course you can, that's your job. You must admit, though, that Anne has an awful lot of explaining to do. Good luck with it." Cargil stood up and gathered his paperwork together. He dropped an envelope on her desk. "You might want to look at these when you get a chance. We're almost ready to go to the judge with this. I hope your client is in agreement."

"Maybe. We'll need to consult some more, and I don't think we need to go to court this soon. I want more information from the forensic accountant."

"Judge Barnum doesn't like to have his cases drag out too long."

Intimate Disconnect

"That's true, sometimes. It all depends on whose case it is, doesn't it? Sometimes he takes an awfully long time, and sometimes he doesn't. Do you know why that is? None of us can figure it out. You seem to know him rather well," Zoe asked sweetly.

"I wouldn't know anything about that," Cargil said evenly. "In any case, I wouldn't give your client any false hope if I were you. Face it, Zoe, she might be a nice person, but she's an incompetent CEO of a corporation as large and demanding as TrendInventions. Do you know she spent $100,000 on tropical plants and another $20,000 on a fountain to build a conservatory in the middle of the building where everyone eats lunch? That makes no sense at all, a total waste of money, and then she kills a multimillion-dollar order and shuts down their R&D budget for at least two months? Face it, she's ruining the company."

"I don't agree. There would be no company if not for her."

"Perhaps, or maybe the company is successful despite her? It all depends on how you look at it." Cargil snapped his briefcase shut. "I will have my paralegal send you the most current paperwork."

"That will be fine."

"How is that guy, anyway? Jimmy? Your paralegal?"

"I wouldn't know. He works for another department. I never see him."

"Oh. I thought he worked for you."

"Not now, he's not on this case. Is there any more fishing you'd like to do before you leave?" Zoe opened the door to the conference room. Cargil smiled, said goodbye, and left. Zoe went to her office and closed the door. She had a headache and her stomach was laced with nervous energy, rebelling over having only had a cup of coffee since seven that morning. It was now well after lunchtime. She opened the envelope that Cargil left, expecting yet another motion that she'd have to answer, and copies of the photos that had been sent to her, showing Nick and Anne in her bedroom, spilled out on the desk. "We're so fucking screwed," she said out loud. She sat in silence for a long time. After a while she took her head out of her hands, picked up her phone, and dialed Anne. After she relayed the news from her meeting with Cargil, she could feel Anne collapse on the other end of the phone. She explained to Zoe about the AmeriMart order, and how it would have bankrupted the company if they'd been foolish enough to try to fill it. She took some money out of research and development, but there was enough left to have them continue to work on anything that was already in the pipeline. Then she explained how she pulled the plug on an item that Michael was trying to rush through to production behind her back that was costly and could have been dangerous. It was far from ready for production.

"We'll play it just like that, then," Zoe said. "All of these items need to be put into writing, especially the contract with AmeriMart, and you need a report from your attorney for the business. I also think we could use a statement from your production manager about that tray that Michael wanted to put into production and anything else you can think of that would argue against their case. I think we can poke a lot of holes in their arguments, but we need to have everything ready, and in very plain language. Judge Barnum can be easily confused when he wants to be."

"Sorry, Zoe, I considered the whole thing simply business as usual, especially with Amory. The man might be a good surgeon, but he doesn't know anything about business. Not that he'd ever listen to anyone but himself."

"It's good that you got rid of him, and it's good that you stopped the contract and pulled the production of something that could be dangerous. But that's not the spin that Cargil is putting on things," Zoe said. "We have to answer all of his contentions. But above all else, you have to be careful that *nothing else goes wrong, nothing at all*. Don't fire anyone or change anything at all with the company for the time being. If anything odd happens that looks like you don't have total control over the situation, that you're anything less than in complete and total charge of your company, Cargil will jump on it, and we will lose. I guarantee it." Zoe hung up the phone and looked at the copies of the photos. Upon close inspection, they looked like they were pictures of the pictures she'd had in her drawer. Grainier, and the whole photo was cropped, like it didn't fit in the frame of the camera that took the picture. Then she noticed a reflection in the corner of one of the pictures, and she called her friend, Detective Pepe.

35

Mary Robinson sat across from Zoe. She had called her in to consult on the Mali case. Zoe liked getting her opinion when she was at a loss.

"Last I heard, Abigail thought she was pregnant," Zoe said.

"Yes, she did." Mary spread her hands out on the desk in front of her before she answered. "The vet told me I had to treat her more like a dog, and that I was treating her too much like one of the family, making her condition worse. Well, I sent her to my mom's for a couple of weeks, and she is much better, her hormones went back in balance and everything else. The vet said she's just fine. So now, when she mopes around the apartment, I take her outside to the park and make her run until she's ready to drop."

"I have a few clients I'd like to do that with. They really need to get over themselves," Zoe said, she paused, "I have a case from hell right now. Wish I'd said 'no' and followed my original instinct."

"I've heard a little about it. Some of it has been in the papers," Mary said.

"I'm doing what I should be doing, but it's not working out, as if nothing I can do will make a dent in their case, and their case is ridiculous. It's ludicrous to think that Anne had nothing to do with the development of TrendInventions." Zoe filled Mary in on the details of the Mali case, just to relieve some of her stress, and maybe get some advice. Mary's eyes narrowed a few times over some of the details, especially the restraining order, and the mysterious photographs.

"Someone on the inside is definitely trying to destroy Anne," Mary said.

"Doing a good job of it, too," Zoe paused. "Maybe I should just advise her to take the offer before it goes to Judge Barnum. God knows what he'll do."

"I know. I had a case against one of Cargil's clients that went before Barnum, and the decision not only went against us, but went against settled law. It literally violated the divorce laws. Barnum cut off my client without any custody or visitation, directly against the decision of Family Court, and awarded most of the marital property to her husband."

"Based on?"

"Nothing, really. He landed on the fact that she'd been in treatment for a problem with painkillers when she'd been in college. She was an athlete and had taken painkillers after an injury. She needed help to stop, but nothing bad had happened. She hadn't failed out of school or been caught buying illegal prescription drugs. It was that she was concerned and sought out some help. There was no evidence that she had any problems since, but he zeroed in on that, more like an excuse than anything else. He rewrote the entire judgment."

"What did you do?"

"We appealed. It took some time, but we had most of his decision reversed by the Court of Appeals. However, the damage had been done. She had been left financially destitute, and her kids didn't see her for a few years. I also ended up doing most of the appeal pro bono. She certainly couldn't afford the fees, which is why Barnum gets away with it. One reason anyway."

"The two of them do seem to get away with a lot," Zoe said. She went over to the coffee machine and made a cup. "Do you want one?" she asked Mary.

"Actually, I could use some caffeine. This day has been a hard one for me to get motivated." Zoe made a cup and fixed it for Mary. She gave it to her and sat down.

"I'm at a real loss here. I spoke to Anne, but she is so wrapped up in her work she can't see this coming. I really think we're going to lose, and lose big," Zoe said.

"Well," Mary started, "it might not be so bad. What I would do is be sure to get everything on the record, everything, even if it's barely relevant. Anne certainly has the money to appeal. You'd think Barnum would realize that. He seems to have gotten a little too arrogant even for his reputation. If he goes too far from an equitable division, he'll need a good reason. Even he should know that. He did go to a first-tier law school."

"I'm beginning to wonder what he did there, or how he was admitted in the first place."

"Family. His dad worked for the State Attorney General's office for years," Mary said.

"It helps if you're from the area to know the inside story," Zoe said. "I'd have guessed as much. Legacy candidate?"

"His dad probably had something to do with his admissions, but he did work hard, and he graduated and passed the Bar. He opened his own practice for a while, but that didn't work out for him. The governor appointed him to his job after someone retired, and he manages to win reelection. Everyone likes to play golf with him, and he's supposed to be fun at parties." Mary was being her usual discreet self. Barnum's incompetence as an attorney was legendary. One judge had sent a brief of his back with the spelling and grammatical errors marked up, instructing him to rewrite it completely and to not bill his client for however long it took. Even now, his law clerk had to tactfully insert changes into some of his decisions so that they weren't completely unintelligible. He was reelected mostly out of sheer inertia running on both major parties. Occasionally, a third-party candidate would run against him, but it was hopeless. Most people who voted for him were highly unlikely to ever have to see him in action as a judge. And even if they did manage to meet him in his professional capacity, to paraphrase a famous judge, "His good friends have nothing to fear from the Bench." He and Cargil were living proof that the system works for the few and the privileged. For all the other people, it was up to lawyers like Zoe and Mary to help.

"Look, Zoe," Mary said, "you're too close to this one. You need to pull back a little and get a larger perspective or Cargil will have you jumping through his hoops. You know that it's going to be iffy with Barnum. Get as much on the record as you will need for an appeal. Barnum isn't so stupid that he won't let that affect him. His record on appeals is abysmal. For his own ego he might not want another loss. Especially for a high-profile case like this. But you need to take a step back, or you'll end up a basket case. I have the same problem. I care too much. You've got to let this one go a little." Mary looked at her. Zoe had sunk in the chair and was looking at the floor. Mary pulled up her chin and looked her in the eye. "Right? Zoe? Am I right?"

"Yes," Zoe said after a few seconds. "I'll work on it." She smiled. Mary scooped up her paperwork and left, but only after getting Zoe to promise to call her in a few days.

Back in her office, Zoe was suddenly tired. It was as if the stress of the past few weeks had suddenly overwhelmed her. Her phone rang. She looked at the caller ID and almost didn't answer it. "Hi Jeff," she said.

"You sound a little bit off. Is this a bad time?"

"No time seems to be a good time," she said. "No offense. It has nothing to do with you. Sorry."

"No need to apologize. I just wondered if you still wanted to go get some dinner this weekend? Saturday?"

"I guess so. Sure. Okay. Why not?"

"I like your thought process. It's fun to listen to. We call it talk-aloud protocols. I get my patients to just talk, and record what they say."

"I remind you of your patients?"

"No." He paused. "Well sometimes. Perhaps. Maybe?"

"Now who's putting his thought process out there?

"Sorry. Look, let me find a nice quiet restaurant for dinner."

"Okay. I'm free this Saturday. My friend Mary told me I'd better go out and have some fun."

"I like her."

"She's nice. Maybe you should date her? She has a lovely Labrador about the size of a minivan. Very friendly."

"Not so fast. I'm trying to date you. Remember?"

"And I'm trying to be on my own for a while. I told you."

"I'm not looking to move in."

"I'd shoot you if you did. I'd have to buy a gun first, but I'd definitely shoot you."

"I'll bet you would."

"Still want to go out on Saturday?"

"Yup. I'll be sure to wear my Kevlar vest."

"You never know," Zoe said. After Jeff was off the phone, she buzzed her secretary and her paralegals, and gave them instructions she knew they would hate, but it couldn't be helped. It would mean more hours of tedious work, but Mary was right. Everything had to be on the court record to get ready for an appeal, and they needed to review all the material to make sure they hadn't missed anything.

36

Detective Pepe met Zoe at her apartment. Zoe had been an assistant district attorney when she had met Naomi Pepe. She had been an officer, and new to the job, and had been charged with police brutality. Zoe was assigned to investigate it. The politicians had decided to offer her up as a sacrificial lamb because there was a race issue involved. Someone had badly beaten a young black man while he was in custody after being charged with burglary and assault in a case where someone had held up a bodega and shot the owner. It later became a murder charge after the bodega owner died from his wounds.

Zoe had not liked the case from the start. The suspect that had been caught and beaten while in custody did resemble one of the men in the grainy security cam video, but he was younger and thinner. Officer Pepe had been with the arresting officers but had never been alone with the suspect. In fact, she went off duty right after the collar because her daughter had been taken to the hospital with an asthma attack. The other officers swore that Pepe had been alone with the suspect, but it was pretty clear to Zoe, and anyone else with a working brain, that they were lying, not to mention the racist symmetry of charging a Hispanic cop for beating a black suspect who was charged with murdering a Hispanic. She had done some research and found that one of the arresting officers had been brought up several times on assault charges, usually involving black suspects, and since he was the nephew of the chief of detectives, nothing had been done. They had handed the case to her as a newbie ADA, thinking she'd be easy to fool. The powers that be had counted on her charging Pepe. There might not even be a trial, and she would take the fall, since they felt that she was just the Hispanic affirmative action appointment anyway. They'd teach Officer Pepe a lesson or two for thinking she could jump to the front of the line just because she was a beaner.

It took Zoe a few weeks of investigation and asking the right questions, but when she was finished, the suspect was exonerated, and the brutal monster, who had no business being on the police force in the first place, and who'd actually beaten the suspect, was charged, and later ended up serving five years for aggravated assault. Naomi Pepe was cleared. However, because the police had spent so much time chasing, and beating up the wrong suspect, and then trying to protect themselves with false testimony, the real murderer was never caught.

The district attorney, a good friend and drinking buddy of the chief of detectives and his sociopathic nephew, was apoplectic when Zoe came into his office after the nephew had pled guilty and been sentenced. The DA was so worked up that Zoe was at first afraid he was going to give himself a heart attack, and then fervently hoped he would, and then was a little disappointed that he didn't. Zoe was promptly demoted in the DA's office and spent all her time in traffic court, listening to endless streams of people complain about parking tickets and speeding tickets, and plea bargaining DWI cases. However, her work hadn't gone unnoticed by the right people, and the firm she now worked for offered her a job soon after her demotion. While she earned the enmity of some members of the police department, Pepe had a lot of friends, and the honest cops gave her their respect and gratitude.

Pepe was in her living room with the photos that Cargil had left her in an envelope.

"Your suspicions were right. Your talents are wasted on being a lawyer. You'd make a great detective."

"Maybe later, after I get fired, I might need a job."

"That bad?"

"Pretty bad."

"Well, these are pictures of pictures, probably yours. The reflection in the photo is of a flat screen monitor. But it could be any monitor." She held out enlargements of portions of the photos that Zoe had given her. "My guess is that the break-in was to get these, and any other evidence they could find for their case. There are no fingerprints on them, other than yours."

"That Cargil is a real piece of work."

"There are more than one of us who'd like to see him nailed, but he's pretty slick. I'm sure he hired some goon to break into your office, someone who owes him big. You'll never find out who he was. And if you do, you won't be able to connect him to Cargil."

"I might not," Zoe said, looking at the reflection in the photo. She looked closely, holding the picture up to her face, and then smiled. "There he is!"

"Who?"

"Egbert."

"Who?"

"Egbert, he's the hard-plastic gecko my brother, Chris, gave me when I first went to law school. I keep him under my monitor. You can see him." She pointed to a spot on the photo.

"Yep. There's just enough light to make him out," Pepe said. "I don't think it's enough to make a case out of this, though. Cargil could always claim he has no idea where the photos came from."

"Oh. That's fine. I just want to use it as a little leverage just in case he's thinking of using them."

"You know that creep you sent me to the first time you got these?"

"Eric?"

"Yeah. The computer guy. I really don't think he took these. He was shocked when he saw them. I gave him the standard line about not doing it again, but I think these are not his." She paused. "But he is up to something, something else, so I'm keeping an eye on him."

"I agree," Zoe said. "Someone from inside TrendInventions sent them to me." She told him about the worn First-Class stamp on the front of the package. Naomi smiled.

"Well, like I said, you can always be a detective if the lawyer thing doesn't work out for you."

For the first time in a while, Zoe felt good about the case, like she wasn't treading water, holding her head just high enough to keep from drowning. She turned to Detective Pepe and asked her about the news from police department and the DA's office. She found out that her case had triggered a State Police investigation of the whole department. It had been stonewalled a couple of years by the previous mayor, but when he lost his bid for reelection, they came in with a vengeance, and the rumor was that there were some major heads that were going to roll, possibly even criminal indictments. There was also a rumor that the investigation had not only found problems with the police but had also moved on to the courts. No one knew exactly what the investigators had found, but several attorneys and other agents from the State Attorney General's Office had been involved in the investigation, and the feeling was that they were about to make their move.

"Wow. You never hear a word about that on TV or in the local paper."

"There's a gag order. I could get fired just telling you this much. It's all rumors, really. I'm certainly not part of the investigation. For a small city they have some real big-time bullshit going on, though."

"How'd you get on the department? You seem so ...," Zoe said.

"Normal?"

"Yes. And smart enough to read without moving your lips," she said.

"Haven't you heard? I'm the affirmative action case. I'm one of the only cops not related to anyone else on the force. After I finished community college with a degree in criminal justice, I took the exam and scored high enough even without the added points to get hired. It pissed them off no end. And after I passed the detective's examination, they were fit to be tied. Of course, I constantly have to prove myself, even to guys who outright failed the test, but somehow managed to get hired."

"Really?"

"Yep. They hire them on a special task force with state or federal grants, usually some anti-drug initiative. They run around and put in a lot of overtime, then bust a bunch of addicts who were dumb enough to sell them dime bags. They never really catch anyone big because it's obvious that they're cops to anyone who is a real dealer, except the addicts of course. They're so stoned that they'd sell a bag to someone in uniform. In fact, one guy was so burnt out that he called the police because someone stole his stash. He actually reported that his dope was missing to the cops." Naomi chuckled. Zoe had read about that in the papers, so she knew she wasn't making it up. "So, we make some headlines and it's a victory in the war on drugs. You know what I'm talking about, the one that's been going on for about fifty years now. In any case, they use the grants so they can bypass the list and hire whomever they want and designate them as special officers. Some of them are okay, but some of them are real idiots. Like the moron who had a high-speed chase in the middle of the day on Murphy Street, plowed into the car he was chasing, totaled two other cars parked on the side of the road, and tore the porch off a house, not to mention totaling the police cruiser. The guy he arrested had stolen two hundred dollars from a Seven-Eleven and had a quarter of an ounce of marijuana. The cop did about two hundred thousand in property damage to catch him. The cruiser had been a special pursuit vehicle that cost over seventy thousand."

"I read about that in the paper. They really left a lot unsaid in that article as I remember."

Yup. And that fool gets to carry a gun. Makes you wonder if you should walk around in a bulletproof vest."

"That's the second time that's come up in conversation today," Zoe said.

"I hope you're not superstitious."

"Not usually," Zoe said. Pepe got up from the couch.

"Sorry I couldn't be of more help. I owe you big time."

"No. You don't owe me anything, and you told me what I needed to know."

"I'm glad I could help."

After Detective Pepe left, Zoe sat on her couch wondering if she had anything in the refrigerator she could microwave for dinner. The news had made her anxious but exhilarated at the same time. She felt like there might be some hope after all, that something good might happen. She knew she had no reason to rationally believe it. She knew it was like a drowning woman grasping at a piece of wreckage, but she'd take it.

37

John Baxter knocked on Zoe's office door, and she waved for him to come in. She was on the phone but ended her call quickly. Baxter was the newest partner in the firm, and like many who took the express to the top, was as ambitious as he was spineless. He had been the most in favor of the firm taking on the Mali case when it looked like they'd get plenty of free publicity, but now was the one leading the charge against Zoe. He had been the big rainmaker and had brought in some of the firm's top clients, which he had stolen from his former law office. He had never liked the whole family law part of the practice because it usually didn't bring in a lot of money. The older partners, though, could remember when the business and real estate divisions were deeply in the red because the economy was in such a bad way that many of their corporate customers were in Chapter 11, and while this recent downturn hadn't been quite so bad, they still liked the idea of a diverse, general practice firm that did a few things very well, rather than specialize in any one form of law. They all, however, knew that Mali v. Mali wasn't going well for Zoe.

"Hi, Zoe, have a moment to talk?"

"Sure, John, how are you?"

"Fine." He sat down across from her. "I just stopped in to see how the Mali case was coming along, and to see if you needed a little help."

"I'd be lying if I said that everything was going well. We've had a few setbacks, but I think we'll present a very good case."

"I'm glad to hear that," Baxter said, not changing his expression. "I've heard that there were some issues."

"Cargil is playing tough, and I'm trying to keep him honest."

"That can be a tall order." Baxter smiled. "Some of the partners are a little worried that this could—"

"Go down the tubes and give us a black eye?"

"Well. It would be bad to have a poor result on such a high-profile case."

"We knew that going in. Rest assured that we are covering all the bases."

"Meaning?"

"That we can take this to the Court of Appeals if necessary. It won't be the first time Barnum was reversed on appeal."

"But he won't take it very well, and we have plenty of cases before him or friends of his on the bench every year," Baxter said, his eyes narrowed, and his head sunk a little into his shoulders. "The partners would like to avoid any form of appeal if possible."

"The partners, or just you?" Zoe said. She knew that Baxter had several cases ready to go before the court and would most likely draw Barnum on at least one of them.

"We are all in agreement."

"I'm sure you are but enlighten me. Agreement on what?"

"Talk to your client. Let her know the consequences of a long appeal. I'm sure she wants to get this over with soon."

"She's not about to walk away from a business she built just to keep you and the partners happy," Zoe said.

"I think you need to keep her best interests in mind."

"Even if they conflict with yours?"

"That's not the point," Baxter said, his eyes even narrower and his pale complexion getting a little red.

"Then what is? Why are you here? Do you think I don't know there are problems with this case? I'm getting everything on record so we can be ready for an appeal. I hope we don't have to, but with things being the way they are, then I think we need to plan on it and be pleasantly surprised if we don't need to file." Zoe was getting angry. Baxter had never been among her favorites of the partners, and he was moving to the bottom of the list very quickly. He was thoughtful.

"Well you must represent your client with all due diligence but be careful of where that can lead."

"I usually am. Careful, that is," Zoe said evenly. Baxter looked as if he was about to say something, but instead, just opened the door to her office and left. He didn't slam the door, he was far too professional for that, but he did give it a crisp snapping shut. Her phone rang and Cargil was on the line. She almost told her secretary to tell him she was out but took the call instead.

"What's up Tim?" she said. He was quiet for a minute. Her friendly greeting threw him for a moment.

"Did you get to look at the package I left for you the other day?" he asked. Zoe was not surprised by his superciliousness.

"Yes. I was wondering where those photos came from."

"I got them from an interested party, someone who thinks we need to see justice served. Now. How well do you think those photos would go over if they were a part of the public record?"

"You'd have to ask the police."

"What?" His voice betrayed him for the first time since the case started.

"Of course. Why else did you give them to me? Obviously, someone is stalking my client, so I turned them over to the authorities. Thanks for bringing them to my attention." There was a silence on the other end of the phone. "By the way, I was wondering where you got them, because they're photos of photos. The police can tell those sorts of things you know. Amazing what they can figure out today with forensics." There was still silence at the other end of the phone. "Tim? You still there?"

"Yes. I'm here," he replied.

"Well. The real funny thing, Tim, is that you can see that someone took those photos on my desk. Right in front of my monitor. How in the world could that have happened? You have any idea? The police seem baffled."

"I wouldn't know."

"Well the photos are in good hands, and I'm sure that you will find out as soon as I do what the police discover. Odd, don't you think, that Anne would have a stalker peering in through her windows like that?"

"Odd that you had the photos in the first place." Cargil was recovering and trying to turn the tables back to his advantage.

"Now, Tim, did I say I had any photos? I think I said that I can prove that the pictures were taken on my desk, and did I mention that we had a break-in a week or so ago? I don't remember saying that they were mine in the first place. You need to be more careful what you say. I hope that no one else sees those photos. It would be messy for all of us, don't you think? An awful lot of explaining for sure for everyone involved." There was a long silence at the other end of the phone. Zoe could hear Cargil breathing.

"You'd better warn your client then. A stalker could be dangerous," he said.

"Thanks for being so concerned," Zoe said. "Is there anything else?" Cargil said, "No," and then they both hung up. It was a real rat's ass of a victory, but Zoe was pleased with it. For the first time in the whole case, Cargil didn't have a comeback.

38

The road to Chris's house had recently been repaved, and the town workers had taken the opportunity to widen it a little. Chris didn't mind since the road had been a bit too narrow in places, but he hadn't liked the fact that they didn't let him know. He would have been happy to cut down the trees lining the road and would have made sure to leave the logs long and not cut up in firewood lengths. He liked building with the native woods, and they had cut a large white oak up into short lengths, too short to do anything with now but burn in a woodstove. He would have preferred to leave them eight or ten feet long so he could have them cut into planks a few inches thick. They would have made great shelves or mantelpieces. He was tossing the wood into the bed of his pickup when he saw his sister's car coming up the drive. Zoe never just stopped by. She always called, so he knew this was a significant visit. She stopped across from his truck and rolled down her window.

"Hi, Chris."

"Hi. What's up?"

"Can't a sister visit her brother once in a while?"

"Sure." He paused, "I'll finish up here in a few minutes. The door's open." She drove up to the house, and went in. Then she went to the gazebo and sat down, listening to the quiet of the forest.

Chris drove up and unloaded the wood under an overhang attached to the toolshed. He already had a few cords stacked up. He'd spent several years on projects around the country working on various modes of energy efficient houses. He applied everything he could to this one. There was a large woodstove, but he also had a very efficient furnace that provided hot water and heat. The heat for the house emanated from the floor through specialized plastic pipes that were embedded in the subfloor. He also had solar water panels on his roof that collected heat and pumped it into a large water storage tank in the basement. The hot water then went to his high-efficiency boiler where it was heated and used for domestic hot water or heat. He was saving up for a photovoltaic array. Just the design made his house use one-quarter of the energy of a similar-sized conventional house.

After he unloaded the firewood, he made a few phone calls, mostly returning calls related to his business. He noticed his sister still sitting on the swinging chair in the gazebo and knew her well enough to leave her alone. The last time she had come to him unannounced was when she had decided to leave her husband and accept an offer to go to law school. She really didn't come to him for consultation, and he never really gave her advice. He would never insult her that way. He just reminded her of what she already knew. She did the same for him, and he was grateful when Zoe had helped him when his ex-girlfriend had decided to achieve enlightenment on his credit card.

Chris disappeared into the house. It was past suppertime, and he rummaged in the refrigerator for some leftovers to reheat. He made a large tossed salad and warmed up the stew he'd had the day before. Chris always made too much when it came to stews or soups. There was no way he could cook just enough for one serving. Lily had been away for the week at a conference in Boston, so he'd been pretty much alone, which was fine with him, although he was a little surprised at how much he had missed her. He could cook and clean up after himself and wasn't a man who needed or looked for a "mommy" as a companion to take care of him. He wouldn't even dream of going out with a woman who'd try to treat him that way, although he knew of relationships that were like that and seemed to work. He knew of marriages where the wife acted more like a mother, or sometimes a nurse, and the husband needed to be taken care of, or nursed because of an illness and read somewhere that this was called "the disease model" of love. Different strokes, he figured, and he knew with his track record of melodramatic, self-indulgent earth mother types, he couldn't point fingers. He wondered what sort of pathological love that was. Maybe the term would be "ditz dependency" or something like that.

The stew was hot, but Zoe seemed to still be deep in thought, so Chris ladled some into a bowl, tore a piece of bread from the loaf he'd gotten from the bakery, and sat at the table with his newspaper. It had been a long day, and he hadn't had a chance to read the paper. It was always pretty slender, about ten pages, and he'd usually finish it off in a short while. There were rumors about a big developer who wanted to build a casino complex near town. People were about evenly divided on the issue. It would bring jobs, but also could bring crime and other social difficulties that casinos preyed on. You can't blame the casinos for the issues themselves, Chris thought. People are fallible, greedy, and sometimes very stupid. Gamblers have trouble controlling themselves. Chris knew a wonderful guy who literally lost a multimillion-dollar construction business at the racetrack, and that was long before anyone talked of casinos. The man's gambling personality had led him to build a huge construction company by taking a risk on a cluster of single-family houses a few miles outside of the city. The houses sold faster than he could finish them. But the same risk-taking aspect proved his undoing at the racetrack. Building a casino complex seemed to concentrate some of the worst aspects of gambling in one small area. However, Chris knew many of his neighbors were unemployed, and many lived at the poverty level.

Zoe was staring off into space. She hadn't planned on driving to her brother's house, just got on the highway and ended up there. It was a weekday afternoon, so Chris needed no one to explain to him that something must be wrong. She stared off into the woods and saw movement from the corner of her eye. She turned quickly to see rustling of some bushes and a red fox ran into the underbrush a few feet in front of her. Zoe stared at the moving bushes where the fox had disappeared, wondering for a moment if she'd really seen it, when her nose found the scent of Chris's cooking, and she made her way to the house.

Zoe ladled up some of the stew and took the end of the loaf of bread to dip in it. She also took a plate of salad, and then sat down across from Chris. He was just finishing, and he folded his newspaper and put it on the table next to him.

"I have no idea what the hell I'm doing."

"What do you mean?" Chris asked.

"I'm a total poser. I took this case and can't figure it out for the life of me. It looked straightforward. Now it's become a total mess, and we could lose, and lose big." She ate a little, and Chris just let her talk. "I became a lawyer so I could help people. Now all it seems that I'm doing is playing a weird game of 'gotcha' with a total asshole—two assholes, really. When did the law become the refuge for the incompetent and the alcoholic?"

"I think you're overstating things a little," Chris said.

"Maybe." She paused. "But I'm thinking of quitting after this case. I just can't deal with this crap anymore." She stopped for a minute. "I didn't sign up to deal with this kind of bull. I wanted to practice law, not spend my life dealing with a bunch of snooty, puffed-up morons who, for the life of me, I can't figure out what they are so arrogant about. It's not like they're smart. What gives them such egos?"

Chris looked at his paper with renewed interest. He knew better than to challenge her. She was still too upset to listen anyway, and she was a lot faster than he was when it came to thinking up a comeback. He also knew that she wasn't about to quit anything.

"You could help me," he volunteered, smiling. "I need a gopher to lug my tools and mix concrete and stuff like that. In fact, I'm thinking of taking on a big project and will need laborers, framing carpenters, and subcontractors. How are you at plumbing?"

"I can swing a hammer," she said, pointing at him with the crust of bread that was in her hand.

"Shows what you know. We don't use hammers anymore, not for a long time. Pneumatic-nailers and screw guns." He added, "In your state of mind, I don't think I'd trust you with a hammer, or with power tools for that matter."

"You're right." She paused. "I'd start with that arrogant jackass Cargil, then Barnum, and then on to Baxter. In his case it would be a mercy killing. How long can you live without a spine anyway?"

"What about the other two?"

"Justifiable homicide. I would just need a jury made up of people whose lives those two have ruined."

"That might be a few more than twelve."

"They'd be flocking to the courthouse." She sat back. Chris had an odd expression on his face.

"I remember someone in third grade—" he began.

"You're not going down that road, are you?" Zoe threw the last bit of the crust of bread at him. He ducked.

"What was that kid's name? Bobby Meisler? I remember walking down the hall to my class when I saw you pounding his head against the floor. It took me a minute to realize that the girl pounding on the boy in front of me was my little sister. I also had a hell of a time peeling you off him."

"He tried to take my lunch money."

"He didn't make that mistake again, did he?"

"I had to spend the next week in detention, and they made me go home that day to cool off."

"Poor Mom, she never had a clue how to deal with you. Getting sent home for fighting was my specialty."

"I know." Then Zoe smiled, "Remember when Principal Meyer tried to keep me from getting my perfect attendance medal that year because they made me go home that day? God that man was a jerk."

"And you argued him into giving you the medal? Yes, I remember it. I think the whole school heard you yelling at him—something about taking it to the School Board, as I recall, or maybe the Supreme Court?"

"Your sixth-grade room was right next to the main office. Don't give me that crap. It wasn't the whole school," she smiled.

"So, Zoe, what do you think you're supposed to do? Cargil is a bully. So's Barnum. Go after them."

"It's not that simple."

"It's never that simple, except in grammar school."

"Not even then," Zoe said. She yawned and realized she was very tired. Chris picked up on it and made up the bed in the spare room.

The next morning, Zoe showered and put on the clothes she had worn the previous day, with the exception of borrowing one of her brother's work shirts. She stopped at her apartment and changed, then checked her email on her phone. There wasn't much that was new. The paralegals had made some progress with their research, but nothing that Cargil couldn't turn around and use against them with his passion for "alternative explanations." However, she would include everything she could think of because she knew this one might very well have to be appealed, despite, or even without the benefit of, her partners. She had come to a decision after all.

39

April drank a cup of coffee and looked out over her backyard. While it was a large house and a very ample and beautiful lawn, April wasn't happy with the house or her yard. She would often comment to her husband, explaining how they really should consider moving to Shady Delta, a gated housing tract twenty minutes farther up the highway. Not far from where Anne Mali lived, or at least used to live. Michael was there now, in that huge house all by himself. The houses there had yards measured in acres, and there was a community swimming pool and tennis court. The whole project was surrounded by a golf course. She didn't swim or play tennis, and neither April nor her husband had ever owned a set of golf clubs, but she found the lack of these resources at her present housing tract becoming more and more intolerable. If she had a nice pool or golf course handy, she was certain that she'd take advantage of them. It was her inability to have these as conveniences that made it impossible for her to pursue a gratifying and enjoyable life. A life she deserved, if only she made more money, if only she and her husband hadn't been so poorly paid for their work. They were both indispensable employees, but their bosses were ungrateful swine, just like all of them. If they only made what they deserved to be paid, then they could be happy like all the people in Shady Delta must be. How could they be otherwise? What more could anyone want out of life but a huge house with access to a swimming pool, tennis court, *and* golf course? She believed they even had a basketball court someplace on the grounds. She thought of how great it would be to have a basketball court, although it was another sport she had never played. April had wrangled a couple of invitations from some people she knew who lived there. But they'd never been invited back. More evidence of ungrateful and ungracious people, she assumed.

She was happy that some people, one in particular, appreciated her for what she knew and understood what she'd been going through all these years. Tonight was her husband's bowling night, and she hoped that her friend Guy would call. She'd met him a few weeks ago when she had gone for lunch to her usual deli. He seemed to already know her and claimed that they'd met before, but she couldn't remember where. Guy had been so charming, and she was immediately attracted to him. She'd mentioned the two of them going out some evening, but he seemed to always be busy. However, he was usually at the deli whenever she had lunch, and customarily insisted on buying her sandwich, like a real gentleman. Then they would talk for a couple of hours. He was such a good listener. Her husband hardly listened to her anymore. That's why she decided to let Guy know that Wednesday nights were *really good* for her; she was alone until after midnight, and he could come over any time after seven. So far, he hadn't come over or called. She hoped he might stop by tonight. Not only would her husband be gone, but the meddlesome old bitch with no life who lived across the street had been gone for a couple of weeks now, visiting her son in Chicago. She tended to mind everyone's business and to voice her unsolicited opinion on it. April hated that in a person.

    She opened her handbag, took out her wallet, and pulled out the card that Guy had given her. He worked for a small data firm. She had noticed the sign out by the highway exit. They were in one of those tiny malls just off the main highway, the kind that always seemed to have new tenants. So many that they had trouble keeping the sign at the main entrance up to date. They might advertise a Chinese restaurant that had closed months before right next to a computer repair shop that had just opened. There was always a huge Space for Lease sign right on the road. She took the card and called the phone number. It was Guy's cell phone. The call went to his voicemail. She left him a message reminding him that she'd be free tonight after work. If he couldn't make it tonight, then they could still have lunch at the deli. She'd be there at her usual time. She then placed the card in her wallet and put the wallet back in her handbag next to her nine-millimeter Walther PPK. While the gun is usually associated with the quiet, sophisticated macho of James Bond, it's really a very small, almost toy-like weapon that can easily be concealed in a handbag. The only thing that gives it away and attests to the fact that it is a serious weapon is its heft. While James Bond favored the gun because it didn't disturb the lines of his Seville Row suit jacket, April liked the fact that it fit snugly in her purse. She had a license for it, and never left the house without it.

Intimate Disconnect

Guy looked at the text on his phone and rolled his eyes. This bitch won't take no for an answer, he said to himself. He then called Cargil. After hearing the latest, Cargil chuckled.

"Looks like you've got your work cut out for you."

"No way. I didn't sign up for this."

"We need to keep her quiet and keep her from getting suspicious. She's not stupid, you know."

"Not me," Guy said. "Pawn her off on someone else."

"It's you she's got the hots for."

"I don't care. This was not part of the deal."

"The deal is what I say it is." Cargil's tone was threatening. "I have your other indiscretion well documented." Cargil had found that Guy had lied on his Private Investigator's license application and that the state would pull his license in an instant if they knew of a felony charge he'd had as a minor. The record was supposed to have been sealed and the crime was dismissed, but those records are never really sealed, not for a prick like Cargil who knew where to dig. Guy had never screwed up like that again, but it didn't matter. He'd even forgotten about the issue and never thought he needed to put it on his application, but that's not how it would look. While it wouldn't have kept him from getting his license in the first place, it now could get his license pulled because it would look as if he'd lied on the application.

So, he did some occasional "dirty work" for Cargil in order to continue to be able to earn a living. He would get some information with a quick break-in. Law offices and doctor's offices never had serious alarm systems, and they rarely locked up information. It was mostly there for the taking. Having lunches with a talkative, self-centered, self-absorbed woman like April, who needed almost no prodding to give him all the information he needed was not really illegal, although the fact that she had no idea that he was a PI working for Cargil could be thought of as unethical. He recorded almost everything she told him because he would zone out for long periods of time while she went on and on about how hard she worked and how she was so unappreciated. How she really had built the business, but Anne and Michael had taken credit for it. Guy at first had no idea if she did or didn't, but she was certainly convinced. The more he listened, though, the more he realized that she wouldn't have the chops to build a business like TrendInventions.

Listening to her was like listening to the same chorus of a popular song repeat over and over again, but every now and then she'd dribble out a few facts that he could check. Like when the business almost went into Chapter 11 because a gadget didn't sell and the company was undercapitalized, or when Anne went to a psychiatrist because of depression. He'd heard some real wild stories about Michael, too, but Cargil wasn't interested in them of course. At this point he really needed almost no new information from April, just a few confirmations on some dates. Guy could get the information with a few quick questions. After he ended his call with Cargil, he sent a text to April. Maybe a lunch would buy him some more time. He did know that this was her husband's bowling night. She'd said it enough, and he'd played stupid for some time now. He suddenly felt sorry for the poor guy, trying to imagine what it must be like being married to her. His phone chimed, telling him that April had sent him a text in reply.

40

Anne and Zoe were in a strategy session. There were empty coffee cups and takeout containers on the table along with stacks of papers from the business. The air smelled of stale perfume as the two women pored over some paperwork. Zoe had filled a couple of legal pads as she catalogued individual incidents and points she wanted to make and answer. They were building a very strong case in Anne's favor, but Zoe knew exactly what Cargil would say at every turn. She anticipated his responses and detailed her counterclaims, making sure everything was cross-referenced. They both knew that the chances of getting a favorable settlement from Barnum might not be good, and that they would have to appeal.

"Here's something," Anne said. "I just barely remember this." She pulled out a file that was about an inch thick. "An inventor sued us because one of Michael's products looked something like an item he'd patented. I can't even remember what it was." She handed the folder to Zoe, who opened it and started to browse through the papers. "This was basically a nuisance suit," Anne explained, "and not the only one we had. Some people make a good living filing a bunch of patents and then suing anyone who files a patent for anything that remotely looks like what they've patented. They never actually develop anything, just sue. Usually they go away if you waive a few thousand dollars at them." Zoe looked through the paperwork.

"That's a lot for a nuisance suit," Zoe said, pointing to the figure.

"That was my mistake. I took Michael to the deposition. After the guy accused Michael of stealing his idea, Michael flew across the table and started pounding on him. He broke the guy's nose and knocked out a few teeth before we could pull them apart. To avoid an assault charge, I had to agree to five times what they were asking for plus medical expenses." She paused. "Do you think we can use it?"

"Maybe. It shows that he has a temper, and that he's put your company in jeopardy, more than once it seems. Was everything sealed?"

"Yes, but the police were called, so there is a charge someplace, at least a police report should be on file," Anne said. Zoe took some notes to give to one of her paralegals.

They had pieced together a picture of Michael that would run counter to anything that Cargil claimed. She knew that he'd be able to put anything she had that showed Anne working hard and growing the business into the worst possible light, so she had come up with a different strategy, showing Michael to be the spoiled, pampered little monster that he was, and they were mining the records and Anne's memory for specific moments when his temper got the best of him, or when he put the business in jeopardy or cost them money by being an idiot. So far, she had at least fifty separate instances of Michael doing something incredibly stupid and Anne cleaning up after him. Most of the cleanup had to do with giving people large sums of money, or writing off an expensive mistake. Even Barnum wouldn't be able to ignore the evidence, or he would ignore it at his own peril. Anne certainly had the money, the will, and the power to fight his decision, something neither he nor Cargil were used to, as they tended to prey on the weak and the powerless. For the sake of his ego alone, Zoe was counting on him to offer an equitable distribution in the divorce decree in spite of Cargil.

It was past midnight when they quit, and Zoe left a legal pad full of instructions for her paralegals. The two of them went to the parking garage together, and Anne got in her Mercedes. She had her window down and they spoke a little before she drove off. Zoe went to her car and drove to the security gate, right behind Anne, used her pass to open the gate for her, and as it opened, she noticed a silver Corolla pull out right behind Anne's car. Zoe wasn't sure, but it looked like he was following Anne. She pulled out and followed him, taking down his license plate number. Zoe followed both cars at a distance, and, just before Anne turned into her condo garage, the Corolla continued down the street. Zoe pulled over and waited to see if he came back, but he didn't. She sent a text to Detective Pepe with the description of the car and his plate number, but she had a good idea who he was already.

Eric headed home after escorting Anne safely to her condo. He made sure that she got home okay every night. He felt it was the least he could do, since she was obviously in love with him. After her divorce, he was sure that she'd come back to him. She was simply playing it cool for now, and he knew that Anne understood. He even knew that she fired him to make sure no one was suspicious. It had taken him a while to understand all this, but he now could tell from all the clues she'd been leaving on his cameras—certain looks and gestures she made, little signs—that it was obvious that she still loved him, not to mention the fact that she had gotten rid of that asshole, Nick. That alone should have been enough for him to figure things out. He had been a fool to doubt her; he knew that now. He went upstairs to his apartment. There was a past-due notice on the door. His landlord was threatening to evict him. He took it off, ripped it to shreds, threw it on the floor, and then unlocked the door. He'd changed the locks so that landlord couldn't snoop around. A small camera he'd placed in the hallway showed him that the landlord had tried to get in several times. Eric sat at his computer console and looked at his monitor; Anne had gone right to bed and was asleep. He checked all the cameras that he had installed around her house, making sure she was safe, and then returned to the bedroom camera. He fell asleep in his chair, staring at her image on his screen.

41

The normal smells of the café were nauseating Zoe this morning. She hadn't slept well. A bad case of nerves kept waking her. By the time she realized that sleep was going to be a problem, it was far too late to take a sleeping pill. The smells of the omelets, eggs, and fried breakfast meats going by her booth as the waitresses walked by did little to help her already anxious stomach. She sipped a coffee and picked at a pastry while she watched Jimmy inhale a breakfast that would give a hungry trucker pause. She was amazed at how much he could eat and remain as skinny as a model.

"What information are you looking for this time, Zoe?" Jimmy asked between bites.

"You get right to the point, don't you?"

"Have to. If I stay in corporate much longer, I won't have a brain left. It will be Swiss cheese. Reading those contracts can burn a hole right through your brain. They did a study on it at Johns Hopkins."

"I'm sure they did."

"Honest. They lined up a bunch of corporate lawyers and x-rayed their heads," he orbited his fork around his head, "nothing but holes."

"And you wonder why no one in that department likes you."

"Hell, they love me in corporate, that's the problem. It's like trying to get rid of an earnest lover that you sort of like, but not that much, that maybe you had a little fun with for a long weekend. You know, and you want to let him down easy, but he insists on taking it the hard way."

"Got it," Zoe said while she swallowed two painkillers with her coffee.

"That bad?"

"Yep."

"What can I do?" He was serious now.

"I need another angle. Nothing I have so far will keep Cargil from tearing it apart or turning it around and making Anne look like an incompetent manager who's in way over her head. Even her extramarital affairs will count heavily against her, which is the epitome of hypocrisy."

"You mean that the law is hypocritical? Really? No!" Jimmy said and sipped his coffee. "I love you Zoe, but you're such a Girl Scout sometimes. Grow a set and deal with the asshole." He had some more breakfast. "You think Cargil is missing his breakfast today? Do you think he gives two shits about the truth or what's fair? He's going for all he can get for his client. You need to get something that will make dear little Michael look like the spoiled shit that he is."

"Which is why I'm here. There are hints in his past where he was violent or messed up, but that was usually covered up, or took place a long time ago. I need something recent, something that happened in the past few months."

"To counterbalance all the issues with Anne?"

"Yes."

Jimmy was thoughtful as he finished his breakfast. The waitress came over and filled their coffee cups. It was beginning to rain outside and Jimmy looked out the front window of the café. It faced the highway entrance, and a gas station. He spotted the waitress picking up a tray of food.

"That's it," he said.

"What?"

"That tray he was working on. So you could keep your beer cold while in a hot tub?"

"Right."

"He rushed it into production."

"I know. Anne pulled it."

"Right. She was supposed to." He smiled and looked around for the waitress to refill his coffee cup. Jimmy drank at least five cups of coffee every morning.

"What?"

"Yes. He and Amory had worked it all out. He would use it as an excuse to bounce her out of the CEO seat and put Michael in charge. Didn't quite work out that way. Now, *she* definitely has a set and a half. Bought Amory out and pulled Michael's budget, just like that. One big flip off to both of them."

"How do you know that she pulled his R&D budget?" Zoe asked. "You're not still seeing him, are you?"

Intimate Disconnect

"No way," Jimmy said, insulted. "Like I said last time you bought me breakfast. This one's on you, too, I assume. Hell, I could get good money for this information," he smiled, and she nodded. "I already told you that I have a friend who does April's work for her while she moans to her husband all day long about how hard she has it. You know, Anne's personal secretary since forever? He saw the memo. Now *he's* the type I'll be going out with. Blond, suntanned, and gorgeous, we have a date this weekend in fact. We're heading out to the island for some nude sunbathing, where we can hang out at a beach full of adults."

"I went to a nude beach when I was in Italy for a semester in college." Zoe paused, "Sometimes clothes aren't such a bad idea."

Jimmy laughed. "You've got a point there."

"So the little prick knew the tray wasn't ready for prime time?"

"Apparently."

"I wonder where he got the idea?" Zoe asked, but Jimmy knew she already knew the answer. "Well we need to prove this, can't just accuse him. Where would the proof be? I know that Cargil is too smart to leave a trail, but I'm not sure about the other two."

"I might have a bunch of emails in my account that could help. He kept sending me stuff long after we broke up."

"He mentioned it in emails?" Zoe was incredulous.

"You'd be surprised what people will put in an email."

"Yes. I know. Had a case where a client's estranged husband admitted that he'd charged an advance of twenty thousand against their credit cards and hid it. He figured she'd have to pay half of it and wrote all about it to his buddy. We got the records. The judge was not amused." She finished her coffee. "Can you get the emails and forward them to me? I'm getting ready for court."

"When do you meet the judge?"

"Next week."

"Ready or not," Jimmy said, and then added, "Even Judge Barnum will see that Michael's a shithead, and that Anne made a serious contribution to that business. Hell, even Steve Jobs wouldn't have made it without his team. No one can do it all."

"His team fired him, and Apple almost went bankrupt," Zoe said.

"True. Michael is no Steve Jobs, though."

"I was thinking of Anne."

"Look. You're making a strong case, Zoe. As long as nothing bad happens at TrendInventions that shows Anne is not a good CEO, there shouldn't be a problem. What could go wrong in a week?" He looked at his watch. "I, for one, am not on salary. I have to get to work ten minutes ago." He got up and kissed her on the mouth. "You need to get some sleep one of these nights, Zoe. Take a happy pill and let this go for a while."

***

The emails were in Zoe's inbox by the time she got back, and they were perfect, showing Michael at his spoiled and immature best. Because he was so thorough in laying out the plot that he'd hatched with Amory, there was nothing left to the imagination at all. The only problem with them was that Michael was so egotistical that he never mentioned that the idea might have come from someone else, even though it had Cargil's cunning all over it. Zoe didn't mind, there was enough to throw plenty of doubt on the narrative of a naïve, creative, innocent man who was being exploited by a greedy wife. Even if Barnum was inclined to want to rule in Michael's favor, this was something that would sink him on appeal, and he was smart enough to know that. No judge liked to be overturned. For once, Zoe began to feel upbeat about this case. She just might be looking at a good result from Mali v. Mali. Her cell rang, and it was Detective Pepe. The plate number had been traced to Eric. It was enough to charge him with stalking, and there was still a restraining order on the record from two years ago, although it was expired, so he couldn't be charged with a violation, but there was more than enough to get a warrant for his arrest on the stalking charges. Pepe was going to go over to his apartment this afternoon and arrest him.

"That should straighten the little creep out," Pepe said.

"I hope so. He could cause some problems with the case, not to mention that I have no idea why he's following Anne."

"He's just a creep," Pepe said. "Doesn't really have to have a reason, he'll make one up."

"He could have mental health problems."

"I'd be surprised if he didn't," Pepe said. "I could encourage the judge to recommend twenty-four-hour psychiatric observation. It might help. He seems like a basket case to me, though."

"That's too bad. He really needs some serious therapy."

"Well, it's the best I can do."

"I know, and thanks for giving me the heads up."

"No problem."

After Detective Pepe hung up, Zoe called Anne and told her about Eric and then filled her in on the e-mails between Michael and Amory.

"Too bad about Eric. I feel a little responsible for that," Anne said.

"It's him, not you. He's making all the choices and none of them are good."

"I know. Good news about the emails. Won't Michael, the Little Prince, be shocked? He always thinks he's being so smart when it comes to technology." She paused. "I wonder who he'll blame for this one? It could never, ever be his fault."

"We'll see. In any case, be careful over the next week. You're not supposed to know about Eric, and you know better than to let anyone know about the emails. I want it to be a surprise, before Cargil and your husband can come up with an explanation of why it's all really your fault."

Zoe got off the phone with Anne, and then she went back to the pile of work on her desk. She suddenly thought of the gazebo at her brother's house, and then she remembered seeing something moving out of the corner of her eye while staring off into the woods, something dark and cold. The thought first sent a chill through her, and it was a moment before she could return to her work, but then an idea came to her, an idea that would put Cargil off balance, something he would never expect. She picked up her phone and hit redial.

42

Eric was in his usual place in his apartment, sitting in front of his computer. He was arguing with someone in Kansas on a conspiracy blog about how the moon landing was faked by the same people who had shot Kennedy and later killed Martin Luther King Jr. Eric thought that the faked moon landing had nothing at all to do with the Kennedy assassination and that they should be treated as two completely separate global conspiracies. The Kennedy assassination was obviously conducted by a global organized crime network, or possibly a consortium of right-wing white power groups, while the other had the clear hallmark of the Masons, with the help of Hollywood experts of course. He even knew the site in New Mexico where the whole thing had been staged. He was searching through his computer files, looking for the satellite photo he'd downloaded about a year ago to help make his case. There was a sharp knock at his door.

"Eric? Open up, it's the police, and we have a warrant!" Eric shut down his computer, ignoring the second and third knock, which is when the police broke in his door. Eric just stood while the police came into his apartment. Detective Pepe read him his rights and sat him down on the couch.

"This is a warrant to search your apartment for evidence of stalking Anne Mali." Naomi showed Eric the paper. "We can do this the easy way, or the hard way. It's up to you. Will you please turn on the computer you just shut off?"

"No. I don't have to do anything," he said, "and you can't touch my computer."

"Okay. If that's how you want things to go." Pepe turned to the other police officers. "I want his computer and all of this equipment impounded and tagged as evidence," she said, motioning to the desk. Eric broke free from Pepe's grip and launched himself at the men who were moving toward his computer. Pepe recovered quickly, tripping up the man and slamming him to the ground. She pulled out her handcuffs and put them on Eric's wrists. "Look, asshole, I gave you a chance. Did you think I was bluffing? That I'm playing a fucking game here? You are forcing me to impound your computer, and I know you think you're clever, Eric, but we have some pretty clever people, too, and they might not be too particular as to how they get to the information on your computer."

Eric smiled, confident that they wouldn't be able to get anything from his PC because it was hidden behind so many security walls. It did bother him, though, not being able to do anything when the police unplugged all his equipment and packed it into evidence boxes. Pepe told Officer Salvatore to search the bedroom for any evidence of photos, a journal, anything that would make the case for stalking. Sal sauntered out of the crowded living room and went into the bedroom. He did a cursory search while muttering under his breath about the fucking spic detective who thought her shit didn't stink.

Sal entered the bedroom and noticed the sour, pungent smell of very dirty sheets and overdue laundry. He pawed under the bed and found only cobwebs, and then he rummaged through the drawers. He found a bottle of oxycodone in the sock drawer that was still half full. He slipped it into his pocket in one quick motion. Sal haphazardly rifled through the balled-up and wrinkled clothes in the drawers, making more of a mess than actually trying to find anything. Except for a hundred dollars in twenties, which joined the pills in his pocket, he found nothing more that was either evidence against Eric or worth stealing. Wandering aimlessly back and forth across the bedroom, Sal conducted a spotty and piecemeal search, never noticing the loose floorboard near the window. He did, however, find a nice pocketknife on the floor of the closet and an LED flashlight that he also pocketed before leaving the bedroom. After Sal went back into the living room Pepe caught his eye and inquired. Sal shook his head.

"Clean," he said. "No pictures, no notebooks." Pepe nodded and went back to supervising the others who were collecting evidence. In his search of the bedroom, Sal had walked directly over the floorboard that concealed Eric's assault rifle and ammunition cache a total of twelve times.

It took a police computer expert about half an hour to find the video files of Anne on the hard drive. Detective Pepe called Anne told her of the cameras Eric had somehow placed in her apartment. She then turned the case over to an ADA. Since there was no proof that Eric had broken into Anne's apartment to place the cameras, the best that he could be charged with was Class B Misdemeanor, stalking in the fourth degree. Most stalking laws are written to go up the scale from misdemeanor to felony based on repeated offenses. They are meant pretty much for domestic abuse issues or for a stalker who, once brought to the attention of the justice system, repeatedly stalks the same or similar victims, such as an ex-spouse or lover. Repeated offenses will make the potential charge go up the scale of misdemeanors to felonies. As far as the system was concerned, this was a first offense for Eric, so the strongest charge was the first level of stalking.

The judge was concerned enough to throw him in jail and require $50,000 in bail but did not feel there was enough evidence to order a psychological evaluation. Part of her decision could have been based on the fact that the county's budget for prisoner medical care was running in the red because of an unusually high number of county inmates who needed expensive medical care. Most were old and homeless, victims of the current recession and the cutbacks in social services. With little food and constant exposure to the elements, many of them had contracted serious lung infections, TB, liver disorders, kidney problems, or had developed anemia. There was simply no money to have a psychological evaluation of Eric or anyone else who might come before the bench prior to the end of the fiscal year, and it would have been unusual to order an evaluation on a first offense, even if there had been a flush health care budget.

Eric was alone in a cell wearing an orange jumpsuit and sitting on the edge of a cot when he heard his name called. The guard opened his door and motioned for him to come out. He followed the guard to a locker room where he was given his clothes. After he dressed, he was then led to another room where another guard listed the valuables they had taken from him, including his wallet, watch, and car keys, and as she retuned each item she checked them off a list that was stapled to the manila envelope she was slowly emptying.

"You have a lady friend who made your bail. You owe her a lot," she said.

Eric stared at her to see if she was making some sort of joke. Then he mumbled incoherently, confused, upset, disoriented, but then his mind became clear. *It had to be Anne,* he thought. Obviously, it had to be her. Who else would have come here to help him out? A disturbing and disturbed smile crossed his face, arranging his features in sharp relief, making his eyes very bright and wide open. Everything suddenly became crystalline to him; everything made sense to him now. All seemed to be lit up inside and outside of his head, including the fluorescent light that was scintillating off the stainless-steel counter, and he saw an unmistakable knowing smile on the guard's face and could read the message coming from her small brown eyes through round wire frame glasses. He knew that she knew. The guard motioned him to the door.

"Just sign this receipt and you're free to go." Eric signed the paper in an illegible scrawl and walked to the steel door with a bulletproof glass window interlaced with steel mesh. The guard pushed a button, and the solenoid buzzed as it pulled back the bolt. He pushed open the door and went into the waiting room. He could see her standing at the other end of the room. Her back was to him.

"Anne," he said. "I knew you'd come." The light from the window flashed across her face as she turned around.

"What the hell's wrong with you, Eric?" April said. "Anne was the one who had you arrested in the first place and she is plenty pissed off about all those cameras you put in her apartment."

April directed Eric to her car. He walked as if he were a zombie, exhausted but dangerous, and was passive while April led him to her car and unlocked the doors. They drove a while in silence before she spoke up.

"My God, Eric. I send you a bunch of photos showing Anne in bed with her latest boyfriend, hoping you'll come around and see her for the slut she is, and you've got a video ringside seat to her whole life."

"You sent those photos to me?"

"Sure. I sent a copy of them to you and her lawyer. I thought she'd drop the case once she saw who she was dealing with, but she's an idiot, too, just like Anne." Eric winced when she said that. "What did you do with them?"

"Shredded them."

"Thank god. They've already got enough evidence against you and they don't need any more. You'll need a lawyer. I can set you up with someone I know."

"Don't have any money."

"That's okay. I can take care of it."

"No. I don't want you to."

"I want to help you, Eric," she said, and put her hand on his knee. He removed it immediately. She bristled. "Okay. I'll drop you off at your apartment," She said slowly. "And I won't bother you again," she said, trying to draw some guilt from him. It didn't work. Eric sat in the passenger seat in a deep funk, only moving when she stopped the car in front of his apartment house. He unbuckled his seatbelt and opened the door but paused.

"Was she really that upset?" he said

"Who?" April asked.

"Anne, of course. Was she really that upset about the cameras? I thought she'd understand."

"Understand what? That you're hopeless? That you're a nut? That you're a goddamn pervert? Jesus, Eric, snap out of it!" she paused, shaking a little, her face red. Then she looked defeated and said, "Forget it. You're just beyond help." Her expression hardened. "I have no idea why I even bothered with you. Just get out of the car—now! You're hopeless." Eric stepped out of the car, and April rocketed away from the curb the moment he shut the door.

The door to his apartment was padlocked because the police had destroyed the deadbolt when they entered. Eric knew enough to not go to find his landlord for the key since he owed him three months' rent. In another week it would be four. He went to the basement and came back with a short piece of steel water pipe. He slipped it behind the hasp, and with a quick snap, broke it off.

43

Friday, September 28

Zoe was working late in her office. White cardboard boxes were stacked against one wall, almost making another wall in front of it. She had finished her last meeting with the small army of paralegals and temps that had been hired for the case. Their job was finished. The boxes were all neatly labeled and contained copies of all the records for the case. They would be presented to the judge. However, Zoe was more focused on the few sheets of paper in front of her than the stacks of meticulously collected and catalogued data: printouts from an email account that she had subpoenaed. Jimmy's emails had given her enough information to get a subpoena. The conversations between Michael and Amory were enlightening. It showed Michael clearly sabotaging an invention and rushing it into production knowing it to be unfinished, and even possibly dangerous, for the sole purpose of having Anne pull it from production. Their endgame was also clearly spelled out. Lou Amory would ride into the boardroom on his usual mixture of outrage and righteous indignation and bully the board of directors into voting Anne out of the CEO position. He, of course, would then offer his services as CEO, on a temporary basis of course, until someone more appropriate could be found, which probably would be never, Zoe thought, if he had his way.

This could have worked had Anne not bought out his partnership and thrown him overboard. The one disappointing element in the emails was that nowhere did it mention Cargil, although it had his signature all over it. Michael certainly would have deleted the emails from the company server but felt that no one would possibly know about the emails, or how to get to them. Detective Pepe had made sure that her best forensic computer expert was on the case when they exercised the subpoena. Even though Michael passed this scheme off as his idea, it was enough to show that he wasn't the exploited victim of an otherwise incompetent woman and could make him look far more cunning than he really was. In fact, it might work out very well that the record showed that he was completely responsible for the idea, he and Amory. This would further justify Anne's actions in getting rid of Amory and shutting down Michael's research for the sake of the company, or at least Zoe could make a stronger case.

She finished the document, highlighting important parts for the judge to see, and slipped it into a folder. This, along with his arrest report for assaulting Anne a few years back, and a few other examples attesting to Michael's fits of temper, would be enough to throw some doubt on the reality constructed by Cargil. It was at this point that Zoe sat back, and for the first time in a very long time, relaxed. She knew she had a good case, and that even if Barnum went against settled law, like he did every now and then, that Anne had the resources to appeal, although until the appeal was decided, things at TrendInventions could get very difficult because Barnum's decisions could remain in place until the appeal was resolved. As long as everything remained peaceful and calm, even Barnum might have to hang his old buddy Cargil out to dry on this one. Anne wasn't some poor, bewildered woman with an inexperienced attorney who could be blindsided, and who had no funds to appeal. Zoe had experience with this kind of ego. Ego is an unpredictable thing. It makes people think they are somewhat smarter than they really are, and makes them think others are a lot dumber, a fault that has led to more than one major disaster in human history—World War II for instance.

The buzzer from outside the front door made her start. She walked to the front of the offices, saw Jeff through the glass door, and buzzed him in.

"I know we didn't have a date tonight," she said, as he came in the door.

"I know. Just drove by and saw the light on in your office. Took a chance that you hadn't eaten yet."

"Look, Jeff, I told you that I'm not interested in a relationship right now. You need to go out and find someone."

"So, I take it that you have already eaten," he smiled.

"No. That's not the point."

"Okay. I get it. But you're giving off conflicted signals at best," he said, which she had to admit was true, but not to him.

"I'm not sure about that. I've told you right from the start where you stood."

"Yes, but the few times we've been out, we've had a good time, right?"

"That's true."

"So, let's have some dinner and have a good time. That's all."

"Not now, Jeff."

"Okay, when?"

"I'll call you," she smiled. "Isn't that what you say? 'I'll call you,' and then never really get around to it?"

"Maybe," he said, evenly. "I wouldn't know. I never operated like that."

"Sorry."

"No problem." He reached for the door. "Maybe I'll see you around."

"That was mean, sorry," she said.

"What's the problem?"

"This case. It's gotten too much under my skin. I can't leave it in the office."

"Sorry."

"It's me. My OCD personality can't just let me do my job and leave it at that," she said.

"Makes you a good attorney."

"Maybe."

"No. It's true. If I ever get divorced, I'm hiring you. Of course, I'd have to get a married first," he smiled, and then added, "look, I'm here if you want to go out for a quick dinner, nothing special. If not, that's okay, too. I know I just popped in without calling. I have no right to expect you to drop everything and come with me, even if it's Friday and no one else in the whole building is even here. Let alone working."

"I don't handle spontaneity too well."

"I've noticed," he smiled. "I promise never to be spontaneous with you again, never."

"No need to lie. I've decided that you will take me to dinner, but not someplace cheap."

"Fine. Where?"

"The Golden Onion."

"Love it. Great food." he smiled. "I'll drive if you want. My car's in front of the building next street over; there is a meter running." He checked his watch.

"Okay," Zoe said, breaking another one of her rules—*Always take your own car on a date, just in case*. She went to get her handbag from her office and lock up the files she'd been working on. She slipped some papers in her briefcase to look at over the weekend.

At least she was being consistent with her inconsistency, even giving herself mixed signals, she thought as she locked the office door, set the alarm, and followed Jeff to the waiting elevator.

***

Zoe woke up early, disoriented by her surroundings. She was on the wrong side of the bed. The place was warm, warmer than her apartment, and then she remembered Jeff and last night. She smiled and listened to him sleep next to her for a while. As a habitually early riser, lying around in bed bored the hell out of her, so she quietly got up and found her way to the kitchen. The empty bottle of good wine still sat on the counter. She found where Jeff kept his coffee, made a pot with his coffeemaker, and sat in the open kitchen looking out at Jeff's living room. It was a little surprising. She picked him for a neat freak with precise, modern decorations, and exceptionally clean and well-organized furniture with boring and uninspiring wall hangings. Instead, she had found an aesthetic but somewhat cluttered place that was full of decorations from Jeff's many travels, something else she hadn't known about him. From the real African masks on the wall to the Murano glass collectibles on the mantelpiece, his apartment was surprising and intricate. Zoe made a note to ask him if the paintings hanging on the large, open wall that he shared with the apartment next door were his paintings, or if he had bought them. They seemed to have all been painted by the same person. She didn't hear him come in and was a little surprised when he entered the room. She had wrapped herself in a large white robe she'd found on the chair next to the bed and pulled it closer, oddly modest in the daylight. He had on boxers and a t-shirt, and he headed straight for the coffeepot.

"You're up early for a Saturday," Jeff said.

"I usually get up around six no matter what day it is."

"Sometimes I get up early. Usually I sleep in," he said. There was a long pause, but neither one felt awkward. They both felt at ease around each other, but also a little on edge since they were still in the stranger stage of a relationship. In fact, it wasn't clear they were in a relationship, not yet, and Zoe took even more comfort in that. Presently he said, "You like that robe? I stole it from the Caribe Hilton in San Juan while I was there for a conference." He sipped some coffee, dipping a donut in it that he had taken out of the cupboard. "Actually, they added it to my bill. But I liked it too much to leave it behind, so I didn't mind paying for it."

"It's nice and soft," Zoe said.

"At least you're quiet when you get up."

"Lot of practice. My whole family liked to sleep in. They hated it when I got up early, especially Chris. He's a bear in the morning, low blood sugar."

"Me, too. That's why I have to have a donut when I get up," he smiled. He took one out of the wax paper bag from a bakery, "You want one?" She shook her head. Jeff continued, "At least that's what I tell myself, it's a rationalization to eat junky food."

"Nothing wrong with the occasional rationalization," Zoe said.

"I see you are an enabler," he joked.

"No. Just practical. If you want a donut, then you should eat a donut."

"I like that attitude."

"You have to be careful, though. You could get fat and have rotten teeth," she smiled.

"All things in moderation," he said.

"You sure you're an American? I don't see much moderation in the US, not anywhere, not in my job at all."

"You don't see people at their best. I think that affects you," Jeff said. "I know I have to make a conscious effort to realize that some people are mentally healthy and have no real phobias or neuroses. That psychologically they're normal."

"Really?"

"Not that many, mind you, but there are some, not enough to negatively affect my business though." He poured himself another cup of

225

coffee and filled her mug. "I can make you breakfast or take you out if you like."

"I'm not sure I can stay."

"It's Saturday, Zoe. A day off? Maybe you've heard of the weekend? That great invention the trade unions came up with in the beginning of the twentieth century?"

"I know, but."

"Okay. I'll make a couple of omelets, and then you can go. I will not send you out into the world hungry. But you should take a little time off. I think you are about as prepared as you are going to be. Knowing you, probably far more prepared than anyone else in the room."

"Don't kid yourself. Cargil is at least as well prepared. He might be a total asshole, but he's a good attorney." She paused. "This case is consuming me," she said.

"I wonder if that is standard for you. Do all your cases consume you? It makes you a good lawyer, but can make you hard on yourself, maybe you expect too much sometimes." Jeff said this pretty much to himself, but out loud, and not expecting an answer, just stating something that he was thinking about. Zoe listened, but made no comment. Jeff pulled a frying pan out of the cupboard and went to the refrigerator. "You like Swiss cheese or cheddar?"

After they ate breakfast, Jeff dropped Zoe off at her office so she could pick up her car. She had every intention of going upstairs to do some more work on the Mali case, and began walking to the elevator, thinking of using the executive bathroom to take a shower and freshen up, but she turned and headed instead in the direction of her car, the only car in the parking lot. She drove home, took a hot shower, and sat on her couch reading a trashy romance novel. Had Jeff known, he'd have considered it to be a rare victory.

Monday, October 1

Eric was sitting in the middle of his small apartment Monday morning, and while it was cluttered, the absence of his computer and screens left a huge vacant space on the table, a feeling of emptiness amid the chaos. All that was left were the wires and cables used to hook up the missing equipment, along with huge dust clumps clinging to wires and collecting in piles on the empty table. Eric hadn't bothered to clean up anything and had left his apartment pretty much the way the police had left it after their search. He was sitting on his leather desk chair looking at the screen of his old laptop. Somehow the police hadn't noticed it in the bottom of his bedroom closet. They had promised to return his computer and monitors when they were done with them but had been vague on when that would be. They'd already found enough to increase the stalking charges already against him now to a low-level felony but were waiting on some more forensic work.

Eric was reading the news on his laptop, waiting for the pages to load. There was an article about TrendInventions that he read, and then read again with disbelief. He was certain it couldn't be true, but there it was. Nick Mason's stock photograph, with his rugged, athletic good looks full of confidence and with more than a touch of narcissism, smiled at the camera lens, lighting up the pixels as the photons streamed out of Eric's laptop. It was Nick's photo that had caught his attention. The article said that Nick had been named as the next in line to become CEO of TrendInventions. He would be trained for a year under the direction of senior management, but then would assume command of the company, and Anne Mali would step down to the position of CFO. She was quoted as saying that she had been working long enough at two difficult, full-time jobs, and this was a chance to bring newer blood to top management. The article went on in a Q and A interview with Nick. Eric was livid.

This, of course, was one of the strategies that Zoe had come up with to steal Cargil's thunder and help to render his main argument moot. It was far more than a legal game, or a legal ploy. Anne could devote more time to the financial end of the business, which she was very good at, and let Nick run the part that used his talents best. He loved being around people and was excellent at handling pretty much anyone who came along, regardless of how much of a complete fool they might be. Nick had the ability to listen to the most asinine or boneheaded ideas as if they were gems of wisdom. He would simply nod and smile, and then ignore.

Eric was sitting in his chair, his laptop on the floor where it had fallen. His stare was catatonic, not focused on anything in particular. He seemed to be asleep with his eyes open. A noise from the street disturbed him, and he seemed to wake up, not knowing where he was. Then a realization hit him, slowly at first, then all at once, and he was suddenly very clear again, like he had been when he was leaving jail. He sat straight up in his chair as if someone had grabbed him by the collar and pulled him up.

"The bastards must be forcing her to do this," he said to no one in particular. "Anne must be defended. I must help her. She wants me to help her," he said out loud as he tracked back and forth across the apartment in a frenetic pace, kicking debris out of his way. He went to his bedroom, removed the floorboard, and took out his assault rifle. Before Eric left, though, he put clean sheets on the bed and washed the dishes in the sink, just in case a grateful Anne might want to come back with him to his apartment. It would be enough for her just to thank him for rescuing her from those bastards. He chuckled to himself, feeling good about thinking through all the little details. He hadn't felt so good in weeks. Concealing the rifle under his coat, he went down the back staircase to avoid his landlord, and went to his car, which was parked a few blocks away. However, as he reached the bottom of the stairs in the small alcove next to the laundry room, his landlord came out holding his toolbox. He'd just finished fixing the washing machine. Morrie was a large man, and very patient with all his tenants. He'd not really bothered Eric about the rent until he had gotten several weeks behind. A gentle man, he liked to avoid confrontation, but Eric had given him no choice but to start eviction procedures.

"Eric, I was on my way up to see you."

"Sorry, Morrie, I don't have any money for you."

"I thought so. Can't find a job at all? Anything?" He was genuinely concerned. "You're a smart guy. There has to be something you can do with all those computers you've got."

"What do you mean by that?" Eric said.

"Nothing. But I'll have to evict if you don't at least try to make up some of the back rent."

"I'm a little busy now," Eric said. He raised the gun a little, pointing it at Morrie, but kept it under his coat, while his finger found the trigger.

"No job, but he's busy," Morrie said to no one in particular. Then turning to Eric, he said, "You need to pay me the money you owe me, Eric. You give me no choice, and that's not fair to you or to me. I hate throwing people out in the street. God, if I knew anything about computers do you think I'd be doing this?" He rattled the toolbox. "Had to dig a bunch of grease and hair out of the water pump in the washing machine, took me all morning. God knows what they put in the damn washing machine to do that." Eric stood in silence, obviously preoccupied, obviously not listening. Morrie stepped aside to let Eric pass. Eric lowered the gun and scooted out the door. Morrie shook his head. "Such a waste. All those brains in his head and he acts like an idiot."

Eric got in his Corolla and drove to TrendInventions. It was a familiar route, but instead of ducking into a side street just before the entrance to wait for Anne as he had done for months, he drove up to the main parking lot and parked his car. He got out and walked to the main entrance. Since it was late morning, most people were already at work. A retired police officer who'd been hired a few months ago was on duty at the security check point. He knew Eric but had not been there the day he'd been escorted out of the building.

"You can't come in, Eric," he said.

"Anne sent for me. I have an appointment," Eric replied. The security guard was skeptical but looked at the screen of his notebook to check and see if Eric had an appointment.

"Sorry, Eric. You're not listed here as a visitor. Maybe they made a mistake? Do you want me to call upstairs and see?" He sat in front of his notebook but made no move to pick up the phone. Eric took out his rifle and shot him through the head. The noise of the shot echoed through the atrium as the guard fell backward and off his chair. Some people came to the railing to see what was going on and Eric shot up at them, emptying a thirty-round clip and hitting six people in the spray of bullets. They stampeded back into their offices. Over fifty calls to 911 went out in the next ten seconds. Eric reloaded as he ran up the stairs to the fourth floor and down the hall to Nick's office suite. The door was locked. It took him a few minutes to kick it in, and he found himself staring at Nick's terrified secretary.

"Where the fuck is he?" Eric demanded.

"Mr. Mason is out of town on a business trip," she said. Her eyes focused and narrowed on the assault rifle.

"Out whoring at company expense as usual and they promote him? This is pure bullshit! Is he fucking you yet?" And then he turned and kicked open the door to Nick's office only to find it empty. He immediately shot the place up, emptying the next thirty-round clip into Nick's desk, PC, sales reports, and for good measure took out the window overlooking the parking lot which was rapidly filling up with police cars as they prepared to assault the building, along with a huge number of fleeing employees running out of every exit. The terrified secretary had taken the opportunity to run down the hall and was hiding in a stall in the bathroom, but Eric wasn't interested in her. He was there to protect Anne, so he ran upstairs to her office. As he rounded the corner, a security officer was there with his gun drawn.

"Put it down, Eric." He had his pistol out at arm's length and made the mistake that many people do in the same situation. He acted as if Eric was rational and would drop the weapon once he figured out that there was no place to go, that the police had surrounded the building and were on their way up the stairs. However, Eric had left rationality long before he even got there. Eric shot him, unleashing about ten shots in the direction of the guard. The guard got off one shot that grazed Eric's left shoulder. Then Eric finished the clip on the locked door and reloaded before going in. Anne was standing in her office behind her desk, April was across the room.

"Hello, Eric," Anne said as calmly as she could.

"I came to protect you," Eric said.

"I know. That's nice of you to think of me," she added.

"They're not being fair to you, Anne. They don't know you like I do."

"I agree, Eric, but you didn't need to bring the gun. Maybe you should put it down?"

"How else will I be able to protect you? How else will you know that I love you? That's my job. You've been asking me to protect you for all these months. I saw it in your eyes."

"I know, Eric," Anne said. He listened to her, and something relaxed in him for a moment. He dropped his guard and lowered his weapon.

"Jesus Christ, Eric," April said. "You're a dammed idiot if you believe that. She's bullshitting you and you can't see it?" She had gotten her Walther PPK out of her handbag and was pointing it at Anne. "You can't see that she's playing you to save her own skin? She doesn't give a shit about you. She's just waiting for the police to get here, which is going to be very soon, judging by all the noise downstairs." Eric looked confused. Anne was astonished.

"I'm here to protect Anne," he said after a minute.

"Get real, Eric. You're such an idiot." April paused. "You need to shoot her. Can't you see that?" April said. Anne was still dumbfounded. April looked directly at Eric but was misreading him in a very dangerous way. "You shoot her, or I will, and they won't even suspect me," she said. "You're the nut with the gun in here, not me." She looked at Anne, who was completely paralyzed. At this point, much to her own surprise, April's gun went off. She'd had kept her finger on the trigger with the safety off and getting angry with Eric had made her tense up her muscles, clenching her jaw and constricting her fingers. She could have used a lot more practice with the pistol than she'd had. The bullet went right through Anne's forearm, missing bone and artery; the force of the injury spun her around and she fell to the floor behind her desk. Eric instantly unleashed half a dozen rounds in the direction of April. The noise of the shots was enough to prompt the police to come running in through the door, guns blazing. They fired over one-hundred rounds in about twelve seconds. Twenty-one of them ended up in Eric, fifteen in April, some of course came from Eric's gun, which was about a twenty percent hit rate, a little above normal for a police shootout. The rest of the rounds ended up in furniture, books, walls, office equipment, just about anywhere. Luckily for Anne, April's poor shooting skills knocked her to the ground behind her heavy steel desk, and she was okay except for the through-and-through in her arm, which was bloody, but not life threatening.

Across town, Zoe and the rest of her staff watched the television in horror as the local news copter hovered over the TrendInventions headquarters, showing clips of heavily armed police officers near their vehicles, and office workers standing in large groups far away from the building talking on cell phones. Ambulances were driving out of the parking lot at top speed. The breathless announcers broadcasted every rumor, anecdote, and wild speculation as if it were fact, at one time reporting that a group of Islamic terrorists had been seen in the area. The man who reported seeing the terrorists was part of a local white power neo-Nazi survivalist group. It turned out that he'd seen two Sikhs on their way to work at a local gas station. Why any Islamic terrorists would want to attack a company that chiefly made overpriced toys for people with disposable income was a question no one seemed to have the time to ask in the heat of reporting on the rumors. No headline grabbing journalist could be bothered with rationality, or the truth, at a time like this.

Zoe was nauseated with worry about Anne. After a while she couldn't watch the TV news anymore and decided to wait until the story was sorted out. While she worried about Anne's safety, and hoped fervently that she was okay, her professional lawyer persona worked its way through the concern and injected her with some cold, clear, harsh reality. Zoe knew full well that their case was now utterly, completely, totally, and absolutely screwed.

44

Cargil had trouble containing himself, and Michael was even worse. He seemed to vibrate with satisfaction as he squirmed in the chair, literally popping out if it occasionally with delight. It was all that Zoe could do to not reach across the table and smack him to knock the smirk off his face. Anne still had her arm in a sling, even though it had been a few weeks since the shooting.

The press had developed a bottomless interest in what they called the "deadly love triangle," and seemed to have an endless supply of very private information, which they could distort, twist, or embellish ad infinitum. After they dropped the terrorist angle, the love triangle became far more fruitful, and needed even less corroboration. Any rumor would do; no source could be too untrustworthy. The two dead security guards and half-dozen casualties provided heart-wrenching human-interest stories that alone could fuel the infotainment industry for a month, let alone the stories of April and Eric, who both became the topics of numerous mini-stories. The facts of the affair that Anne had had with Eric seemed to be known to the press in minute detail, even if they were misleading and distorted, and had been pretty much spun from whole cloth by the press on a particularly paltry amount of evidence. Zoe didn't think they needed to look too far to find the source of the information.

The worst part of it was the spin that the press had put on the whole tragedy. This is where they left the facts far behind and created as many speculative fictions as they possibly could. There were endless speculations about Anne's private life, and every possible sexual permutation that they could think of that could have happened between Eric, April, and Anne had been fully explored in the pages of the newspapers, weekly news magazines, news blogs, social networks, talk radio, and TV talk shows. The shootings had been a bonanza, a gold mine, of opportunities to tell cheap jokes, and on TV, radio, or the Internet no joke was too cheap. It was a rare event to have a quadruple homicide and a handful of victims with so much potential for inspiring gruesome humor and righteous indignation.

One heavily Christian TV station run by a famous self-appointed conservative guardian-of-all-that-is-good-and-holy had no fewer than fifteen televangelists draw a staggering number of lessons from this one multiple homicide, often leaving the facts of the matter far behind in an effort to make a titillating point, and to increase their donations. They knew, like everyone else, that sex sells. As consummate salesmen, they understood that while there had been an endless supply of money in Jesus for the past 2,000 years, sex couldn't hurt. Zoe had been astonished at how much the story had grown from a local tragedy to a national pastime. She knew it was bad when it had happened, but had no idea how far it would go in a slow news cycle, with little happening on the world scene, and the US Congress, in a rare moment of cooperation, boringly doing the job they were elected to do without any grandstanding. It seemed that only an invasion of some third-world country, a natural disaster, or maybe a juicy sex scandal in Washington could knock this off the evening news. Although it was starting to run its course and was becoming old news simply because of media saturation, at least it was no longer a topic on the late-night talk shows, but the televangelists were still crushing it for all they could.

"As you can see," Cargil said after they had begun their pre-trial hearing. "We've modified our terms." That was an understatement. They were now demanding that Anne immediately resign from TrendInventions, that Michael be appointed as CEO, and that a search be conducted to hire a suitable CFO, whereupon Anne's resignation would take full effect. She would be left with her stock in the company and one year's severance pay. Michael would get the house, cars, property, everything. She would get to keep her downtown apartment and her Mercedes. There was little that she could do but agree to the terms. After the papers were signed, she was alone in the room with Zoe. Cargil and Michael had sailed out of the room on a cloud of self-righteousness.

"I guess it's over," Anne said.

"I'm so sorry," Zoe replied.

"Not your fault. You're one hell of an attorney." She paused. "Maybe it's a blessing. I had no idea how much of my time and energy that business was taking from me. Maybe I'll go and do something else for a while. At least I won't have to fight anymore."

"We can appeal this after the nonsense calms down. For one thing, Barnum should have given you a much longer break than a few weeks."

"At this point I don't care."

"Yes, you do, and so do I. Want a glass of wine? There's a nice place around the corner."

"I don't want to be in public. I get recognized and then everyone starts pointing. It's too annoying."

"I understand," Zoe said. Anne got up and left the room and Zoe went back to her office. She worked for a short while, but her mind wasn't on anything she looked at. She read documents repeatedly without understanding them. She decided to leave and as she headed for her door, took a cheap vase that had held flowers the partners had given her for her birthday and smashed it on the floor.

***

Zoe was asleep on her couch, an empty wine bottle near her head, and the TV turned to the movie station. She was still in her work clothes from the day before and dreaming of thunder and Thor from the comic books she'd consumed by the gross when she was a kid. He was standing on a mountain with his long blond hair streaming behind him, looking like the actor in the B fantasy movie she'd been watching when she dropped off to sleep, actually passed out from the wine. Then his face suddenly changed into Jeff's face, and his hair turned red and curly. She woke up suddenly, and with a wine hangover, slowly realizing that the thunder was someone pounding on her door. She went across the room, one hand on her head, and flung the door open, ready to kill. Jimmy was standing in the hall.

"Jesus, Jimmy. Can't you leave the dead in peace?" She had both of her hands on her head and turned to go back into the room.

"Zoe," he said, barging into the apartment and turning the station on her TV. "I've been trying to call you all morning."

"I shut my phone off for the first time in years."

"Well this time you should have left it on." He fiddled with the remote and landed on a twenty-four-hour local news station. Zoe at first couldn't focus on the TV and realized she hadn't put her contacts in. She put her face up close to the screen and could make out Cargil. He was wearing handcuffs. Jimmy turned up the sound. The announcer was starting the top of the story. "Local Attorney Tim Cargil and Judge Franklin Barnum were both arrested today as the result of an ongoing corruption investigation. The two were charged with soliciting bribes from Cargil's clients for a favorable verdict from the judge. Michael Mali of TrendInventions was recently represented by Cargil, and reportedly paid a six-figure bribe for a favorable verdict in his divorce case from his wife Anne, one of the survivors of the recent shooting at TrendInventions." They cut to a clip of Barnum being led out of his office in handcuffs, Detective Pepe was holding his arm and guiding him to a waiting police cruiser, she had a deadpan look, but there was a slight smile on her face.

"Holy shit," Zoe yelled, and hugged Jimmy, picking him up off the ground. "Holy shit." She said over and over.

"You do have a way with words," Jimmy said, while straightening up his clothes and patting his hair in place. "I thought there was something funny about those two. Didn't I tell you?" The two of them watched more of the report. Zoe wanted to make sure it was real, that they wouldn't suddenly come on and say that they had made a mistake. But the news looped through again with the story, and it was on all the local stations and was getting picked up by the networks, and cable. Zoe made coffee, and she and Jimmy each had a cup.

"Notice how she's now a 'survivor' of the shootings," Jimmy remarked.

"She was always a survivor. Poor Eric was just out of his mind. My guess is that April just got in the way, wrong place at the wrong time." Anne had never mentioned a word of what had really happened in her office that day. Everyone assumed that Eric had shot her, or that she had caught a stray bullet during the shootout.

"Maybe," Jimmy said. "Have you heard from Anne yet?" Zoe picked up her phone. It was still off from the night before. She turned it on, and as it powered up, it chimed for over a minute with messages and texts before settling down. Most were from Jimmy, but two were from Anne. She called her, and Anne answered on the second ring.

"Does this mean what I think it means?"

"The divorce will be null and void. In fact, Michael could face bribery charges, maybe even jail time for bribing a judge."

"Wow."

"My guess is they will waive the charges for his testimony," Zoe added. "You're back in charge of your company."

"Not sure I still want it."

"Don't make any hasty moves."

"I won't," Anne said. "Thanks, Zoe."

"For what? They did it to themselves."

"For sticking with the case. I know that your bosses were probably trying to get you to make my case go away. Especially after—"

"Something like that. They're not long on courage," Zoe said. She didn't bother to tell her that Baxter had, in his best toadying and smarmy manner, asked for her resignation right after Anne had left her office. Zoe and Anne talked for a little while and decided to get a new agreement as soon as possible before Michael could get stupid again. Zoe hung up the phone and said, "God I need a shower." Let me get cleaned up and I'll buy you some breakfast," she added.

"Look at the clock, Zoe. You can take me to a late lunch, though, and not at a diner either. I'm not a cheap date."

"That's true," she said, as she headed for the bathroom. "You might want to come back in an hour and get me," she shouted to Jimmy from the hallway. She knew that Chris would yell at her for wasting energy, but she was going to take a shower until the hot water ran cold.

Epilogue

Zoe looked at the door of her new office and read: Peters Law Offices, Family Law, Zoe Peters, Attorney at Law. She'd rented an office in the same building where she had worked. She turned to Jimmy. It had been his idea to rent the space there so that her old bosses could see the business they would be losing.

"Here goes nothing." She opened the door to the smell of fresh paint and new construction. Zoe had resigned the day after the corruption investigation had made the news, even though the partners had taken back their demand. It didn't take much to persuade Jimmy to come along. Anne had helped finance the new office, and Chris had done most of the renovations. She was excited and terrified at the same time, but it felt good, like it was finally right. Jeff had been a tremendous help to her, giving her the confidence to make this move. They were still going out together, but no one dared called them an "item," including Jimmy.

Anne would stop by later that day but was guiding Nick through his first board meeting as interim CEO. After a year, he'd become *the* CEO. Anne was already thinking of travel plans. Michael had been chagrined by a close brush with jail time. He was under probation for five years and had to do about a million hours of community service, but he was still the prime mover for research and development and was now working on a customizable laser pointer that would project someone's name or company logo, or any image they wanted.

As slick an attorney as Cargil was, the best deal he could get for himself was two years in jail by basically blaming everything on Barnum, who got six years, which was unprecedented for someone with his connections and family ties. It just seemed that no one was willing to go to bat for him this time around. While corruption was usually permitted and acceptable up to a point among his inner circle, he and Cargil had gone way over the line, even for well-connected men. Michael managed to avoid any real penalties by giving as much evidence as he could about Cargil and his methods, which launched another investigation, and Cargil was possibly facing even more charges. He had already been disbarred.

Zoe and Jimmy entered the office suite and were admiring Chris's carpentry. The built-in cabinets were inlaid with mahogany and other exotic woods he took from his private supply. Zoe's desk was a masterpiece, and the reception area was a work of art. The two were absorbed when the phone rang. They looked at each other for a minute as if neither was sure of what to do, and Jimmy answered the phone. "Peters Law Offices, Jimmy speaking." He listened for a minute. "I'll have to check her calendar to see if she has an opening. She's terribly busy this week." He looked up and smiled at Zoe, pausing for a few moments with his hand over the mouthpiece of the phone, and then took his hand off.

"She has an opening on Tuesday at 9:30 a.m., will that work for you? Fine. I just need your name, phone number, and the reason why you want to see the attorney." He typed the information into the calendar of the brand-new computer on his desk.

About the Author

Joe Zeppetello has published two novels, *Daring to Eat a Peach*, and from All Things That Matter Press, *These Truths,* along with various short stories and nonfiction. He also has a keen interest in photography. *Intimate Disconnect* is his third novel.

Joe was an adjunct lecturer for ten years at several colleges in the Hudson Valley. After finishing his doctorate, he worked as a faculty administrator in charge of the writing program and writing center at Marist College, where he currently teaches English.

Intimate Disconnect was inspired by the fact that it is extremely hard today for people to initiate and maintain an intimate relationship—there are just too many factors that conspire to disrupt and end them.

Joe lives in the Catskill Mountains with his wife and is presently working on another novel.

ALL THINGS THAT MATTER PRESS

FOR MORE INFORMATION ON TITLES AVAILABLE FROM
ALL THINGS THAT MATTER PRESS, GO TO
http://allthingsthatmatterpress.com
or contact us at
allthingsthatmatterpress@gmail.com

**If you enjoyed this book, please post a review on Amazon.com and your favorite social media sites.
Thank you!**

Made in the USA
Middletown, DE
24 July 2020